A WEEK TO REMEMBER

★★★★★

'What a **fabulous** book. **Gripping and unputdownable.** Well worth a read! Ruth, please write more books, they are fabulous and realistic.'

★★★★★

'Fantastic read, **loved this book** so much, could not it down and was disappointed when I finished it as I wanted more. Can't wait for her next book. **Highly recommend** reading this book.'

★★★★★

'I read this in 5 days on holidays. Such a **beautiful and inspiring** story. Makes me want to book the Camino for my own journey.'

★★★★★

'Just finished this **thoroughly enjoyable** book. **A brilliant read.** Loved the characters and twists in this book. Definitely will be reading more books by this author.'

★★★★★

'Outstanding. Absolutely one of the best books I have read in a very long time.'

THE WEEKEND BREAK

★★★★★

'Brilliant book. It had me laughing out loud and also shedding a few tears. I really **did not want to put it down,** it's such a brilliant story.'

★★★★★

'Excellent read. Twists and turns and shocks, made me gasp out loud at one point. **Would absolutely recommend.'**

★★★★★

'A fabulous debut. It is a **beautifully written** story, wonderfully told and skilfully structured. You will fall in love with the characters and root for each of them. **Ruth O'Leary is an author to watch.'**

★★★★★

'Could not put it down. **A heart-warming story** to remind us that we all have flaws. **Wonderful.'**

★★★★★

'Brilliant. Very easy to read and I felt part of the friendship group. Full of laughter.'

The Last Week *of* Him

RUTH O'LEARY

POOLBEG

This book is a work of fiction. References to real people, events, establishments, organisations, or locales are intended only to provide a sense of authenticity, and are used fictitiously. All other characters, and all incidents and dialogue, are drawn from the author's imagination and are not to be construed as real.

Published 2026

by Poolbeg Press Ltd., 123 Grange Hill, Baldoyle,

Dublin 13, Ireland

Email: poolbeg@poolbeg.com

A catalogue record for this book is available from the British Library.

ISBN 978-1-78199-655-3

www.poolbeg.com

ABOUT THE AUTHOR

Ruth O'Leary, an *Irish Times* bestselling author, lives with her family beside the sea in Dublin, Ireland. When she is not writing about the imaginary people in her head, she works as a freelance movie extra, playing a variety of roles in TV dramas and full-length movies.

Ruth's other passion is travel writing. She writes a monthly Travel Blog called Rambling Ruth, which can be found on her website .

Her book reviews and author interviews are published on Writing.ie. She also writes short stories that have been published in Irish national publications and online.

She is very active on social media and can be found on Instagram, Facebook, Threads, Bluesky, TikTok and Substack as rutholearywriter.

The Last Week of Him is Ruth's third novel with Poolbeg Press, Ireland, the previous two being *The Weekend Break* and *A Week to Remember.*

ACKNOWLEDGEMENTS

Writers spend a lot of time alone, walking around with imaginary people in our heads for months. We talk to them, ask them questions, and figure out how they will react to the situations we put them in, all the while creating the world where their stories unfold. We mould, chop, and change until it becomes a story with a beginning, middle, and end – but it takes a team to transform that story into the book you now hold in your hand.

For their help and guidance, I would like to thank my sister, Barbra, who is always the first person to read my manuscript. To my agent, Kate Nash, who is the next to read it and always offers thoughtful advice, and to Paula Campbell of Poolbeg Press, whose expertise and guidance I deeply value. I then hold my breath while my editor, Gaye Shortland, has her first read, and together we work on any changes needed. Finally, thank you to David Prendergast, who generously welcomes my input and ideas and ultimately creates book covers I adore.

As we lost our beloved golden retriever, Rusky, this year, after sixteen and a half wonderful years, I am especially grateful to have a Golden Retriever on the cover. It is a tribute that means the world to me.

Thank you to every member of my online writers' group, Writers Ink, under the leadership of Vanessa Fox O'Loughlin, aka crime writer Sam Blake, and business mentor and journalist Maria McHale. Because of them, I continue to learn about this writing life and the publishing industry. Included in this group are my fellow Poolbeg authors, Lucy O'Callaghan and Sharon Black. Thank you for the great chats, the support as we navigate this writing world. Writers Ink really is 'my tribe'—a place of support and encouragement from the nicest, book-mad people!

To the people of Belmullet, County Mayo, who so generously answered all my questions – my heartfelt thanks. And to the hugely talented Orla McConnon Bakeberg, who wrote the beautiful poem that appears at the start of this book – it is perfect for this story.

Thank you to Deirbhle Healy and all the staff at the beautiful Áras Inis Gluaire Arts Centre in Belmullet town, on the Erris Peninsula, for their very generous welcome. Being invited to speak at the Focal Chosta Literary Festival was one of the highlights of my year, and I look forward to returning for the Mayo launch of this book.

Thank you to the booksellers for stocking my books, and to you, the reader, for purchasing them. I am so grateful every single day that I get to do this.

Finally, to my mum and dad, my sister Barbra, and my brother Peter – thank you for ongoing support. And to my husband Hughy and my sons Jack, Michael, and Tim – let's keep the adventure going.

Listening to the sound of the sea,
Even the coastline has rhythm.
Waves crashing like drums,
The breeze whistles in tune,
Soaring seagulls add a little harmony.
Lives reunite,
Watching and listening to the sound of the coast.
From afar to the near,
Where the coast has rhythm.
The sound of the coast,
The rhythm of the sea.
Life connections, forever altering its tone.

© Orla McConnon, Bakeberg
Orla@orlaphotography.ie

CHAPTER 1

Thursday 30 May 2024

NORA

"Penny! Penny come here!"

Nora shielded her eyes from the sunrise and pushed a strand of her long, straight, red hair behind her ear as she scanned the sand dunes of Dollymount Beach for her Golden Retriever.

It was a beautiful May morning. The cloudless sky was a perfect palette for the wonderful dawn colours of red, orange and purple before the sun peaked over Howth Head, spreading its golden light across the calm sea waters and along the rippled sand.

Behind her, Dublin's famous Poolbeg Chimneys stood tall overlooking Dublin Bay and, in the distance, the first ferries of the day were leaving Dublin Port for the UK.

Nora loved walking at this time of the day and had done so ever since Penny was a puppy, so she was used to it too.

"Penny!" Nora looked around again.

Up popped Penny's sandy head, panting as she looked around. Her ears perked up the moment she caught sight of Nora, before bounding towards her.

"Get in there, missus!" Nora smiled as she patted the open back door of her jeep.

Penny shook the sand from her long golden hair before leaping up into the back of the vehicle. She then turned around, sat down, and waited for her hug.

"There's a good girl." Nora scratched Penny's back as she leaned in to her. "Right, let's get you home – I have work to do."

Shutting the back door of the jeep, Nora pulled the sleeve of her green work-fleece down over her hand and wiped away the sand covering her business website address and logo painted on the door.

"That's better," she said, standing back and admiring the artist's lettering for Ladylandscapers.com. No point in having a niche business if nobody can find you, she thought.

Her heart swelled with pride every time she looked at her jeep. Starting her female-only landscaping business five years ago had been terrifying, but every day she thanked her lucky stars that she had taken that leap of faith. The business took off immediately and she now had three jeeps on the road and a team of six women who she could trust to represent her company well.

How different my life is now, she thought. It was just over six years since Greg walked out. He left the divorce papers on the table and his sports car in the driveway before leaving for good this time. The parting gift of his beloved sports car covered the cost of her first jeep and some of her business start-up costs, so at least something good came out of her four-year sham of a marriage.

It wasn't until two months after he left that she discovered she was pregnant. She was so worried at the time that the stress of the divorce and having to sell the home she loved might have affected her unborn child but, thankfully, Millie was perfect.

"Are we going back home now, Mummy?" Millie asked from the jeep's passenger seat.

"Yes, we are. Time to get you ready for school," she said, smiling at Millie who was wiping the sand off her shoes with a towel in her child seat.

"Can't we just stay here and play?" Millie said, tilting her head.

"Not today, sweetie. Mummy has to build a garden for a nice lady and, anyway, don't you have Irish Dancing today?"

"Oh yes!" Millie clapped her hands, happy now.

Sitting into the jeep, Nora had started the engine when her phone buzzed in her work-trouser pocket. Someone is up early, she thought as she opened her phone case. She looked at the number, not recognising it, and then gasped when she saw the message.

She read the WhatsApp message over and over.

"*No, no … no …*" Her voice trembled and her hand shook as the words started to blur through her tears.

"What's wrong, Mummy?"

"*Eh …*" Nora took a deep breath and wiped the tears away as she was dragged back to reality. "Oh, nothing, baby, I think I just got some sand in my eye." She shook her head. "I'm okay now."

She drove home quickly, gave Millie her breakfast and then took her to school in a daze. Dropping her into her classroom, she kissed her on the head before quickly exiting. In the schoolyard, a class mam approached her and started to say something to her about Sports Day but Nora couldn't reply so she simply kept walking. She pulled herself together just enough to call in sick to work, something she had never done before and luckily Annabelle, one of her experienced landscapers, was free to cover for her.

Once back in her jeep, a phone call to her mother back in Belmullet, her hometown located on the northwest coast of County Mayo in the West of Ireland, confirmed the awful truth.

As soon as she got home, she curled up in bed and cried for most of the morning. She felt like a knife had been plunged into her heart. It took all her strength to get up to collect Millie from the after-school service she attended and, even at that, she had to fake a dose of hay fever to explain her puffy face, flushed and red from crying. She felt like her veins had been filled with cement as she dragged herself around for the rest of the day.

How can this be true, she kept asking herself in disbelief as she gave Millie her tea and then put her to bed. Lying down on her own bed, she clutched her chest. The pain in her heart deepened as she sobbed into her pillow until finally falling asleep fully dressed.

CHAPTER 2

FERN

Fern couldn't help but smile as she crossed London's Millennium Footbridge. St Paul's Cathedral rose behind her and the iconic Globe Theatre stood proudly in front of her. She could hardly believe it was the final performance day. A gust of wind swept up from the Thames, pushing her long, curly, brown hair across her face. Grabbing hold of it, she twisted it with her hand and held it to one side as she quickened her step across the bridge.

It was a beautiful sunny day but, despite the high temperature, Fern stuck to her usual uniform of a black pinafore and her trusty Doc Martens, just exchanging one of her many long cardigans for a colourful embroidered waistcoat.

From the very first time she visited the Globe Theatre as a first-year drama student, her dream was to perform there. A big ambition for a girl from the wilds of West Mayo. Back then, anything seemed possible in this big city full of opportunities, as long as you knew the right people and hung out with the right crowd.

When she first arrived from Ireland, she lived rent-free with her mother's sister, Joan, in London's chic Marylebone area, for her first year in Drama School. Like Fern's mother, Aunt Joan was a talented artist. She led a bohemian lifestyle entertaining fellow artists and colourful characters all hours of the day and night.

Once she made her own friends, Fern moved into a damp terraced house with five other drama students for her second year of college and she absolutely loved it. The rent was manageable but only by working in a Mexican restaurant in Covent Garden two nights a week and covering flatmates' shifts at a local King Cross café when they had auditions to attend or were too hungover to work. Those early days were so exciting, living day to day.

She loved acting in college plays surrounded by others who shared the same dream: either to act in theatre or film or to be involved in making scripts come to life on stage and screen. Competition was always tough for acting parts and sometimes you got the part because you matched the image the director had in his head for the character, rather than the acting CV in your hand.

Working as a background actor or extra on films and TV dramas brought in some money too. That work had been a godsend, allowing her to meet the right people and learn more about the industry.

And that was how she met Max. She was an extra in a TV drama and he was an assistant director trying to gain experience on set and make his way as a young director in London. Twenty-three years later, they were still very happy together. She smiled, thinking back to those early days. Through hard work and persistence her dream of appearing on the famous Globe stage had come true.

Arriving at the theatre, she stopped to take a final photo of the poster.

Much Ado About Nothing

Hero played by Fern O'Malley

She sent the photo to her son Otto with the words: **My last day! Are you up? Can you let Slinky out before you leave for class and make sure to lock up? I will be late home, wrap party at Leo's. Love you. Mum X**

She waited for Otto's usual reply to appear: a thumbs-up emoji, the standard reply from any twenty-year-old, she imagined.

She then forwarded the photo to Max.

My last day! I hope the heat isn't too intense today. Good luck on set. I'll send you some photos from the wrap party. Love you. X

He replied immediately. **On a break. Started at five this morning. One of the stunt guys fell off a horse so we have to reshoot the whole scene without him in it. The last thing we needed today. Break a leg tonight and top tip: don't let Leo anywhere near a piano when he's had a few. Honestly, it's horrendous! Later gator X**

Max and Leo, Fern's director in the play, had met while attending Film and Drama College and were both now highly sought-after directors, Leo in theatre and Max in film. Currently in Morocco filming a medieval TV drama for Channel 4, Max's work took him all over the world. Fern felt so excited to be joining him on set in a few days' time.

Although he'd be working long hours, Fern was looking forward to lying by the hotel pool in Marrakesh and checking out the famous souks for herself.

"Morning, Fern!" David, Fern's father in the play, held the door open for her.

"Morning, David, how are we today?" She smiled as she passed him. "Oh sorry, my phone is buzzing here."

Fern pulled her phone out from her pinafore pocket. She didn't recognise the number immediately but saw the name **Ballycross College, Belmullet**, so she opened the message.

"*Oh my god!*" Fern gasped. Her hand flew to her mouth and she stumbled backward and bent over as if she had been punched in the stomach.

"What's the matter?" David asked, still holding the door open.

"It's ... just ..." Fern gasped, trying to get the words out.

David put an arm around her waist to steady her.

"It's a message from home ... a friend ... *oh my god!*"

"Let's get you inside," David said, waving to an usher to help him as he led her to a seat in the foyer.

CHAPTER 3

CLO

Clo's Yellow Cab driver beeped the horn and muttered some curse under his breath as they made their way through Manhattan's busy streets. There was never a good time to arrive from JFK airport – the city was always busy but Clo loved it. The scent of New York, a mix of subway fumes and hot dogs from corner stands, and the busyness of Manhattan, were like an injection of energy into her veins.

She had messaged Rory as soon as she landed. He was finishing up his work at the office so that he could be there when she arrived.

The cab pulled up outside the familiar brownstone building on 7th Avenue. Clo reapplied another layer of her new bright-pink lipstick and tossed her blonde, spikey, pixie haircut into shape before swinging her legs to the side and stepping out of the cab.

The exclusive apartment building's doorman opened the door for her. "Welcome back, Ms Kennedy."

"Thank you, Jake, good to see you."

Clo walked ahead of him, her six-inch heels echoing around the very grand foyer.

Clo had been coming to this apartment block for about five years now, ever since Rory's divorce. His ex-wife and two daughters stayed in the family home in Scarsdale, a wealthy leafy suburb in upstate New York, but Rory had purchased this apartment downtown, preferring to live in the city near his business.

Jake pressed the elevator button, placing her small suitcase into it when it arrived, and Clo went up to the 10th floor. Her excitement rose with every step she took along the long corridor. Stopping at his door, a grin crossed her face. She knocked twice.

Rory answered the door immediately and his face lit up as he looked her up and down, taking in her tight pencil skirt and high heels.

"Hello, beautiful!" He smiled and her knees went weak. "Let me make you a little more comfortable ..." He took the suitcase from her and placed it on the terracotta tiled floor.

She stepped towards him into the hallway.

Peeling her blazer from her shoulders, he leaned in and caressed her neck, closing the apartment door with his free hand.

Clo moaned, breathing in his expensive cologne, and dropped her handbag to the floor before reaching out and moving his head up to look him straight in the eyes, before kissing him deeply.

"Want to move to the bedroom?" he asked, breaking away.

"I don't think I can wait another minute," she said breathlessly as she opened her blouse, revealing her new hot-pink, lace, see-through bra.

"I see," he said, his eyes widening as she unzipped her skirt, letting it fall to the floor, revealing her matching hot-pink thong.

Pulling his T-shirt over his head, he threw it aside and then quickly released himself from his jeans.

"Leave the heels on," he whispered as he pulled her to him. Pressing her back gently to the wall, he took both of her hands and held her wrists over her head as he began kissing her neck again. He then moved slowly down to her breast.

"*Oh god!*" groaned Clo as she threw one of her legs up around his waist.

Just then, her phone buzzed in her bag at the same time as Rory's phone buzzed in his abandoned jeans.

"That's a coincidence," said Rory, pulling away for a second.

"Ignore it," Clo said, directing him back to the job at hand.

Then both their phones went off again.

Rory raised his head. "That's just too much of a coincidence, no?"

Clo sighed. "Okay, check your phone," she said, lowering her leg and bending over suggestively as she picked up her bag.

Rory looked at his message. "*Oh my god!* Did you get the same message?"

Clo nodded but couldn't answer. She was staring at the phone in her hand in shock.

It is with sadness that the board of the Past Pupils Committee of Ballycross College, Belmullet, Co Mayo, announces the passing of Danny O'Connor, age 49, in a tragic accident. Gone too soon. RIP. Condolences to his family.

CHAPTER 4

Thirty Years Earlier

January 1995

Fern, armed with notebooks, a pen between her lips, and her heavy schoolbag hanging off her shoulder, found an empty desk at the back of the school library of Ballycross secondary school in Belmullet town. She sat facing the wall because some lads from the football team were at another table, messing around instead of studying, and she didn't want to be distracted by them.

The poor librarian kept telling them to *shhh*, which worked for a short time before their murmuring got louder again.

"*Nice legs, shame about the face!*" a lone voice sang out, followed by childish laughter from the rest of the group.

Fern turned around to see Clo swanning across the floor, her skirt rolled up as short as possible, sticking her middle finger up to the lads.

"*Immature feckers!*" she said, loud enough for them to hear as she pulled out a seat beside Fern and plonked herself down, stretching out her long bare legs for them to eye up.

Fern smiled. Clo didn't give two hoots what anyone thought of her. Her school shirt was buttoned down just low enough to see the colour of her bra. She was always getting into trouble with the teachers over it.

"Is this the play?" she said, leaning forward and picking up one of the loose pages in front of Fern.

"Yes, most of it anyway." Fern sighed. "I thought I had it all sorted but then Kevin pulled out so I'm probably going to have to rewrite it."

"What's up with him? Why did Keanu pull out?" Clo asked, casting a glare at the table of lads to see if they were still looking at her legs. She was the one who christened Kevin 'Keanu' due to his likeness to the actor Keanu Reeves. He hated it although many of the lads in his school would have loved that comparison.

"His Christmas exams didn't go as well as he wanted so he wants to put his head down and study for the Leaving Cert without any distractions."

"Does that include you?"

Fern blushed.

"Sorry, I shouldn't have said that." Clo tilted her head apologetically. "Well, he needs a lot of points for psychology and I suppose it does suit him ... Mr Deep, Dark and Moody."

"Stop!" said Fern, laughing.

The librarian shushed them so they lowered their voices.

"Well, you can put myself and Rory down for a part," said Clo.

"Oh, that's great – I haven't asked him yet."

"Neither have I but he'll do it. Anyway, I can't stand to spend a minute longer than I have to in my own house of misery, so I'd be delighted to hang out in your gorgeous place. And it gives me more time to snog the face off Rory."

"It's rehearsals, not a snogging session, and I haven't written in any kissing scenes yet."

"I don't care, I can snog him on stage or off – I'm multitalented!" She cocked her head and gave a cheeky smile. "Right, I'm off. See ya later!" She swung her legs around and sashayed her way back out the way she came.

Fern shook her head and smiled. Clo was such a good friend with a little bit of crazy on the side.

As she turned back to her notes, she felt someone standing behind her. Turning around, she started.

"Sorry, I didn't mean to creep up on you there."

Standing at her shoulder was Danny O'Connor, a fellow 6th-year student, who happened to be the best sportsman, the most popular and the best-looking boy in the school.

"Eh ... hi," was all Fern could mutter.

"Can I sit down?"

Fern looked around, checking to see if he was on his own and he was.

"Sure," she said but she was very confused.

He smiled. "You look confused."

"*Eh*, I am. Is there something wrong?"

Danny O'Connor had never sat beside her except for science class because he came in late on the first day and that was the only seat left.

"I know this might sound strange but ..." he hesitated, "I was wondering if I could have a part in your play?"

Fern sat up straight and looked around the library. The football lads had gone and only one or two other students were studying quietly on their own.

"Are you taking the piss?"

"No!" Danny said, looking directly at her.

"You want a part in my play?"

"Yes," he nodded.

"Why?"

Danny took a deep breath. "This play is the last play I will ever get a chance to be in. I have always wanted to try it but rehearsals clashed with training and ..." He paused, looking down at his feet and then back at Fern. "I didn't have the balls to do it before."

"Seriously? This isn't a prank?"

"I'm very serious. Before, I would've been too worried about what other people thought, you know, the lads on the team and that ... but I don't care about them now. This is our last year, our last play and I won't get a chance to try it again."

"Danny, you have never shown any interest before ..."

"Yes, but I've wanted to try it for years. I was too much of a ... I don't know, too self-conscious. Will you give me a chance or an audition even? And if I'm shite, then ... grand."

This is ludicrous, thought Fern. Danny O'Connor? But she could see in his eyes that he really meant this. Jesus, those eyes! No wonder the girls threw themselves at him. When Danny O' Connor looked at you, it felt like you were the only girl in the world.

"If you commit to this," Fern said, stabbing the page in front of her with her finger, "you absolutely cannot back out."

His face lit up. "I won't."

"And it means rehearsals in my house after school or at night, I haven't figured it out yet."

"I'll be there." Danny nodded, looking deep into her eyes.

Fern bit her bottom lip. With Kevin dropping out, this would save her a total rewrite or, worse, having to hold open auditions.

She smiled. "Okay, you're in."

Danny's eyes lit up. He stood up and, looking down at her, placed his hand on her shoulder. "Thanks so much, Fern. I won't let you down."

"You'd better not!" She smiled as he headed for the library door.

What have I done, she wondered, as she placed her hand on the spot his hand just left, her body still tingling from his touch. And what on earth will the others say?

CHAPTER 5

NORA

It only took a day before Danny O'Connor's death notice appeared on the national website that announced all deaths and funeral arrangements in Ireland. Nora thought there would be a delay in his burial. Given how young Danny was, she presumed that the hospital would want to do a post-mortem and they would need to allow time for Danny's younger sister Audrey to book flights home from Australia.

How awful for her, thought Nora – such a long and lonely flight from Melbourne. I hope she has someone with her. Will anyone else make the trip from Australia, she wondered?

The death notice confirmed that Danny O'Connor would be reposing at his family home at 6pm on Tuesday the 3rd of June, the day after the bank holiday weekend and the funeral itself would be at 11am the following day in the Church of the Sacred Heart in Belmullet.

That same day, the Ballycross College Secondary School board of management announced, via social media and through the past pupils' WhatsApp group, that a memorial service would take place on the following Saturday, the 8th of June, before the school shut for the summer break, at which they would plant a memorial tree in Danny's honour and rename the school's sports hall the Danny O'Connor Sports Hall.

Feck it, thought Nora when she read that message. Belmullet was just under a five-hour drive from her two-bedroomed, red-bricked terrace cottage on Dublin's Northside.

Millie's school was closed for two days after the bank holiday due to a teacher training course so taking Millie out of school for the week wasn't a problem.

But can I really afford to take time off work for the whole week? she asked herself.

Sitting at her desk under her living-room window, she opened her work diary to check what jobs she had booked for that week. Luckily she only had three small jobs on. She'd have to check with the others to see how many of these they could do for her.

She had picked up her phone to call Mandy, her longest-serving employee when it rang in her hand. It was a Mayo number, but she didn't recognise it.

"Hello?" she answered.

"Hello, is this Nora Cunningham?"

"It is, yes."

"Nora, this is Mary Comerford. I'm on the Board of Management at Ballycross College."

"Oh, hello."

"Sorry to disturb you but I presume you heard the terrible news about Danny O'Connor?"

Nora's stomach clenched. "Yes, of course. I can't believe it."

"Yes, the town is devastated here."

"It's awful," Nora said, swallowing hard, "I knew him very well."

"Yes, someone mentioned that and that's why I'm ringing you. I was just wondering if you planned to make it down to the funeral?"

"Yes, of course. I was just looking at my work diary here trying to figure out my dates."

"Oh good, good. Did you get the message about the memorial service on the Saturday?"

"Yes, I did, it's a lovely idea."

"Well, the reason I'm ringing you, Nora, is that I believe you have a very successful gardening business now in Dublin and, as the event is happening at the school, we want it to look its best on the day. I'm afraid the front driveway is very bare and barren-looking. And as we're at the end of the school year, any planting that was put down at the start of the year has been destroyed by the kids and their footballs."

Nora could see where this was going.

"So we, the Board that is, were wondering if you were coming to the funeral and, seeing as you are a past pupil, if you might stay on and do some planting to make the school look nice for the memorial event? We're expecting a big crowd, as you can imagine, it being so tragic and everything."

"I see, *em* ... well, like I said, I was just looking at my diary and I can't say right now how long I'll be staying – until I make a few calls. That would mean a week away from my work here."

"We would pay you, of course, and you'd have Pavel to assist you."

"Pavel?"

"Yes, he's the school gardener. He sometimes has his son helping him but Alek has gone back to Poland to his mother for the summer so we were hoping you might be free to do it."

"Mary, can I ring you back? I need to ring my work colleagues and ..."

"Of course, Nora. I know it's short notice but we just want the school to look its best for Danny."

Nora sighed. Emotional blackmail, great.

"I'll get back to you today, Mary."

"Thanks very much. Goodbye now."

"Bye."

Nora put the phone down and sat back in her chair. She could get the girls to cover her; it was always quiet after a bank holiday weekend.

But, the question was, did she want to spend a week in Belmullet? She tapped her fingers on her desk. She didn't want to go home at all. Going home makes everything real, she thought. The funeral is going to be horrific ... I don't know if I can face this.

"My poor, poor Danny!" she sighed. Leaning forward, she placed her elbows on her desk and rested her head in her hands. Every time she thought about him, it set her off crying again. She wiped a tear away with her jumper sleeve.

Okay, I need to pull myself together, she thought, sitting up and shaking her head. Gathering her long hair in both hands she pulled it back in a tight ponytail and secured it with a large wooden hairgrip.

"Okay, first things first – where on earth am I going to stay? Not with my mother anyway," she said, turning to Penny who was sprawled out on the couch after her walk.

Penny raised her head, wagged her tail and then went back to dreamland.

"*Hmm*, you're no help," said Nora.

How can I get around this one, she wondered. Her mother would be delighted to have Millie stay with her and Millie would love being spoilt by her grandmother. And her mother had already presumed they were staying with her when she rang after the details came out about Danny's accident. "I'll make up a room for you and Millie. I can't wait to see her," she'd said. Nora didn't have the energy to protest at the time but she definitely didn't want to stay there.

A year after her husband's death, her mother Margaret had met a German named Ralf, on a Rhine River Cruise in Germany. Two months later he came to visit her in Belmullet and never left. Nora presumed that a dark bleak winter spent in the furthest corner of West Mayo would have him running back to Germany but, no, he loved it and two years later he was still there. She was happy for her mother and it was clear that Margaret and 'the German', as Nora preferred to call him, were in love – but it was hard to watch. Nora adored her father and missed him so much, so it was hard to watch her mother and Ralf act like teenagers, always touching and kissing each other. She really didn't want to stay there.

On a practical level, there wasn't that much space for herself, Millie, and Penny there but she knew her mother loved making a fuss over Millie on their rare visits. It would be difficult to think of a reason not to stay there. Her brother lived in Belmullet too, just outside the town, but he had young kids himself and it was a very full house. She would have to think of something else.

She was last in Belmullet over Christmas and they were due another trip. She loved the wild walks with Penny on the beaches on both sides of the Mullet Peninsula and up around Erris Head, where the wind would nearly knock you over if you weren't careful. Millie loved all the attention from her grandmother and loved playing with her cousins so she'd be happy to go back for a week.

Her mind went back to the last time she sat with Danny. She had popped into McDonnell's pub on her way home from town for a quiet drink when Danny came in. Catching her eye, his face lit up and she felt safe and happy when he gave her one of his bear hugs.

"If it isn't yourself!" he'd said, brushing a strand of hair away from her face.

She remembered she felt dizzy, looking into his bright-blue eyes.

He then took her gently by the elbow and directed her to the snug at the back of the pub. Sitting her down in front of the fire, he bought her a fresh drink.

"It's great to see you, Nora – now tell me everything you've been up to."

She smiled, lost in his blue eyes. Danny O'Connor had a way of making you feel like you were the only woman in the world.

CHAPTER 6

FERN

Even the sound of two Solpadeine fizzing in the glass of water hurt Fern's head.

When will I ever learn, she asked herself as she sat at her kitchen table, staring into space. The sun shining in through the kitchen window lit up the orange walls. Fern loved colour and every room in the house was painted a different colour but today everything felt too bright. Even her blue kitchen cupboards did little to ease the glare today.

The memory of throwing up in the bathroom at 4am made her wince. The final show went fantastically well. The audience reacted to every laugh and gave a standing ovation at the end. She should have been elated but the message about Danny's death cast a shadow over everything. She just couldn't get his face out of her head. He was only forty-nine, for god's sake! And what a way to die.

News had come through from her mother that Danny was found collapsed beside his car, with a head wound caused by hitting his head against a rock. He had gone out alone, to take down his father's election posters. The local elections had recently taken place and Danny's father had retained the seat he'd held for as long as Fern could remember. Danny had just removed a poster from a roadside pole – it was found lying under his body. It appeared he may have stood on top of a low wall to reach the poster and had fallen from there. A passing motorist found Danny unconscious on the quiet rural road. The motorist called the ambulance service, but it was too late.

Such a sad way to go, thought Fern, at the side of the road – and how long had he been lying there, alone? She sighed, staring into her glass.

"Oh god, Mum, you were in a right state last night," said Otto as he entered the kitchen.

"Never spend the whole night drinking wine. If you learn nothing else from me, learn this," Fern said as she lifted the glass of Solpadeine to her lips. "Have you classes this morning?"

"No, not till this afternoon, and then I'm going to a gig so I might be home late or I might crash in someone's flat."

Otto's college year had finished and he was taking a course in film production for a few weeks before joining Max on the film set in Morocco in a few days' time, for some work experience.

Fern smiled, remembering the days when she could stay up all night drinking with her college friends and function perfectly well the next day. She couldn't do it now. And *wine*! Her body repeatedly showed her that she just couldn't drink it anymore. Bloody menopause!

"Why don't I get you a coffee – would that help?" Otto said as he slipped his feet into one of the many pairs of sliders he left abandoned around the house.

"Oh yes, please, nothing too milky though. An americano would be perfect."

"And will I get you an almond croissant?"

"Oh god, yes. You are a darling." She watched him walk down the hall. "You are worth every one of my stretch marks, you know! Have I told you that?" she called after him.

"Yes, Mum, a hundred times." He shook his head and laughed as he went out the door.

Fern smiled. Her heart felt full. I'm so lucky to have him, she thought for the millionth time. I wasn't even sure I wanted a child after ... She shuddered, pushing that thought away.

I'm having a lazy day today, she decided, as she folded her arms over her floral-patterned pyjamas. It was a beautiful sunny morning but her hangover was giving her the chills. Drinking the last of the Solpadeine, she stood up and rinsed her glass in the sink. Reaching up, she pushed a loose strand of her hair back into place. Her long, curly, brown hair was tied up on the top of her head in a loose bun, held in place with a scrunchie to keep it away from her face. I must look a sight, she thought.

Slinky the cat rubbed against her legs as if sensing her delicate state.

"*Aw* ... are you giving Mummy a hug?" Fern asked, bending down to pick up their three-year-old black tabby.

Slinky accepted her hug and then squirmed in her arms, signalling that that was quite enough of that, thank you.

Walking to the back door, Fern opened it and put Slinky down, releasing her to explore their unkempt back garden. Their three-storey, red-bricked London terrace had a long narrow back garden. Fern had planted grasses along the winding pathway that led to a seated area at the back and thrown in a few seed bombs of mixed wildflowers to create a meadow effect. She wanted a reminder of the wildness of her home near Elly Bay beach, on the Mullet Peninsula in North West Mayo.

"Home," she whispered. "I'd better book my flights today, but for how long?"

The message from the school board about the memorial service meant that now she would need to go home for a week. She was supposed to be flying out to Morocco to meet Max in two days' time so she needed to ring him to cancel that.

She sighed as she watched Slinky scratch her back against a wooden patio chair before skipping off into the long grass for an adventure.

Leaning against the doorframe, she closed her eyes, feeling the sun's heat on her face. Danny O'Connor's face as an eighteen-year-old came to mind. Fern had thought he was joking when he approached her about appearing in the 6th year school play, thirty years ago, to be staged just before the Easter Holidays. He had never been interested in the drama group before so she thought it was a prank – after all, he was the football captain, one of the most popular boys in school, and one of the best-looking too. But he was very serious and, to everyone's surprise, he was great too. He could have become an actor if his dad had allowed him to make his own choices in life.

Fern remembered his beautiful blue eyes. She used to scoff at the girls who followed him around, hanging on his every word, but she understood it when he held her gaze. Because, when Danny O' Connor looked directly at you he made you feel like you were the only girl in the world.

Fern closed her eyes and took a deep breath. She had no idea that day, the day he joined the drama group, that he would play such an important role in her life. She felt the tears coming. No more texts on a particular day of the year. No more eyes across a bar room at home. No more shared secrets. It was just so sad.

CHAPTER 7

NORA

Nora was busy on her laptop, looking up rental properties in and around Belmullet, to see if she could afford to stay for the whole week. She needed a pet-friendly house as Penny was coming along too. She was just about to confirm a townhouse in the centre of Belmullet when Fern's WhatsApp message came through.

Hi, Nora and Clo, I am about to book my flight home. I'm flying solo as Max is in Morocco filming and Otto will be joining him there. I'm booking a flight for tomorrow Sunday and staying for the week. My parents are in the South of France for the month which means I'll be on my own in the house. So I was wondering if you two would like to stay with me and keep me company? It's been so long since we did that. I'll understand if you need to stay with your families but, if you want to stay out in the sticks with me, I'd be delighted. And Nora, both Millie and Penny are more than welcome to stay too. F x

"*Yes!*" Nora punched the air in delight.

Fern's parents had a beautiful house on the Mullet Peninsula right beside Elly Bay beach. It was originally a traditional stone cottage but Fern's parents, both being artists, added an extension of an identical stone cottage, with a glass walkway joining the two buildings. The newer cottage had a living room with floor-to-ceiling windows overlooking the sea, three bedrooms downstairs, and a top floor that was a huge studio space for her mother's art. Her father had his own woodwork workshop in a converted shed out the back. He specialised in carving bogwood into beautiful ornaments and furniture.

Nora quickly sent her reply: **Fern, you are a lifesaver! I was just looking up some Airbnbs for myself, Millie and Penny to stay in but I would be delighted to stay with you instead. Thank you so much. XX**

Clo's response came quickly after that: **Oh god, thank you so much. You have saved me from the House of Misery!**

Fern replied: **Fantastic! We are well overdue for a catch-up. Arrive when you want and stay as long as you want. I can't wait to see you both! It will be just like old times. Has anyone heard from Rory or Kevin? F x.**

No, came the reply from Nora.

Me neither, replied Clo.

Nora had wondered about Rory and Kevin too but she hadn't kept in touch with either of them. She knew from her mother that Rory still lived in New York. He had married an American and had two daughters but was divorced now. Rory and his girls had holidayed in Ireland a few summers ago and his wife and daughters returned when Rory's father had died in November. She didn't meet them herself then. She couldn't go home for the funeral as she was away with Millie visiting her ex-husband Greg in Italy but she sent a Mass card to his mother as soon as she got home.

As for Kevin, well ... the last she heard he was in Australia but he didn't keep in touch with anybody. His family moved to Waterford that last school summer and he had never returned to Belmullet or Blacksod after that or she would have heard about it from her mother.

During their schooldays, the gang of five hung out all the time. They loved listening to music and making mix tapes from recording American Music stations on the radio. Fern's house was where they usually hung out. Her parents were bohemian artists, always travelling to visit a new exhibition in Dublin or in some European city. Fern, being an only child, had so much freedom and her parents were so welcoming to all her friends. Nora loved going there. They hung out in her mam's art studio mostly and that's where they rehearsed for the 6th year play.

Nora gazed out the window as her mind wandered back to that time. "No, it wouldn't be like old times," she whispered. "It wouldn't be like old times at all."

Penny's nose nudged her knee, bringing her back to the present.

"I know. I will take you out but I just have to send a few texts first," she said, rubbing the dog's head.

First, she sent a text to her mam.

Hi Mam, the Ballycross school board has asked me to do some landscaping to get the place ready for Danny's memorial service so it looks like me, Millie and Penny will be coming for the week.

Fern has asked us to stay with her as her parents are away, so I might go between her house and yours, if that's okay with you. Fern could do with the company and we wouldn't be under your feet. Nora. X

Her mother answered immediately: **Ah, that's a pity. We were looking forward to having Millie staying here.**

Well, I was hoping I could drop her in to you every day that I'm working? Nora replied.

Oh well then yes. She could stay over a few nights too."

Nora smiled at her mam's response. It was clear who they wanted to see the most. In fairness, they loved having their Dublin granddaughter stay with them and Millie would be delighted with the attention.

That would be a great help, Mam, thanks.

Okay. Text me when you leave Dublin.

Nora sent a thumbs-up emoji.

That's sorted, she thought. I don't know how much work there is to do, so having Millie stay with Mum some nights will be very handy.

Then she sent a text to Mary Comerford from the school board saying that she would arrive on Monday and could she set up a meeting with Pavel for Tuesday or pass on her number to him. She had already sorted out the week off with the other lady landscapers and they would have her back covered for the week.

"Okay, Penny," she said then. "Walk first and then the wholesaler's."

She needed to pick up some plants and a special tree suitable for the memorial and somehow find space for everything in the jeep as well as her clothes for the week, gardening gear, and everything Millie and Penny needed.

It was going to be a difficult week but she needed to keep it together. She'd had a crush on Danny O'Connor all her life. From the time she started school when he sat next to her, and all through their school days. He was always sweet to her and, as they lived close to each other, they would often walk home together. When they were alone they could talk about anything but she feared during the school years that he never saw her as anything more than a friend.

Being a bookworm and an introvert, she could never compete with the confident, good-looking girls that surrounded him. But, still, he always took the time to talk to her. After she left school he still sought her out if he heard she was home for a visit, making sure to catch up over a coffee or a pint. He was always kind and she just knew he valued their friendship.

That last year of school, when he joined their little drama group and she got to spend so much time with him, was her happiest time at school. It was hard watching him with other girls, especially Fern, but she liked to think of it as him just playing around until he was ready to settle down. She could wait. She knew they had a special connection and she believed that in time he would see how real that connection was. There was no doubt in her mind that one way or another they would be together someday. And then he got married ... but she still hoped ...

But now he was gone and it was too late. She felt all over the place. She had been tethered to that dream for so long. Now it felt like it had been violently ripped from her future. Everything had shifted.

Oh god, I have to stop this! she berated herself as the tears came again. I can't be like this when I go back there. I'm going to have to reimagine my whole future without him. Nobody knows the plans I had, and I have to find a way to cope with this grief alone. I need to pull myself together, take each day as it comes when I'm back home and try to enjoy my time with the girls in Fern's house. It will do me good to stay there and feel their support. But how long can I keep up a front? How long can I hide my feelings from the girls and everyone else who will be home in Mayo for the funeral?

She rubbed her chest to try to ease the pain that was lodged there since she'd read that awful message, and sat there staring out the window, not bothering to wipe away the tears as they fell.

CHAPTER 8

CLO

"*Oh, for fuck sake!*" Clo sighed loudly as she looked at her WhatsApp message.

"Something wrong?" Rory rolled onto his side and faced her, his head propped up with his hand.

"They're only going to have a memorial for Danny in the school on the Saturday!"

"*Hmm*, that's a nice thing surely?" He stroked her ribcage with the fingers of his spare hand, moving upwards till he reached her nipple.

Clo smiled. "Are you trying to distract me, Mr Darcy?"

"Maybe I am," he said, moving his hand to her other bare breast.

"Seriously though," she said, picking up his hand and placing it back on his side of the bed, "this means I will have to drive down on Tuesday for the removal and drive back late on Wednesday after the funeral only to drive back down Friday so I'm there in time for the memorial service on Saturday."

"Or stay for the week – that's what I'm going to do."

"Are you serious? You're flying home for it?"

"Of course. It's Danny."

"When was the last time you spoke to him?"

"I always met him for a pint when I was back home and he used to send me bits of news from home on WhatsApp. He was very good when Dad died too, calling in to Mam and that."

"I ... didn't know you kept in touch," said Clo.

"Ah yeah, he was good company and he'd a lot of life to live. His poor kids!" Rory said, shaking his head.

"So you're going for a week?"

"Maybe more, if the girls want to come for a few days to visit their grandmother. It's a quiet time for me workwise so I can switch one or two meetings online and Zoom from over there. I might add on some extra days. Anyway, this will bring people back from all over the place, like a huge school reunion. You never know who might show up. I haven't been home since my dad's funeral in November so I'm due a trip and Mam will be delighted."

"The golden boy returns," said Clo with a smile.

"Very funny. Come on, stay for the week too. We could –"

"We? No, Rory." Clo's face was serious now. "You know there is no 'we' back home."

"Sorry." Rory lay back on the bed, folding his arms over his head. "Will Pierre be there?"

"No, definitely not. I'll need him to run the shop for me if I'm gone that long."

"Or ... are you afraid he will notice something if he sees us together?"

"Yes, that as well. I don't want to rock that boat until Sophia does her Leaving Cert and goes off to college."

Clo didn't like talking about her long-term partner and the father of her only child Sophia when she was in Rory's bed completely naked.

She had told Pierre years ago that she stayed in a company apartment belonging to one of her suppliers when she travelled to New York, and he never once questioned it. Also, with smartphones, he and Sophia could contact her anytime they wanted.

"Look at the time," Clo said, changing the subject. "I need to get to the other side of town for a meeting in an hour so I'm hopping in the shower." She pulled back the black silk sheets.

"Oh no, you don't," Rory said, reaching out and grabbing her hand. "You need to build up a sweat first, gorgeous."

Clo laughed as she let Rory pull her back down onto the bed. He threw his leg over her and, taking her other hand, he drew both her arms over her head.

"You have fifteen minutes," she said, smiling up at him.

"Start the clock," he said as he placed his mouth on her neck and she moaned in appreciation.

Standing under the huge showerhead in Rory's wet room, Clo's thoughts turned to her family home in Mayo. She would have to go for the week. The drive from her home on Dublin's southside to her family home outside Belmullet took over four hours on a quiet day but could take up to five if there was any congestion on the motorway, so going up and back home again in the same day was unrealistic.

But the thought of spending a week in her family home with her mother and father didn't appeal either. Her parents either fought or didn't speak to each other for most of her life growing up. Instead of divorcing, they stayed together, sleeping in different rooms, and only spoke to each other when necessary.

When, at around sixteen years of age, she asked her mother why she didn't leave, her answer was: "Sure, where would I go? And anyway, your dad needs me on the farm."

Her dad spent his time working on the farm, or in the nearest pub. They were both miserable and insistent on staying that way. Her mother's answer had infuriated her. She vowed there and then never to get married and become trapped like her mother and father were.

She couldn't wait to leave that miserable house and move to Dublin to study Fashion Design at college. When she returned for the odd holiday she usually rented a house in the town for herself, Pierre and Sophia, and visited her parents while they were there. But she didn't have any excuse to rent this time when it was just herself visiting.

"*A whole week in that bloody house with my parents!*" she groaned as she turned off the shower. Running the towel over her pixie haircut, she resigned herself to a week in her old bedroom which hadn't been changed since she left thirty years ago.

It's worth it for Danny, I suppose, she thought. The most popular boy in the school with the most beautiful blue eyes. And then he joined their little drama group in their final year of school.

She shivered when she thought about that summer. Although she kissed many other boys, Rory was always faithful to her. He put up with her wild ways. She knew Danny O'Connor was out of her league but that didn't stop her from feeling hot and sexy when he was around. He made her feel a lot of things she shouldn't, because when Danny O'Connor looked at you he made you feel like you were the only girl in the world.

CHAPTER 9

Thirty Years Earlier

January 1995

"Danny O'Connor?" Clo's mouth fell open in shock.

Clo, Rory, and Kevin were standing in front of Fern's house, having got off the school bus.

"Yes, I know," Fern said with a shrug. "That's exactly what my reaction was."

"And when did this happen?" asked Rory.

"In the library, just after you left," Fern said, looking at Clo.

"And you didn't think to tell us on the bus?" Kevin's face was like thunder.

"No, I wanted to wait until we got off because I figured this would be your reaction!" Fern snapped back at him.

She knew he didn't like Danny. He was always giving out about him, even though to Fern's knowledge they'd never even had a conversation.

"I can't believe you said yes to that asshole," scoffed Kevin.

"I don't know what your problem is with him," Fern said, feeling irritated by Kevin's predictable reaction. "Have you ever spoken to him? Because we've been in school with him forever and he's not that bad."

"Ever since I came here it's been him and his football pals that have made snide remarks about all of us, calling us nerds and geeks and weirdos just because we're not neanderthal football dunces like they are."

"Okay, okay," Rory said, trying to diffuse the row. "He's not that bad, but Kevin's right, his cronies are arseholes. Are you sure this isn't a wind-up?"

Fern let out a deep breath. "Look," she said calmly, "I was just as surprised as you are but he seemed very sincere to me."

"Unless he actually is a great actor!" Clo said, laughing. "Sorry."

"This is ridiculous, letting him into the group. He'll make a mess of everything," Kevin said, shifting from one foot to another.

Fern was getting fed up with his attitude. "If you hadn't dropped out I wouldn't have a role for him, but you did. We need an extra male and he fits the role. The play is about two rival football teams after all."

"Yeah, sure look, there's no harm in giving him a chance," said Clo.

"Rory?"

"Look, it's not ideal and maybe he'll be shite and it won't work out so, yeah, I'll give him a chance."

"We'll find out soon enough. First read-through is here tomorrow after school," Fern said, nodding towards her house.

"Oh, so it's a done deal, is it?" Kevin said, glaring at Fern.

"As a group, we're giving him a chance," she said. "Otherwise, I have to rewrite the play or write another one and I just don't have the time."

"Well, I'm having nothing to do with this," Kevin said in a huff.

"Fine!" said Fern. "You lost your opinion when you dropped out of the play!"

Kevin opened his mouth to say something and then changed his mind.

"I'm going inside," Fern said. "It's freezing out here. Are ye coming in for a bit?"

"No, I'm going to Rory's," said Clo, linking his arm. "See you tomorrow?"

"Yep, see ya tomorrow," Fern said. "Are you ..."

Kevin didn't wait for her to finish her question. He just marched off down the road in the direction of his house.

Once inside, Fern plonked herself down at the kitchen table and put her head in her hands. Have I made a mistake with Danny, she wondered.

Kevin did have a point that those football lads were the bane of their lives in school, bullies slagging anyone who wasn't sporty or in their team, and the girls that hung around with them weren't much better. But, although Danny was their golden boy, it was never him doing the slagging and in class he always seemed nice.

And he did help out at the Christmas charity fundraising event she organised.

Oh, she sighed, am I just clutching at straws?

One thing was certain: as Danny was the captain of the football team Kevin hated him. And this might be the thing that finishes us, she thought. How do I feel about that? Kevin's dark brooding ways and love of literature had attracted her to him when he first joined their school but she never knew what was going on in his head. Lately, he'd been so moody over his Christmas results that he took all the energy out of a room. Anyone else would have been delighted with his marks but not Kevin. If she thought about it, did she really look forward to seeing him anymore?

The next morning Fern waited at the school gate for Danny to arrive. As usual, he was surrounded by a group of lads but he separated himself from them to go over to her.

"Hey!" he said cheerily.

"Hey," said Fern. "First rehearsals at my house at seven tonight. Is that okay?"

"Sure, yeah. My dad lets me drive the car on the minor roads so, yeah, I'll be there."

Fern nodded and headed into the school. Of course the local politician's son would let him drive on a learner's licence! She was learning to drive too but she had to wait until her mother or father had the time to take her out for practice. Well, at least he'll have no excuse for being late.

There was no sign of Kevin this morning. She looked down the corridor and checked the classroom. Usually they would meet up five minutes before class started just to say hi. The bell rang and everyone poured into class.

At the last second Kevin came in, walking slowly, not in a rush at all, and took a seat at the back two rows away from Fern. Well, there's my answer, she thought, determined not to turn around. She was open to talking with him but it was clear that he did not want to talk to her. Fine, she thought, message received.

The rest of the day flew by. She felt oddly aware of Danny all day, despite having shared some classes with him for years.

Today she had asked her mam to collect her as she wanted to get home as quickly as she could. She wanted to change her clothes and go over the play.

I never felt self-conscious about my work before, she thought, looking out the window of her mam's car as they drove out of Belmullet and turned off towards Blacksod.

Was it a mistake inviting Danny into their group if she was going to feel this awkward about it? No, everything will be fine, she decided.

Danny was bang on time. Fern jumped up out of her seat to let him in and was then mortified when her dad stopped to ask him about the football.

"Will those Kiltane lads give you any trouble this weekend?"

"No, we have them sussed," Danny answered politely.

"I used to play myself, you know, and –"

"Dad!"

"Sorry, I'll let you kids get on with it," her dad said, turning to walk back to his seat by the open turf fire.

"I'm sorry about that. He has no men in this house to talk football with," she said.

"I don't mind. It's the one subject I know something about."

Fern smiled. She knew that Danny wasn't top of the class academically and he certainly wasn't worried about his upcoming exams. His dad owned a big quarry company in North Mayo and, as Danny was his only son, he had a guaranteed job there.

"Wow!" Danny stood in the doorway of the attic studio. "This is some place!"

"Yeah. My mam paints here. It can be a little crazy if she has an exhibition coming up. But I love it – you can get lost for hours up here."

"I bet you could," he said, looking around, taking it all in.

Fern heard voices downstairs.

"That must be Clo and Rory," she said but Danny was too busy gazing at her mother's paintings on the wall.

"*Em* ... I'm making tea or would you prefer a coffee?"

"Tea is grand, thanks," he said, without turning around, his eyes fixated on the artwork.

Fern ran down the stairs to see her dad talking to Rory about football.

"Is he here?" whispered Clo.

"Yes. Help me bring up the tea, will ya?" Fern asked, switching the kettle back on. She had already put mugs and a plate of biscuits on a tray before everyone arrived. "Rory? Will you go up to him?" She nodded toward the art studio. "While me and Clo get the tea ready?"

"Yeah, sure."

Rory headed up and, as soon as the kettle boiled, Clo and Fern followed with the tray of tea and biscuits.

"Now," Fern said, placing the tray down on a big wooden table in the middle of the room. "Help yourselves while I explain the play."

They all sat down at the table.

Clo poured out her tea and milked it, all the time watching Danny. Fern kicked her under the table to get her to stop.

"So it's basically *West Side Story* but between two rival football teams here in Mayo, Belmullet versus Kiltane."

Everyone nodded and Fern continued with the storyline.

"So it opens outside a disco. I've gone out for air and Danny follows me and we get chatting and he asks to see me again. But he's the captain of the Belmullet team and my brother is the captain of the Kiltane team so we arrange to meet in secret."

"Oh, I love it!" said Clo.

"Clo plays my friend," Fern tells Danny, "and she tells me not to meet you because it will end in trouble and, when I won't listen to her, she goes behind my back and tells my brother."

"Jesus, I'm a right bitch!" said Clo.

"Rory is my brother and he threatens Danny and tells him to stay away from me and he bans me from seeing him." She looked at Danny. "Danny, we continue to see each other in secret but at the county final match Rory finds out that we are still seeing each other and fouls you on the pitch, resulting in a big fight between the two teams, and you lose the sight of one eye and can never play again. Rory, you are banned for life. Danny, we can't stand all the rows between the two families and the two communities but vow to stay together so we run away to London, not telling anyone where we have gone. Our families are distraught, but we can finally be together and be happy."

Fern looked around and smiled but nobody said anything. Her smile faltered.

"What? What is it?"

Danny was the first to speak, "*This ... is brilliant!*"

"Oh, I'm so relieved!" Fern said, letting out a big breath.

"No, Fern," Clo added, "it's *really feckin* brilliant!"

"She's right," said Rory. "You've outdone yourself."

"*Aw* thanks, guys, you're making me blush. It means a lot to me, you know?"

"That drama school in London will be delighted to get you," said Clo, dunking a fig roll into her tea before eating it.

"London?" Danny asked.

"Yes, I've been accepted into a Drama College in London." Fern felt herself blush again. "I went over for a weekend in November, attended a workshop and an audition and I had to give them a CV of all the productions I was in here and I included a play I wrote too. And ... I got in."

"That's ... incredible," Danny said, genuinely impressed. "You have a whole new life ahead of you away from this place ..." His eyes clouded over and he looked away.

"I know what you mean," Clo said to him. "I can't wait to get up to the capital and go wild without everyone knowing my business."

"What are you hoping for?" Danny asked her.

"Enough points to get into the College of Art and Design in Dublin, to study fashion design."

"Rory?"

"Business in UCD, I think. And yourself?"

"Business. Not in Dublin though – god, I'd love that. UCG for me."

"Why not Dublin?" Rory asked.

Danny sighed. "When your dad is a local politician, you need to be near home to deliver leaflets and shite like that. It's all about him. The furthest he'll let me go to college is Galway."

An awkward silence followed.

"*Em*, do we have enough people, Fern, for the match part," Rory asked, changing the subject.

"Yes, we do. Let me go through the cast list by scene. The first scene is just me and Danny outside the hall so we'll have a doorway prop in the school and we'll have disco music coming out from the doorway. Then, there's the bedroom scene where Clo tells me to stop seeing him. Then you, Rory, stop Danny in the street and threaten him. I have third-year students who can be players or onlookers for the fight scene. And then, the aftermath will be you and Clo telling the audience that it was too much for us and that we ran away together. Then the final scene is a shot of me and Danny in a window in London kissing ... or hugging." She cursed herself for blushing as she read out those words.

Danny smiled at her. "You have it all planned out, very professional."

"Well, the idea has been living in my head for months and I've gone over the scenes a hundred times on paper, so I think it's ready now."

Oh god, he really is gorgeous when he smiles, she thought, looking into his blue eyes.

"Right, let's do a run-through," she said, pulling herself together.

CHAPTER 10

Fern opened all the doors and windows in her parents' house as soon as she arrived, letting the breeze from the Atlantic Ocean blow through.

Her parents had left for the south of France two weeks previously so it felt good to open the house up and let the air in. The smell of the sea, the sounds of the rustling grasses in the garden and the nesting birds in the distance brought a familiar feeling of calm to her as she stood on the back patio.

When her parents travelled abroad, they drove their car to Belmullet and parked it off the main street where there was free parking. They then took the bus to whichever airport they were flying out of. If they were at home her dad would usually pick her up from Knock Airport but this time she took the bus from the airport. She had a spare set of keys to her dad's car so when she got off the bus in Belmullet, it was only a fifteen-minute drive home. She would leave the car back in town where she found it and get the bus back to the airport on her return.

A car was vital to living out on the Mullet Peninsula. Fern's family home was about halfway down, just before Elly Bay beach, and although it was only a fifteen-minute drive from the main town of Belmullet, it would take you two and a half hours to walk it. There was a local shop about an hour's walk or a fifteen-minute cycle away and Fern didn't mind walking or cycling there at all when she came home for visits. Coming from London, the fresh air, wild winds and the quiet was pure bliss.

When Otto was young he loved visiting Grandma and Grandad and running wild on the local beach. He had friends in the area his own age and, as a teenager, he went to the local disco with them. Every summer secondary-school students, from the age of twelve to seventeen, travelled from all over the country to spend two weeks at the local Irish College and watersports centre down the road. Some stayed in rooms at the college but most stayed with families in the Irish-speaking area for immersion in the language. The Irish language College, called Uisce, Irish for *water*, was still particularly popular with Dublin students. The students learned to improve their spoken Irish-language skills through water sports.

Fern was fifteen when the college opened down the road from her house and she remembered the excitement of having boys coming from Dublin and Cork and Galway to their tiny part of the world. Herself, Nora and Clo had practised their kissing skills on many a student passing through for their two weeks of Irish college.

She had laughed when Otto as a young teen came out from his bedroom stinking of Linx Africa, saying he was going out to play football with the locals. She knew he was doing the same thing she had done at that age.

Max also loved the area. He could really switch off when they came here. He loved the long coastal walks and the boat trips out to the nearby islands. He was determined to make a movie in the area someday as the scenery was so unique to him as a London city boy. It meant a lot to Fern that Max and Otto loved spending time in her home place and they tried to get home for a two-week stretch each year if their schedules aligned.

The summers were lovely if you got good weather, although it wasn't uncommon to experience four seasons in one day regardless of the month. But the winters were hard. As an only child, Fern got used to her own company from a young age. She spent many hours looking out the window at the wild sea – but she loved writing and drawing while her parents lost themselves in their own art.

They also travelled a lot, the three of them, as her mother was regularly invited to exhibit in art exhibitions abroad. Her parents had many friends in the artistic field and they visited them in their homes in many European capitals. Equally, people paid good money to come to their house to paint the West Mayo landscape under her mother's instruction. Her father also ran workshops in bogwood sculpturing. The workshops paid for them to travel and, by the time Fern left for London, she was well-travelled and independent.

Bringing the last of the groceries from the car into the kitchen, she put water in the kettle and switched it on. She had stopped at the big Eurospar in Belmullet and filled a trolly with the basics of food for a day or two, some wine and snacks, and some children's comic books for Millie.

I just need to change the sheets in the bedrooms, she thought, as she gazed out the window waiting for the kettle to boil.

"This view," she said, aloud. "It's like an oil painting today."

Her eyes followed the green grass of the back garden down to the stone wall that divided the garden from the sea, which was a beautiful turquoise colour today. That same sea could also be a dull grey, matching the fog that often sat over the bay for hours, lowering her mood. But not today. The sky was clear and the sun was out and the sea was beautiful.

If only I could paint like my mam, she thought as the kettle noisily came to the boil.

After making her tea, she looked around. Everything was spotless. Her mother Angela always got a cleaner in to clean the house when she was leaving it for a while as she liked to come back to a clean house after her travels.

She smiled as she put the groceries away. The girls would be back together again. How long had it been since the three of them were together, she wondered.

Nora and Millie had come to visit her in London two years ago and she had met Clo for lunch a few times when Clo travelled to London to buy stock for her shop. But the three of them all together? It must have been Nora's wedding – which was six years ago now. Fern sighed as she placed her mug in the sink. Poor Nora, we never did get the full story there, she thought. That girl really deserves to find some happiness.

She wondered who else would turn up, as some white clouds moved slowly across the sky. She was sure people would come out of the woodwork for the funeral of Danny O'Connor. Her chest hurt when she thought of him. He would always have a special place in her heart.

How different our lives could have been if … A tear rolled down her cheek. I must keep it together, she thought as she rinsed her mug out and wiped the tear away.

Clo was debating whether to call in to her parents' house to say hello before going to Fern's or put it off until later. She shook her head as she watched the coffee pour into her keep cup at a service station on the N5 motorway. She knew the answer: she had to call in to her parents first. The worst thing about coming home to a small town was someone else telling your mother they saw you before your mother got to see you. Her mother's voice rang in her ears, remembering making that mistake when she came home from college one Christmas. "*The whole town knew you were home before I did!*" Of course, that was because she had been avoiding going home like she was doing today, but it had to be done.

In fairness, she was the only daughter they did see. Her sister Angie escaped to nursing college in Dublin and fled to Australia where she married an Australian policeman and was very settled there. Deirdre, her younger sister, met some lad on a vegan yoga retreat and they both now worked in a holistic centre in the Orkney Islands, so she rarely came home either.

Being raised in a home where their parents barely spoke and showed no love for each other was suffocating. Coming back through the door after school drained every bit of joy. When she was very young she thought everyone's family was like that. In fact, when she visited other girls' houses she thought their parents must be putting on an act, pretending to like each other. But as she got older she realised that it was her house that was unusual and other homes were normal. Her parents' dislike for each other felt like a dark cloud over the house and it sucked the life out of both of them. The three daughters couldn't wait to leave.

She had wondered on more than one occasion if growing up in that house was one of the reasons for her ongoing affair with Rory and that somewhere in her subconscious there was a fear of committing herself one hundred percent to one man for life, after seeing how miserable that made her parents. She was definitely commitment-phobic when it came to relationships.

In college, she often had a few men on the go at the same time. Although he was reluctant, Clo convinced Rory to agree to an open relationship while they were in college. She knew he deserved better but he always came back to her.

Leaving a small town in the west of Ireland for the capital city of Dublin was exciting and being in the fashion world gave her access to parties and clubs she could have only dreamed of as a teenager. She wasn't going to let any opportunity pass her by and was very promiscuous.

It wasn't the lifestyle for Rory so they eventually went their separate ways and he moved to New York while she moved to Paris. Eventually, he met his American Beauty and settled down and she met Pierre. She hated coming home as it reminded her of her childhood, trapped in a house with no love or warmth, which had tainted her view of relationships for decades.

The beeping of the coffee machine brought her back to the present. Taking her coffee cup, she picked up a cake in a box from the petrol station selection and went up to the counter to pay.

No, I'd better go straight home, call in to the folks for a cup of tea and then head on to Fern's, she decided. I can't wait to sit in her beautiful house again and sip a glass of wine looking out onto that fabulous view and reminisce about Danny. About how things changed for their gang of five when he decided to join their little drama group. How all their lives changed because of one school play.

CHAPTER 11

Monday

"*Hello and welcome!*" Fern waved as she walked barefoot from the front door of the stone cottage to Nora's jeep, wearing a baggy purple jumpsuit with a bright-green crop top underneath.

Nora was happy to see that Fern's fashion sense hadn't changed. Her thick, curly hair was piled on top of her head, held together with a green scarf. She knew Millie would love her.

"Good to see you," Nora said, stepping forward to hug her friend. "It's been too long. Let me get Millie."

Opening the jeep door, she unbuckled the child seat and helped an excited Millie jump down onto the gravel.

"Hi there! You've grown so much since I last saw you." Fern smiled as she bent down to Millie's height.

"Can my dog come in?" asked Millie.

"Of course! She can stay here too."

Nora opened the back of the jeep and Penny jumped out. She rushed up to sniff Fern's hand and then walked over to some grass, sniffing around before picking a spot to empty her bladder.

"Okay, let's grab these bags and get you guys inside," Fern said, walking to the jeep.

"Thanks," Nora said, handing Fern a sports bag while she picked up Penny's rolled-up bed along with her food and bowls.

"I have dinner ready. Do you eat lasagne, Millie?"

"Oh yes, I love it. We had it in Italy, didn't we, Mummy?"

"Yes, we sure did."

"Italy? How exotic! Well, I hope you like this one too," Fern said, leading Millie into the house.

"Daddy's friend made it. He's Italian and he's a great cook."

Nora looked away, taking the last bag from the back of the jeep. She hadn't counted on Millie mentioning Greg so soon. She hadn't said much to Clo and Fern about the breakdown of her marriage or her arrangement with her ex-husband.

Although Clo and Fern were her best friends growing up and both had been bridesmaids at her registry-office wedding, the reality was that now they only kept in contact via their WhatsApp group and rarely had the time to see each other in person. The last time Nora saw Fern was two years before when she and Millie stayed with her and Max on a little holiday to London. And although Clo lived in Dublin, she was so busy with her travels that they usually only managed to meet for the odd coffee and lunch at Christmastime to catch up.

I should have put more thought into how much I want to disclose about Greg, she thought while unloading the jeep, but I don't want to censor Millie either. Things were much easier when she was a baby, she thought with a sigh.

Closing the jeep door, she followed Fern, Millie, and Penny into the kitchen.

"Oh, this is fabulous!" Nora let out a deep breath as she placed the bags down on the floor. The kitchen table sat alongside a floor-to-ceiling window that looked out over the bay. The boundary wall at the end of the garden had a gate that led to the water's edge. Fern's parents had a wooden sauna cabin in the garden so it was possible to go for a dip in the sea and then warm up in the sauna.

Today the temperature had reached 22 degrees and now at seven it was still in the late teens. And as they were far in the west of Ireland it would be bright until after ten.

"Why don't you put your things in your room," Fern said. "It's the second door on the right."

"I'll do that now," Nora said, feeling at home already.

She picked up the bags and headed to the bedroom. The double bed had soaps and towels folded neatly at the end of the bed and bottles of water on the bedside lockers, just like a hotel. A big window looked out onto the back garden and the sea beyond.

I just know I'm going to sleep well here, she thought.

Her small cottage in Dublin had no front garden and opened straight out onto the footpath. Out the back was a small courtyard with space for a small table, two chairs, a bar-b-que, and a small shed for her and Millie's bikes.

It had broken her heart to sell her house in Rathmines, with its beautiful gardens that she had worked on for years, but that was the deal. With her half of the sale money, she couldn't afford anything the size of her old house. Everything was so expensive, so she felt blessed when she found the small two-bedroomed cottage near the sea in Clontarf on Dublin's Northside, to start a new life as a single mum to Millie and dog-mother to Penny.

It turned out to be ideal for their needs. Millie's school was only a ten-minute walk away and the neighbours on the quiet cul-de-sac were so kind and friendly. The older neighbours in particular loved Millie and she, being a little chatterbox, loved to stop and talk to them too and tell them about her day at school.

Coming back out to the kitchen, she took out Penny's food and water bowls while Fern took the lasagne out from the oven and brought it to the table.

"This looks delicious, Fern."

"Oh, I just picked it up in the supermarket as well as some bags of salad and a loaf of garlic bread so not much cooking involved," Fern said, putting a small portion of lasagne for Millie in a bowl to cool.

"I'll just give Penny some water. Where will I put her bed and bowls so she's not in the way?"

"Anywhere you like. I'm delighted to have a dog in the house again. We can't have one in London because we both travel for work and Mam and Dad didn't get another dog for here after the last one died. I think they plan on spending more time in the house in France."

"Well for them!"

"It is indeed. They have been going there for so long now the neighbours know them very well and of course it helps in France if you speak French fluently, as they do."

Nora placed Penny's bed and bowls in a corner of the open-plan kitchen and sitting room. After filling her bowl with water, she joined Millie at the table.

"Did you wash your hands, Millie?"

"Yes, she showed me," she said, pointing at Fern.

"You don't say 'she' – it's Fern, remember?"

Fern laughed. "Don't worry, Millie, it's a funny name, Fern. I'm named after a plant!"

"Really?" Millie's eyes widened.

"Yes! Now here's your lasagne," she said, placing a small bowl down in front of Millie. "I've let it cool down a little but test it first."

Millie began to blow on her lasagne.

"And now for the grown-ups," Fern said, walking to the fridge and opening it. "I have this cold white," she said, holding up a bottle of wine, "or I can open a red. Which would you like?"

"A cold white would be gorgeous, thank you. I have done enough driving for today so I will enjoy this."

Fern opened the bottle, poured the wine and joined Nora and Millie at the table.

Then she raised her glass. "To absent friends!"

"To Danny!" replied Nora, feeling her chest ache and the tears well up. She turned away, closed her eyes, and took a sip.

Just then Penny jumped up and barked as a car pulled into the driveway.

"Oh, this must be Clo," Fern said, standing up from the table.

"This is Mummy's other friend," Nora said to Millie.

Through the front window, she could see Clo step out of a very nice two-seater BMW convertible. *Hmm*, she must be doing well, she thought as she watched Clo embrace Fern.

"Hi there!" Clo smiled as she walked into the house with a designer suitcase and matching shoulder bag. Despite having driven for over four hours, she still managed to look pristine in navy trousers, a multi-coloured silk blouse and matching high-heeled shoes. Her spikey blonde hair gave her extra height.

"Wow, you look great!" Nora said, standing up to hug her. "This is Millie – it's a while since you saw her."

"Hi, Millie!" Clo smiled and gave her a little wave. "You are so grown up! I haven't seen you since you were three but I have seen so many photos of you. You are so tall now! And you have your mummy's beautiful hair."

Millie ran her hand over her long ginger hair which matched Nora's shade perfectly.

"Do you want to drop those bags in your room or ..." asked Fern, holding up the bottle of wine.

"Oh no, they can wait!" Clo said with a laugh. "I'm dying for a glass of wine."

She put her suitcase and shoulder bag over by the wall. Bending down, she patted Penny on the head and kicked off her high heels before taking a seat at the table.

"Oh thank you so much, I need this," she said as Fern handed her a large glass of wine. She took a big sip. "That's better! It's so good to see you guys and I had forgotten how beautiful this house is."

Clo looked around at the exposed grey-brick kitchen-living-room. The forest-green presses were lightened by the stainless-steel appliances and warmed by the copper lighting. A multi-coloured rug in front of the fireplace brought colour to the stone floor. Light flooded in from the huge kitchen window and the skylights up overhead.

Clo looked up at the skylight. "Remember when we used to lie on the floor in the studio in the dark and look at the stars?"

"You can do that if you feel like it," Fern said, putting a plate in front of her. "There is no street lighting outside our house, so you can still see the stars very clearly out here."

"This house is a breath of fresh air compared to the dark dreary house I've just left," said Clo.

"And how are your parents?" Nora asked.

Clo shrugged. "Just as miserable as ever, no change there."

She had stayed long enough for a cup of tea and for her mother to complain about the cost of the cake she had brought. Her dad joined them at the kitchen table and when he finished his tea he sat back by the fire, picked up his newspaper, and didn't say another word to anyone.

"Finished, Mummy!" Millie smiled with a pasta sauce ring around her lips.

"Good girl," Nora said, wiping the sauce from her face with a napkin.

"Would you like some ice cream?" Fern asked.

Millie nodded excitedly.

"Right – come with me."

Millie got down from her chair as Fern got up and opened the freezer.

"Now you choose," Fern said.

Millie chose an orange split.

"Can I eat it on the swing?" she said, pointing to the egg chair on the terrace.

"Oh yes, of course, but it's not a swing. Let me show you."

To Nora's surprise, the floor-to-ceiling window was actually a sliding door. Fern slid it open easily and took Millie's hand as they walked over to the egg chair.

"Let me lift you up. There now. It's not a swing but you can sway on it." Fern gave it a little push and Millie giggled.

"Thanks," Nora said as Fern walked back in.

"She's adorable. She's the image of you."

"I suppose she is."

"Thank you so much for inviting me here," Clo said. "I could not have spent a night in that house. I get the creeps when I walk into it. I hate it there. You'd want to see the charity-shop ornaments that my mam has on every surface, the crochet toilet-roll holders and of course the picture of the Sacred Heart over the fireplace staring down at me. That picture used to frighten the life out of me as a kid. Nothing has changed since I left, even the bloody tea towels! I mean who keeps tea towels for thirty years!"

Nora laughed at Clo's horrified face.

"Seriously, though, it's like a time warp over there. They sit in the same seats and eat at the same time every day. They go nowhere so they have no news and nothing to say. They are in their early seventies but it's like they have been living like eighty-year-olds for the past twenty years. I don't know how either of them can stand it. So thanks again, Fern. It would have been very difficult for me to come up with a reason not to stay there as I'm here on my own."

"No problem. I'm delighted to have you both. When was the last time we had a sleepover?"

They smiled at each other.

"Oh god, it was that last summer, wasn't it?" said Clo.

"Before you moved to Dublin," Fern said to Clo.

"And before you went to London," said Nora to Fern.

Fern winced at the memory.

"Danny burnt the sausages and we ended up throwing them at each other," said Clo.

Nora laughed and then started to cry.

"Oh, I'm sorry," said Clo.

"It's fine," said Nora. "I just can't believe he's gone."

"I know, honey. And from something so simple as a bad fall. He must have fallen from a height," Clo said, reaching out to squeeze her friend's arm. "It's shocking how these things can happen. Pierre had a friend who came off his bike when it went over a bump in the road and he died instantly. He was only thirty-five. No doubt this week will be difficult and it is going to throw up all kinds of memories, good and bad, but we're here to support each other if anything ... you know, unexpected comes up."

"You don't think it will, do you?" asked Fern anxiously.

"I ... I don't know. Hopefully not. I guess it depends on who shows up," Clo said, picking up the bottle of wine and refilling everyone's glasses.

CHAPTER 12

Tuesday

NORA

Nora opened her eyes and stretched her arms over her head. The navy-velvet curtains in the backroom Fern had prepared for herself and Millie blocked out all natural light, aiding a deep, deep sleep.

Checking her phone, she was shocked to see it was eight thirty already. Normally, in Dublin, she woke at six. The house was dead quiet so most likely everyone else was still asleep, she reckoned. It had been a lovely evening. Fern had made everyone feel welcome and it was like their old schooldays again, sitting around her kitchen table, except this time they had exchanged mugs of tea for glasses of wine.

After dinner, they had all taken Penny for a walk on Elly Bay beach, returning when a light drizzle fell. The change in weather wasn't unusual for the Mullet Peninsula. The clouds could hang over the peninsula for days, covering everything in a light drizzle when it was clear and sunny in Belmullet just fifteen minutes away.

Millie was tired from the journey so Nora headed to bed with her when they returned from the walk.

I'd better get moving, Nora thought. She had things to do today. She was due at the school at ten to meet Mary Comerford from the school board and Pavel, the school gardener, to discuss the planting in preparation for the memorial service. Nora had already drawn up plans but she hadn't been to the school grounds in many years so she had based her drawings on Google map images of the school and grounds.

She had asked her mother about Pavel during their last phone call and it seemed everyone knew him around the town and he was widely liked. He worked on many gardens in the area and her mother said he was a dote to deal with, whatever that meant. According to Nora's mother, they had come to Mayo as a family but his wife returned to look after her elderly parents and decided to stay in Poland. The marriage didn't survive the distance and she had remarried over there. But his son, having grown up in Mayo, wanted to stay and that's what they agreed.

"He's as Mayo as any young lad around here," her mother explained, "and a fine football player too."

Nora shifted her weight as quietly as she could to the edge of the bed, so as not to wake Millie who was still asleep beside her. I'll take Penny for a quick walk and then drop the two of them to Mam's, she decided.

Pulling on her work gear of green combat trousers with padded knees and a matching khaki T-shirt which she'd left on a chair beside her, she tiptoed to the ensuite where she quickly splashed her face with cold water and applied some deodorant and sunblock. Then she left the bedroom, closing the door gently behind her. She planned on having a shower in the afternoon. If the school board were happy with her plans, she could make a start today and would need a good scrub afterwards before they all headed out to Danny's wake.

Danny's wake. She felt sick when she thought about the night ahead.

As she walked into the kitchen, Penny raised her sleepy head from her dog basket and yawned as she stretched her long body before getting up and walking over to Nora.

Nora picked up her lead and some doggie bags and headed for the double porch that held coats, hoodies, shoes and boots. Pulling on the trainers that she'd left in the porch the previous night, she grabbed a hoody and headed out the door.

Stepping outside, she stopped for a moment, taking in the beauty of the morning. To her left, the tide was out and the sun was up, shining along the sand. To her right, green fields with detached one-storey bungalows lined the winding road that ran from Belmullet down the peninsula to the Blacksod lighthouse. Closing her eyes she took a deep breath. The scent of the warm sand and grasses was different to the scent of the beach near her in Dublin.

Sometimes you have to go away to appreciate what you've had all your life, she thought as Penny bounded down the garden and onto the beach.

When Nora returned to the house Millie was sitting up at the table and Fern was buttering some toast for her.

"Hi, guys!" Nora kicked off her sandy shoes and left them in the porch.

"Mummy, Fern has yellow jam! Yellow jam!"

"I hope it's okay?" Fern asked.

"Of course and thank you. I didn't expect you to make breakfast for her – she was fast asleep when I left."

"It's just a bit of toast and juice. And I'm sure you'll be spoiled by your Granny Margaret, Millie," Fern said as she poured some orange juice into a colourful glass.

Millie beamed as two slices of hot buttered toast topped with lemon curd were put down in front of her.

"*Yum*," she said as she took a big bite.

"Are you sure I can leave Penny here while I'm out? I don't know how long I'll be."

"Of course. She's such a dote and I miss having a dog around the place."

Penny walked over to Fern as if she knew she was talking about her and rubbed her head against Fern's thigh. "Aren't you a beautiful girl," she said, scratching Penny behind her ears. "Sit down and have a bit of breakfast. Help yourself." She nodded to the worktop where different breads and cereals were laid out. "There's tea in the pot but I'm out of coffee, I'm afraid."

"Tea is grand."

"I can't believe we don't have coffee in the house, even the instant stuff, but there's plenty of places in town open early now if you need a caffeine hit."

Nora poured herself a mug of tea and, picking up a side plate, took a slice of brown soda bread, buttered it and then topped it with a sliced banana to give her some fuel for the day.

"Who'd have thought when we were growing up that there would be early-morning coffee shops in Belmullet?" she said, sitting down beside Millie.

"I know. I had a cappuccino in the Bike Café yesterday and it was gorgeous."

"I'll give that a go after I drop Madam off."

"Millie might like to visit the library too. It's in the Arts Centre, Áras Inis Gluaire – have you been?"

"No," answered Nora, "but my mam was raving about it. She has been to so many exhibitions and shows there."

"It's a beautiful building. My mam had an exhibition there last year."

Millie finished her juice and was licking bits of curd off her fingers.

"Go wash those hands, missus," said Nora, "and brush your teeth and then we'll get ready to go."

"Okay," Millie said, sliding off the seat and running to the bathroom, sticky fingers aloft over her head.

"She's gorgeous, Nora," Fern said sitting down at the table with a mug of tea. "She had herself dressed and everything."

"I like her to be independent."

"She's a great chatterbox too and so articulate."

Nora felt her chest tighten. Millie was a chatterbox but there were things her friends didn't know about her break-up with Greg and she wasn't sure if she wanted them to know now. She didn't see Fern or

Clo often enough to tell them everything. Yes, they had kept in touch via WhatsApp with photos and short notes but WhatsApp was not the place to discuss your marriage break-up. But now they would be sharing a house for a week some questions were bound to come up.

I'd better get my story straight, she thought, finishing her breakfast and washing it down with the last of her tea.

"So, any idea what this gardener is like?" she said as she went to wash out her mug at the sink..

"No, I haven't met him," said Fern, "but my mother was raving about him."

"Mine too!"

"Maybe he's an old Lothario getting all the OAPs excited around here."

Nora laughed, wiping her hands on a tea towel. "Well, I'll find out shortly. I'm meeting him at ten."

"Oh, do keep us informed and try and take a sneaky photo!"

"I will not! But, look, I'll be in town for the morning so do you want me to bring anything home for dinner later?"

"I think I have enough here. I have cold meats and cheeses here for lunch and god knows how late we'll be out after the wake."

Nora shook her head. "Jeez, it's going to be tough."

"I know. God help his family. I don't plan on spending much time at the house."

"How old are his kids now?" Nora asked.

"The oldest boy is doing his Leaving Cert, god love him, so he must be eighteen or nineteen," said Fern. "The other lad is near in age –

seventeen, I think, like Irish twins – and then the girl ... fourteen, maybe? Actually, will you check the names and ages with your mam when you see her? We don't want to get that wrong."

"I will, good thinking," Nora said, biting her bottom lip. Going into the family home of Danny O'Connor and having to speak with his wife and kids was not going to be easy. "They must be in shock, the kids. It was so sudden – so hard to believe he's gone." She felt a shiver down her spine so she turned away, putting her mug back in the press to distract herself from thinking about it.

"I was thinking we could go together, the three of us, in my car," Fern said. "There'll be drink at the house no doubt and then everyone will be in the pubs later so, if I have a drink, I can just leave the car in town and we can get a taxi home."

"Yeah, good idea. Sure we've enough cars here to go back in the morning to collect yours, if we have to. I'll have something to eat at lunchtime at my mam's and when I come back here later I'll give Penny a short walk before we head off. Millie is staying with my mam for the next two nights anyway so I don't have to organise anything for her."

"Okay, that's a plan then, we'll meet back here later and go in my car. I'll ask Clo if Rory is back and we'll meet up with him. I think she keeps in touch with him, doesn't she?"

"I have no idea, but I'd say she has his number," Nora said with a shrug. "I seem to remember her saying that she met him in New York for lunch or something, but that was years ago. Right, I better get moving. Millie, let's go!"

Nora checked that she had everything she needed. She had packed a separate bag for Millie's sleepovers with her mam and had a work bag in the jeep too with her plans for the school grounds.

Mam, coffee, school, she said to herself, patting her combat pockets and checking that her keys were there. She was glad to be out and about today as the thought of Danny O'Connor's removal tonight was making her nauseous.

CHAPTER 13

CLO

Clo heard voices chatting from her bedroom but she was too busy replying to Rory's messages to get up out of bed yet. He was home in Drum, just a five-minute drive from Fern's house. He'd sent her photos of his childhood bedroom that, unlike Clo's, had been taken over by his younger sister after he left Ireland for New York. Even though his sister had married and moved out, the bedroom remained pink. Pink walls, pink carpet, and pink duvet covers.

I may be a changed man after a week in this room, Rory had messaged.

You are like Ken in Barbie's bedroom, replied Clo with a laughing emoji.

He replied by striking a topless pose with puckered lips, and adding: **I'm not sure I would have such fond memories of our first time if it had been painted this colour. The first time for both of us right here in this same bed. That's some memory**.

Clo replied with a pink heart. That time was over thirty years ago. He wasn't her first but she told him he was and there was no point in bursting his bubble now.

So let's meet up later, he messaged. **Where do you think is best – a busy coffee shop in town? Just two old friends catching up. Or I could meet you at Blacksod lighthouse for a walk where nobody will see us?**

Hmm. Clo had to think about that. **The lighthouse. It would look more like we bumped into each other there than arranging to meet for a coffee.**

Yes, boss! Say 11 o'clock?

Yes, I might cycle.

Cycle? That's some distance to cycle.

I'm a fit girl!

Oh, I know you are. I'm just thinking about how fit you are right now ...

Cheeky! Gotta go, I'll see you at 11.

Clo smiled and put the phone back in her bag. She carried two phones, and this one was just for Rory.

Pulling back the duvet, she swung her legs out of bed and walked across to open the curtains.

"How beautiful is this?"

Her floor-to-ceiling window looked out over the sea.

Her parents' house was so cramped and dark in comparison. It was a collection of small rooms that made Clo feel claustrophobic. Most people would have knocked down walls or built an extension to let more light in, but not her parents. The place was as dark as their mood. Her father had planted trees around the house so nobody could see in from the road but this meant as the trees rapidly grew the house got even darker.

Clo was blue in the face telling them to cut the trees down. But they wouldn't even talk about it. This meant her mother had the light on in the kitchen all day long. They didn't have anything like Fern's view but, still, they could have done so much to make it a relaxing bright place to live in, if only they could have been bothered. The felt wallpaper of her youth was still on the walls despite some yellow staining from the little sun that snuck in through the glass panel over the front door.

Yuk, enough of that, thought Clo as her tummy rumbled. Time for breakfast.

"Good morning," she said as she wandered out barefoot to the kitchen in her nightwear of silky shorts and a matching camisole top.

"Morning, love, did you sleep okay?" Fern was opening and closing the kitchen presses to see if they needed anything in town.

"Like a log," Clo said, reaching her arms over her head as she stretched.

"Nora and Millie were up and out. Millie is staying with her Granny Margaret for two nights and Nora has to meet the Polish gardener at the school. Toast?"

"No, thanks. I don't eat bread, try not to anyway."

Sleeping with both Pierre and Rory made her more conscious of not going over what she considered the right weight for her. She watched what she ate, worked out regularly and liked to wear tight clothes to show off her hard work.

"Just coffee and fruit for me in the mornings."

"Ah, I'm afraid we have no coffee. I presumed my mam would have some in the house so I didn't get any but I'll pick some up today. But there are berries in the fridge and bananas on the worktop if that's any use."

"Never fear – I have my own coffee supply." Clo smiled as she walked back into her room and returned with what looked like a small picnic cooler bag.

"You brought your own? *Wow!*" Fern watched as Clo opened the bag and took out a French press and two different types of ground coffee.

"Problem sorted!" she said, walking over to fill the kettle.

"Good for you!"

"Well, I do live with a Frenchman and, as I visit New York a lot and I hate American coffee, I made up this little coffee travel bag. Honestly, I take it everywhere with me. Will you join me?"

"I'd love to," Fern said, looking at her watch, "but my dad's car is making a funny sound so I have to drive it into Belmullet this morning to have it looked at in Paddy Storm's garage. Do you remember him from school?"

"Oh yeah! The heavy fella, not so bright?"

"Clo! Well, while he might not have done well in exams, he's no eejit – he owns three garages now and does very well for himself."

Clo put down the bag of coffee she was holding and turned to Fern who was leaning against the Aga.

"Well, good for him. God, this week is going to be full of memories and meeting people we haven't seen in years, isn't it?"

"Yes, it is. I'd say we'll see most of them tonight. It will be so strange though. Most of them thought we were oddballs in school."

"I know ..." Clo looked out the kitchen window into the distance.

"Oh, do you know if Rory is back?"

Clo felt a flush of heat through her body at the mention of his name. The kettle clicked so she busied herself opening drawers, looking for a spoon for her ground coffee.

"Here!" Fern handed her one drying on the draining board.

"Rory? Yes. He's home. He messaged me when he got here."

"Oh great! I don't have his number so will you ask him if he wants a lift later?"

"Later?" Clo felt flustered.

"I'm driving past his place to go into town so I thought we could all go together, you know. Get the gang back together again. I can drive us in and if I have a few drinks I'll leave the car there and we can get a taxi home."

"I ... I have no idea what he's up to." Clo stirred the coffee as she poured boiling water in.

"Oh well, can you ask him, for me? We'll leave here about five."

"Sure. I'll ask him."

"It would be great to go together"

"Yes, it would," Clo said, turning around and placing her French press on the table. "It would be lovely to see him."

"Okay, I'll leave you to do that. I have to go now to catch Paddy so help yourself to anything. There's lunch things in the fridge so go ahead if I'm not back by lunchtime."

"Will it take that long?"

"I don't know, but I have a few things to do in town so I might grab a sandwich there and come back here after Paddy's finished with the car."

"Okay."

"There're spare house keys hanging up in the press here to let yourself in, if you go out," Fern said, opening a cupboard door. "But Penny is walked so she's happy relaxing here."

"When did Nora say she'd be back?"

"She's having lunch in her mam's so sometime this afternoon, I'd say. Right, I'd better get a move on. Make yourself at home."

Fern picked up her handbag from the back of a kitchen chair and headed out the door.

Hearing the car pull out of the driveway, Clo went back to her room. Taking her extra phone from her bag she sent Rory a quick message.

Change of plan. I have a free house.

I see ... he replied. **I'll be there in 15.**

Clo smiled and threw the phone back into her bag. I should probably change, she thought, looking at her reflection in the full-length mirror in her room, with her short silk pyjama two-piece and her messed-up pixie hair. No, I'm perfect just as I am, she decided as she padded back out to finish her coffee.

CHAPTER 14

NORA

"Flat white, please – to go."

Nora looked around the Bike Café, the cute new coffee shop on American Street that Fern had recommended. It had a coffee cart inside the building with a few tables and chairs both inside and outside on the footpath. The display of pastries looked delicious, making her regret eating so much in Fern's. Looking out the window, she noticed all the new shopfronts that weren't there when she was a child. So much had changed even in the last few years.

The pandemic brought dining outside as the council allowed businesses to place tables and chairs outside their properties, to help them survive this difficult period. Tables and chairs outside added to the atmosphere in the town over the summer months and offered people a place to sit and watch the world go by. Many of the shops had brightly coloured exteriors, giving the street a lift, and the planting at Cartar Square was in full bloom and bursting with colour. Nora could see how the wooden flower boxes and newly painted benches around the square would be appealing to visitors and locals alike.

Dropping Millie in to her mother had been seamless. Margaret and Ralf had engulfed Millie in hugs and kisses when she arrived and Millie was delighted with the attention. Their house was a dormer bungalow off the main road out of Belmullet.

"I have lots of plans for us today," her mother had said to Millie. "We'll go into town so I can show you off and we can see if we can spot Donald the Cat."

Donald, a ginger cat, belonged to the whole town. He marched around the town like the King of Belmullet.

"And then this afternoon," Margaret continued, "you can come with me to the seniors' club in the Community Centre and help me give out the tea and biscuits to the older people."

"And can I have biscuits too?" Millie asked, her eyes widening

"Yes, of course! Sure aren't you the helper today?"

She won't miss me, thought Nora as Millie gave her a quick goodbye.

"I'll be back for lunch, Mam."

"Great, see you then," her mother said over her shoulder as she headed into the house.

Millie had always been an easy child and she loved meeting and chatting to new people which was the complete opposite of the child Nora had been. Not for the first time she recognised that Millie got that trait from her father.

"There you go!" the barista said, placing the flat white on the counter.

"Oh, thank you."

Nora picked up the coffee and headed back to her jeep which was parked outside the café. She had walked out onto the road to get into the driver's seat when someone beeped their horn. She almost dropped her coffee with the fright.

The driver pulled up beside her and shouted through his open window.

"*Bloody hell! Watch where you're walking!*"

Before she could shout a reply, he skidded away.

"*What an asshole!*" she shouted after him. "*No need to be so aggressive!*"

And the way he sped off, she thought, looking after him, he's the bloody danger on the road not me!

Hopping into her jeep, she placed her coffee in the coffee-holder and pulled out of her parking spot. She grinned when she saw that the asshole was stopped at the roundabout as a slow tractor went around it. She drove right up behind him.

"So, asshole, you were rushing just to get stopped by a tractor. *Ha!* Serves you right!"

Seeing him looking at her in the rear-view mirror, she stuck out her tongue and then laughed at her own childishness. She could see him shake his head and, as soon as the tractor passed, he revved his Landrover before racing off.

What an idiot, sighed Nora as she drove ahead and then indicated to turn down the road that led to the school.

"*Oh no!*"

Her face dropped when she saw the Landrover asshole indicate ahead of her and turn into the school. Then the penny dropped: *He must be Pavel!*

Nora made sure to park her jeep as far away as she could from his in the car park.

Okay, maybe this isn't him, she thought, looking at him as he got out of his jeep.

She had expected him to be older. Didn't Fern say he was entertaining the OAP's of the area? She presumed he'd be in his sixties, but this guy certainly wasn't.

Nora picked up her coffee and took a gulp of it before putting it back and getting out of her jeep. Shutting the door, she saw Pavel walk towards her.

"Ah," he said with a serious face, "you must be Nora?"

"Yes," she sighed, looking up at him, "and I'm guessing that you must be Pavel?"

"Do you usually stick your tongue out at other drivers?" he said, standing there with his hands on his hips.

"Only the assholes who shout at women," Nora replied, irritated by him again.

Pavel looked taken aback and opened his mouth to reply...

"*Oh, there you are!*" A smiling woman – in her early sixties, Nora guessed – wearing navy Capri pants, white trainers and a long cardigan came walking across the car park towards them, her glasses swinging from a chain around her neck.

"I'm Mary Comerford," she said, putting her hand out to Nora. "It's just great to see the two of you."

"*Humph,*" Pavel replied, crossing his arms across his chest.

"Hello, Mary, I'm delighted to meet you," Nora said, stepping forward to shake her hand.

"Likewise – and you've met Pavel?"

"Yes, I have," Nora answered, putting her hands in her pockets to avoid shaking hands with him.

"Thank you so much for doing this," Mary said to both of them. "Let's go inside and discuss the plans."

Nora nodded and followed Mary into the school without looking at Pavel.

"This all looks lovely," Mary said, looking at the drawings Nora had laid out on the table. "I love the different coloured grasses for the driveway and the heather bed at the front door of the school with the garden seat – that's a lovely idea Nora. It looks so welcoming. What do you think, Pavel?"

"The design looks good on paper and a hawthorn is a good choice for the memorial tree. They do well in windy places ... but these grasses you suggest for the driveway," he said, leaning in and running his finger over Fern's drawings, "they won't last a winter out here so they are completely impractical. They might work for a Dublin garden but not for here."

"I see," Nora said in a calm voice. "These grasses have been chosen particularly for hardy weather." She looked him straight in the eye. "Something I would know about, having lived here most of my life."

"I ... I did not know that," he said, holding her gaze.

"Well, I'm happy with how everything looks," Mary said, sensing the discomfort in the room, "and the board has approved the funding, so I have a set of keys for you, Nora." She took them from her cardigan pocket and put them on the table. "And Pavel has his own."

Nora picked up the keys and rolled up her drawings. "Right, well, we can get started right away, I have some plants in the jeep."

"Today?" said Pavel, looking surprised.

"Yes. Is that a problem?" asked Nora.

"It's just that I have another job on."

Nora shrugged. "Fine. Go. I can get started here."

"I thought today was just a meeting," he said, looking at Mary.

"Oh, I'll leave you two to sort that one out," Mary said, standing up.

"I can get started by myself," Nora said as she stood up, deliberately not looking at him. If Pavel wasn't committed to the project then that was fine with her. She could have done with a bit of help with the digging out of the ground for the heather bed but she wasn't going to let him see that. "I was also hoping to get a bit of work done before the funeral tomorrow. I'll be here from six to nine ... if you're free?"

"I'll be here," he said, standing up and walking with her to the door.

She stood back to let him pass. "See you then," she said as she looked up at him.

"I was told that this was just an introductory meeting," he said, looking down at her, his face softening.

"It's fine, I can manage," she said, holding his gaze.

He opened his mouth as if to say something but Nora turned away quickly. I don't have time for this, she thought, before walking back into the office to go over her plans.

Nora stayed at the school, measuring out the space for the heather bed and the new grass plants, marking them with horticultural line-marking spray paint.

I'll take pleasure in getting Pavel to dig out all those holes, she thought as she stood back to check everything was even. Her rumbling tummy let her know it was lunchtime. Her family home, like many others in rural communities, had the main meal of the day at lunchtime and she was really looking forward to her mother's home cooking.

After locking up the school, she drove the ten-minute distance through the town and out the main road, turning up Tallagh Hill to her mother's house.

Turning into the driveway, she gasped.

"I ... I don't believe it."

Parked there was a familiar jeep.

What on earth is *he* doing here, she wondered as she got out.

She walked around the back of the house. And there he was. He was replanting shrubs, it looked like.

She stopped for a second, staring. Pavel had removed his red-and-black check shirt and had tied it around his waist.

"Nora?"

Nora was mortified to be caught looking at him.

"Following me now?" he said, grinning.

"No! No, I'm not actually."

"*Mummy!*"

Before Nora could say anything else Millie ran out of the back door. She knelt down as Millie ran into her arms.

"Oh, there you are! I see you've met Pavel." Margaret came out the kitchen door.

"Yes, yes, I have."

Nora took Millie's hand and headed over to her mother.

"What is *he* doing here?" she whispered.

"He's doing the garden for me – what does it look like?"

"I could have done that. You didn't need to ..."

"*Arrah*, you are never here and Pavel is a neighbour. He does a great job. Come on, your dinner is ready." Margaret wiped her hands on her apron. "Pavel, dinner is ready."

"Thanks, Margaret," he said, standing up and stretching out his back.

"He's staying for dinner?" Nora whispered to her mother.

"Yes. What is *wrong* with you?" her mother asked. "Go wash your hands."

Nora couldn't believe she now had to sit down and eat with this man.

"Come on, Mummy!" Millie said, pulling her hand. "Time to wash our hands."

CHAPTER 15

"Hi, how did you get on?" Clo asked Fern when she returned to the house.

"Well, not too bad. The rattle is the brake callipers whatever they are, and he has to get a replacement part, but he patched it up and said it should be fine for short journeys. Tea?"

"That's good news about the car anyway and, thanks, tea would be great." Clo was sitting on the couch in the open-plan kitchen-cum-living-room with the back sliding door open. A light sea breeze eased its way around the house, keeping it cool.

"Were you out for a walk? You look flushed," Fern said, filling the kettle and switching it on.

"No, I just did a bit of a workout here actually," she said, turning her face away so Fern couldn't see she was lying, "but I'm going to make a sandwich and then take a long walk."

"Did you not get some lunch?"

"No. Rory Darcy called in so I didn't get a chance."

"Rory?" Fern said, turning around. "How is he?"

"He's great. Doing very well in New York and he was delighted when I suggested we pick him up."

"Oh good."

"Yes, I think he was happy to go tonight as a group and then hang out later."

"How did he look?"

"Oh, very well actually." Clo blushed, thinking of his naked body on top of hers only an hour ago.

Fern made a pot of tea. "Help yourself to anything that's in the fridge." She placed the teapot on the table. "You go to New York a lot – do you ever meet up with him there?"

"Rory? *Em* ..." Clo wasn't sure what to say. She had told them that she hadn't kept in touch with him but she couldn't remember if she told Rory to say the same thing. I'd better double-check with him, she thought, feeling a little panicked. Just then, she heard Nora's jeep pull into the driveway. "Ah, here's Nora!" she said, delighted at the distraction.

We really must get our story straight, she thought as she buried her head in the fridge. They didn't do much talking when he was here. The possibility of someone coming home unexpectedly fuelled their passion. As soon as she opened the door to him, he picked her up and said, "Which room is yours?" before carrying her in the direction she pointed. Clo felt her whole body tingle just thinking about it.

"Hey, Nora," said Fern. "I've just made a fresh pot of ... Is everything okay?"

Nora threw her car keys down on the table and let out a long sigh.

"The bloody gardener!" Pulling out a chair at the kitchen table, she plonked herself down.

Fern grabbed another mug and poured the tea. "What happened?"

Nora recounted the whole story, right from the coffee-shop incident.

"It sounds like you both got off on the wrong foot," Clo said, plating up some cheese and opening packs of Serrano ham.

"It gets worse! When he said he couldn't work today because he had another job I never expected it to be at my own mother's house. And she loves him! She gave out to me for being rude."

Fern laughed. "Sorry, but that's so funny. And you had to eat dinner with him?"

"Yes, and I had to sit there while my mother hung on his every word. He may have charmed the old dears around here, but he's an arrogant asshole."

"And ... is he as good-looking as my mother says he is?" Fern asked with a grin.

"Well ... I suppose ... in a rugged lumberjack kind of way ..."

Clo laughed and slapped her hand on the table. "He sounds exactly your type!"

"*Ha, ha*, very funny. Anyway, I'll have to go in early tomorrow and do a few hours before the funeral."

"How early?" asked Clo.

Nora grinned. "I told him six."

"Oh, you are a hard taskmaster!"

"It was worth it to see his face. So what's happening here? Any news?"

"The car needs a replacement bit but it's fine to drive short distances so we are picking up Rory at five and we'll all go to the house together."

"Rory? He's here?"

"Yes, he called over earlier," Clo said, stirring her tea.

"How is he?" Nora asked.

"Good. He didn't say too much, so we'll have loads to catch up on tonight."

"Great. I must try to keep in touch with him. I always liked Rory," Nora said.

"Did you say on WhatsApp that you had lunch with him last year in New York or was that the year before?" Fern asked, turning to Clo.

"*Hmm*, I can't remember ..." Picking up her fork, Clo pushed the food around her plate, avoiding their eyes. Oh god, I better check my WhatsApp messages to remind myself of whatever story I've told them. "Oh yes, I remember now. It was ages ago. I messaged Rory when I had a free afternoon and he happened to be in the area and we had a lovely lunch in Central Park. But have either of you heard from Kevin?" She needed to get away from this line of questioning.

"*Ooh*, that's a definite no from me," Nora answered.

"And me," said Fern with a shrug. "As far as I know he severed all ties with everyone around here. After his family moved to Waterford, he left for Australia. My mam said even his parents haven't been back as far as she knows."

"They were a strange family," said Nora, "and they moved around a lot, so Belmullet was never really home to him, I suppose. When did he come to our school?"

"Just before we did the Junior Cert so, yeah, I guess they were only here for three summers," Fern said sadly.

"But you guys ..." Nora began.

"I know. He was my first boyfriend," Fern said, looking into her mug of tea.

"Remember, I kept calling him Keanu!" Clo said, smiling. "It drove him mad! Or at least he pretended it did. Loads of lads around here would have loved to be the spit of Keanu Reeves."

"And he really did look very like him," said Nora. "Dark, brooding and mysterious."

"I never really knew what was going on in that head of his. And the way he left ..." Fern frowned.

"Hey," Clo said, reaching across and placing her hand on Fern's arm, "put all that business out of your head, okay? We have to walk into that house tonight united and we will."

"I know, sorry," Fern said. "It's just we'll be seeing all the old school pals tonight. It just brings back memories and poor Danny ..."

"Yeah, I'm dreading walking into that house," Nora said, staring out the window.

"Okay, enough of this. It is what it is and isn't it great that we all travelled here to honour him?" Clo stood and picked up her mug. "Who's coming for a walk with me? We have an hour and a half before we have to leave so I'm going for a 40-minute walk."

"I'll join you," Nora said. "Penny could do with another runaround."

"Me too," said Fern.

"Great! And guys," Clo said looking at both of them, "we can do this. It's going to be hard tonight but we have each other."

She opened her arms and they both walked over for a group hug.

"Right, let's go!" Clo said.

Fern was so glad that the girls were here. Memories of Danny occupied her mind constantly. Small things like airing the studio upstairs brought back the memory of their first kiss, the first time Danny O'Connor leaned over and gently placed his hand on the side of her face and kissed her. The memory was so vivid it hurt.

CHAPTER 16

April 1995

The rehearsals for the play were going very well. Clo, Rory, and Danny got together in Fern's house a few nights a week to rehearse. They also had rehearsals in the school hall with the younger third-year students who would be extras playing footballers from each team and spectators. They were young and giddy but willing to be involved so Fern learned quickly how to motivate and direct them.

Danny turned out to be a great actor and good fun too.

"He's a dark horse, isn't he?" Clo said one night when they were tidying up.

"You mean his acting?" Fern asked.

"Well, everything really. He's taken to this like a duck to water. But he's really nice and I'm surprised, that's all. I always thought he was a dickhead because of those goons he hangs around with but he's not like them at all."

"*Hmm* ..." Fern agreed but said nothing.

"And I think he has a soft spot for you."

"*Shhh* ..." Fern said, looking over her shoulder to where Danny and Rory were sitting.

"Oh my god, you're blushing now!" Clo leaned towards Fern and whispered, "Do you fancy him?"

"Will you stop!" Fern said, getting flustered, avoiding Clo's eye.

"Well, I think you should go for it," Clo said.

"Don't be silly, he doesn't fancy me. I'm not his type at all and you know it."

"Maybe in the past, yeah, but we're seeing a different side to Danny here and I've seen him look at you. Go for it, girl! Even have a fling. He's certainly more exciting than Keanu Kevin."

Fern laughed at this.

"And, besides, half the town wants to ride Danny O'Connor so get in there," said Clo.

Fern picked up a tea towel and threw it at Clo and the two of them burst out laughing.

"What's so funny?" asked Rory.

"Nothing!" the two girls answered at the same time.

"Come on, Rory," Clo said. "These two need to practise the last scene and we're not in it so let's go."

The final scene saw the two main characters embracing at a window after they'd run away together to London.

"Fair enough," Rory said, doing exactly what Clo said, as usual.

After they left, Fern and Danny went back upstairs to the studio. They sat on the floor drinking cans of Fanta orange, with the script out in front of them.

"You are a great actor, Danny – would you not think of doing more of this?"

"Do you really think I'm good?"

"Yes, for someone who's never done this before, you're a natural, seriously."

Danny sighed and looked away. "I'd love to have the freedom to decide what I want to do."

"What do you mean?"

He turned back to look at her. "My dad."

"Oh right. Could you talk to him?"

"No. I tried that. I wanted to take a year out, a gap year to go travelling, to try different things, but he wouldn't hear of it. He wants me to work in the family business as soon as possible. He wasn't happy about me taking a summer job in Uisce either but I can't wait to hang out with the students, helping them with the water sports. He wanted me to start in the quarry straight after school. I mean, Jesus! I know I'm lucky to walk into a job and I know he wants me to take over the business one day but I just feel trapped. Don't tell anyone I said that."

"I won't. But, Danny, you should have a choice in what you want to do."

"You'd think that, wouldn't you? All I get is 'Do you not know how lucky you are?' and I do, but I don't think it's for me. It should be Audrey anyway. She is the one with the brains and she's dying to work in the business. She's working there this summer. It's not fair on her. She'd love to take over the business but Dad is so old-fashioned and narrow-minded, he wants his eldest son to do it. He gets pissed off when I'm not kissing his feet in thanks."

"And what about your mother?"

"She's a snob. She loves all the 'local politician's wife' stuff so she doesn't understand why I'd want to get away for a year and try something different. I want to figure out who I am away from this place and decide what I want to do with my life but that's not going to happen."

Fern's heart broke for him and she thanked her lucky stars that her parents were open-minded and creative.

"You're so lucky with your parents," he said as if reading her mind.

Fern nodded.

"Anyway, enough of that," he said, turning to her. "You and I will have a great summer in Uisce."

"Yes, I can't believe we're both working there. You'll be sick of looking at me."

"No, I won't. That's the part I'm looking forward to, actually."

Danny held her gaze as he said that and they both sat looking at each other.

"So ... what's the story with you and Kevin?" he asked.

"There is no story, we broke up. Why do you ask?" Fern felt butterflies in her stomach.

"It's just that he's been giving me dagger looks for weeks."

"Ah, ignore him. He got the hump when I let you be in the play. Some of your football pals gave him a hard time when he moved here first so he has a bit of a grudge, I suppose."

"I never said a bad word to him."

"Maybe, but you were there."

Danny blushed and looked away.

"Forget about him," Fern said.

"Have you ... forgotten about him?"

Fern looked at Danny and her stomach did a summersault.

"Yes, we are so over."

Danny smiled and reached across to stroke the back of her hand with his finger.

"So, how would you feel about giving this play its proper ending."

Fern blushed and smiled nervously.

"The first day I came here, you read the play and the two heroes kissed at the end, but then you changed it to a hug. How would you feel about doing the original ending?"

Say no, say no, say no, Fern said to herself. He was still running his fingers up and down her hand. She wanted to kiss him so bad!

"I think that's a great idea," she whispered.

CHAPTER 17

"Well, that's some crowd!"

Rory leaned forward in the passenger seat as Fern drove down Tallagh Road, passing the long line of people queuing up at Danny's house to pay their respects at the wake. Clo and Nora strained to see the crowd from the back seat.

"I'm going to have to park down the road a bit," Fern said, passing the entrance to Danny's house.

She parked the car outside a neighbour's house, they all got out and walked back.

"The line will move quickly," Fern said. "Most people just want to pass through as quickly as possible."

"I'm surprised there are so many people here this early." Nora said quietly.

"Well, everyone knows his dad," said Clo, "so there'll be politicians and councillors here too."

When they reached the end of the queue, they were near the gates to the driveway so they could see people coming out. Danny and Rossa's house was within walking distance of Danny's family home on Tallagh

Hill. Their modern detached dormer bungalow was in an elevated position with views of the town and out over the Bay.

Clo walked beside Fern. She had been avoiding eye contact with Rory ever since they picked him up. She had sat behind him in the car so he wouldn't be tempted to turn around and look at her.

"A lot of lads from the Gaelic Football Club too," Fern said.

"I think he was a coach there," Rory added. "I still can't believe it. To go just like that."

"I know," said Fern "from a head injury?"

"It happens," Rory said shaking his head. "I'm sure they did a postmortem. It must have been just the way he fell."

The line of people moved along.

"So what's the plan here?" said Rory as they approached the house. "Do you guys plan on spending time here or –"

"Well, I'm a quick in-and-out person," Clo interrupted. "So as soon as I see Rossa and the kids I'd prefer to go to the pub for a drink rather that have any refreshments or drinks here."

"Me too," said Nora. "Are you all going to go in to see him laid out?"

"I don't think we can avoid it, Nora. This is why we're here," said Fern.

"I'm dreading this part," Clo said.

"How about I go in first?" Rory suggested, as they shuffled along the queue.

"Oh, would you please?" Fern said, putting a hand on Rory's arm.

"Of course." He turned around to them. "Just follow me when we get in there and I'll move along quickly. We can then commiserate with Rossa and the family and leave then."

The first person they met from the bereaved family was Danny's uncle who was welcoming people at the front door.

"You are very welcome," he said, shaking their hands. "Rory, I haven't seen you since your father's funeral last year. How's your mother?"

"She's doing well, Jack, thanks for asking. How's everyone here?"

"Ah well, still in shock as you can imagine. We're all staying strong for the kids and Rossa and this turnout is incredible. The community really comes together at a time like this. Danny is in there," he pointed to the open living-room door, "and you can walk through to the kitchen from there to where the refreshments are."

Nora looked over his shoulder, down the hall to the other entrance to the kitchen behind him.

"There are tables and chairs out in the back garden too." He directed them on their way – his job was to keep things moving.

Rory walked into the room first.

"Oh god," Nora whispered as she clutched her stomach. "I don't think I can do this. I think I'll skip this and go down the hall to the kitchen."

"This will only take a minute," Clo whispered. "I'm shuffling past the coffin and not looking in at all. You can just keep your head down and keep moving."

Nora hesitated. She felt nauseous.

Rory led the way, walking along the side of the coffin. He paused, looked, blessed himself, and walked on. Clo followed close behind him, averting her eyes.

Fern walked ahead of Nora, stopping at the door to look around the room. The modern house was a carbon copy of many other houses she had been in around here. The living room and dining room were separated by sliding doors that were open today. To the left, the front room was narrow but long and a big window looking out onto the garden let the evening sunlight in. A very large TV hung over the fireplace in the living room and a big L-shaped couch was against the opposite wall. Fern imagined Danny lying out on it watching movies with his kids. The walls were covered with photos of foreign holidays and smiling faces on summer days. Kids playing in the sand, ice-cream cones and swimming-pool pictures, images of happy family holidays.

To the right, the dining room was taken up with a long table. The big mirror in the room was covered with a sheet which was the tradition. The table was home to many happy family meals, she imagined, but today that table held the coffin of a husband, a father, and a lover. A shiver ran over her body and she felt the hairs on her arms stand on edge as she forced herself to look into the coffin.

And there he was. Feeling a sharp pain in her chest, her eyes began to fill up.

Oh, Danny, she said to herself. He looked perfect, just like he was sleeping. She almost expected him to smile and open his eyes and say '*Gotcha!*'

How could he be gone when he looked like he was just sleeping? An image of the young Danny holding her face in his hands, gently caressing it, came to mind. She felt dizzy and hot. Since she had heard the news, images of that summer kept replaying in her head.

By inviting the girls to stay with her, she had hoped it would distract her from her thoughts. There was no way she could stay in the house alone with thoughts of that summer replaying in her head. Keeping busy had only gone some way in distracting her. She couldn't show it, but her stomach had been so nauseous walking up his driveway that she almost vomited.

She wanted to reach out and stroke his face but that would not be appropriate. *My beautiful, beautiful Danny. My life changed that summer – all because of you, Danny O'Connor.*

She wiped a tear away and, pulling herself together, straightened up, bracing herself for the next hurdle. Danny's wife and kids were in the kitchen. She could see Rory and Clo shaking hands with them. She took one last look at him before blessing herself and moving on.

Just as she took a step forward she heard a sharp intake of breath behind her, followed by a wailing sound.

Turning around, she saw Nora with both hands on the coffin. Her body was shaking and tears were flowing down her face.

Startled, Fern put an arm around her friend.

"*Oh Danny!*" Nora said between sobs.

"It's okay, Nora, it's okay."

Nora turned her head towards Fern and sobbed on her shoulder.

People behind them strained to see who was so upset. Rory and Clo turned around and stared from the kitchen.

"We have to move on, love," Fern whispered.

Nora's feet felt like cement. She didn't want to leave the coffin. This would be the last time she would see his face. But she had to move, people were queuing behind her.

Fern gently turned Nora toward the kitchen and, an arm around her, led her out of the room.

So as not to upset Danny's wife and kids, head down she led Nora past them, out through the back door to a bench at the end of the garden. People turned to have a gawk at the still sobbing Nora but Fern ignored them.

"Let's sit here. It's quieter down this end," she said, helping Nora onto the bench.

"*Oh god!*" Nora pulled out a packet of tissues from the pocket of the blue-and-white check shirt she was wearing. Her shoulders were shaking. Strands from her ginger hair, which was held up in a loose bun, stuck to the wetness of her cheeks.

After wiping her tears away and blowing her nose, she placed her two hands on her knees and closing her eyes took a deep breath.

"That's it," Fern said, rubbing her back.

"Poor Danny," Nora whispered, "it's not fair." She shook her head. "I'm so embarrassed. I shouldn't have gone in to see him. I hope Rossa and the kids didn't see me making a show of myself like that."

"Ah now, everyone cries at these things," Fern said, glad in one way that she had been distracted from feeling like a little part of her heart was broken too.

"But I should have kept it together. That was careless of me."

"Careless? What do you mean?"

Nora didn't answer, just stared up at the sky.

"Are you okay?" Clo asked as she and Rory walked up the garden to them.

"Eh ... yes," replied Nora, snapping out of her trance. "I just got overwhelmed in there."

"Yeah, well, it was a shock to all of us seeing him in there." Rory shook his head. "He just looked like he was sleeping."

"Yes," Clo and Fern answered at the same time.

"Okay, can we go? I need a drink," Clo said, rubbing her arms and feeling a shiver up her spine.

"Can we leave by the side gate?" Nora asked, nodding to the side entrance of the garden. "I don't want to see Rossa and the kids. I'm ... you know ... a bit shook."

"Of course," said Rory. "They saw the two of you were here and that's the main thing. Let's go."

When they came out the side gate, they saw the queue of people waiting to pass through the house had become longer. Clo said hello to a friend from school and Fern nodded to a few neighbours she recognised, while linking Nora who seemed to be in a daze.

Walking ahead, Rory stopped to talk to some old school friends.

"See ye in McDonnell's," he said to them as he left them to join the girls again.

"Who was that?" asked Clo

"Tommy McGill."

"Little Tommy McGill?"

"Yes," said Rory. "Little Tommy McGill is married with four kids now."

"Jesus, I feel ancient," said Clo.

"But you look fabulous," Rory said.

Clo's eyes widened in alarm before she managed to control her reaction.

Fern looked at Clo's face. Was she blushing?

"You all do, you all look fabulous," Rory added, trying to cover up his slip-up. He walked on but turned back to say, "I'd say everyone will head to McDonnell's pub after a few drinks at the house. And I'd say there'll be a few familiar faces from school back for the funeral too."

"Are you okay, Nora?" Clo moved to the other side of Nora. She had felt Fern look directly at her after Rory's loose comment.

"Yes, I'm just so ... sad. I need a drink."

"We all do," Clo said, linking Nora's other arm.

They walked on.

Then Clo said, "And guess what? Danny's sister Audrey got back in time."

"Was she there?" asked Fern. "I didn't see her."

"No, she was having a lie-down. Apparently she was at the house earlier but, with the jet lag and all, she decided to go back to the hotel."

"The hotel?"

"Yeah, she's staying in the Talbot, Rossa said."

"Why would she not stay in her own house, with her mam and dad?"

"No idea," shrugged Clo.

"But it's strange, isn't it?" said Fern. "There's her mam and dad up there in that five-bedroomed house and instead of staying there she is very publicly staying in a hotel right on the main street."

"I suppose it is," said Nora.

"She couldn't be making any more of a public statement that, even at the worst time in her parents' life, their only daughter won't spend a night under their roof."

CHAPTER 18

Donnell's pub on Main Street was quiet when they arrived. Having left quickly with Nora, they were ahead of the crowd. Most of the locals working in town were only just finishing work and would make their way to Danny O'Connor's house before possibly coming to the pub.

Rory was already at the bar and waved them over.

"What can I get you all?" he said, leaning one elbow on the bar while summoning Padraic the barman.

"I'll have a bottle of Coors," Fern answered.

"I'll have a pint of Bud, thanks," Nora said.

"G&T for you?" he said, looking at Clo.

"No, I'll have a white wine, please," Clo said, staring at Rory. "Pinot if they have it."

"Okay, we'll find some seats," Fern said as she ushered Nora to the back of the pub.

"Will you stop?" hissed Clo at Rory.

"Stop what?"

"You look fabulous? And ordering my usual?"

"Oh sorry, a force of habit," Rory said, tilting his head. "Look, what have you told them – about us?"

"Nothing. I mean, I told you earlier that our story is that we met up for lunch once when I was in New York."

Rory leaned in. "All I remember from earlier is you answering the door in that short silky two-piece. Your nipples were so erect they nearly burst out of that top."

Clo's jaw dropped and then she laughed, looking around her.

"Will you stop it!" She slapped his arm playfully. "We need to play it cool."

Padraic returned with the drinks order. "That'll be twenty-two euros."

Rory handed over some cash before turning back to Clo.

"Look, it's the funeral tomorrow – nobody will be looking at us. I'm going for a run in the morning if you fancy bumping into me?"

"*Hmm* ... how early?"

"Say eight thirty at the lighthouse," said Rory.

"You're on," Clo replied, picking up her glass of wine and walking off to join the others. "Oh, and do not sit beside me," she added, turning back to Rory with a serious look.

"Yes, boss," Rory said, placing the drinks on a tray and following her to the back of the pub.

"They're very cosy," Fern said as she watched Clo and Rory.

"Who?" Nora said, looking up. "Oh, those two – well, they were childhood sweethearts."

"*Hmm* ..." Even from this distance, thought Fern, you could see the sexual chemistry between them.

"Maybe it's being back here and all of us together again," Nora said, watching Rory and Clo approach. "You know, old memories and all that."

"Yes, that's probably it," said Fern.

"Here we go, ladies!" Rory said as he put the tray down on the table and pulled out a stool beside Fern.

"This is a great spot," Clo said, sitting down on the cubicle couch beside Nora. "We can see everyone coming in the door from here."

"I saw a few neighbours at the house but I haven't seen many from our old class yet," said Fern, pouring her bottled beer into a glass.

"Not everyone does the house bit and some might be travelling to get here still," Rory said, raising his pint of Guinness. "To Danny!"

"*To Danny!*" The others raised their drinks and took the first sip.

"Are you okay?" Rory asked Nora.

"Yes, I ... I just ..." Nora stopped and shook her head.

"It's not easy," Clo said and held up her glass. "We'll have a few more of these to ease the pain."

"I'll drink to that!" Nora said, taking a gulp of her pint.

"I was telling the girls about Audrey," Clo said to Rory.

"Oh yeah, she's staying in the Talbot," he said. "I don't think I'd recognise her if she stood in front of me."

"She was only two years behind us in school," said Fern, "but she was very quiet, not like Danny at all."

"Did any of you hear anything about a falling-out?" asked Clo. "Something must have happened for her not to stay with her parents."

"Yeah, it looks odd all right," said Rory. "I'm sure we'll find out by the end of this week, small town and all that."

The pub started to fill up and after a while there wasn't a free seat to be had.

Locals nodded or waved from the bar and a few came over to say hello to them. Some old faces from school appeared and came over to chat, some having travelled to Belmullet for just the one night before returning to their lives elsewhere after the funeral.

"I heard from the bar that there's still a ton of people up at the house," Rory said as he carried a tray with another round of drinks to the table.

"Who's your man, the big fella in the check shirt?" asked Clo. "He keeps looking down here but I don't recognise him."

As they all looked up to see who Clo was talking about, he nodded at them.

"Oh god," said Nora, looking away. "That's Pavel."

"The gardener? Jesus, you didn't tell us he was *that* good-looking! He's a total ride!" Clo said. She didn't notice Rory looking sharply at her remark, his eyebrows raised, but Fern did.

"Don't stare at him, Clo!" Nora sighed. "Oh god, he's coming over!"

Pavel was making his way through the crowd, nodding to people on the way.

"Jesus, everyone knows him!" said Clo, looking him up and down in approval as he approached.

"Nora," he said with a nod.

"Hi, Pavel." Nora forced a half smile to be civil. "Pavel, this is Rory, Fern and Clo. Everybody, this is, Pavel. We're working together on the school grounds."

"Lovely to meet you," said Clo, taking in his broad shoulders and the big rough hand cradling his pint of Guinness.

"I'm sorry for your friend," Pavel said. "I knew Danny well from the football club. He was a good man."

"Yes, it was a shock to all of us," said Rory.

"Do you want to join us?" Clo asked, making room for him on the couch.

Nora shot her a look.

"No, but thank you. I have to be in work early in the morning," he said, looking directly at Nora. "Nice to have met you," he said to everyone before turning and walking back down the bar.

"He seems nice," Fern said.

"*Hmm*, very nice," Clo said, oblivious to Rory's jaw tightening. "I can see why he's popular around here."

"Clo, please!" Nora said, exasperated. "I have to work with the guy."

"Well, he seems friendly," said Fern, "and from what my mother says, he's very good at his job, so maybe you'll get on better with him tomorrow."

"Yeah, maybe." Nora watched Pavel finish his pint and leave the pub. "I'll be back in a minute."

She stood up and inched her way down the pub, pushing through the crowd to the front door.

It was still bright outside. Squinting in the brightness, she looked up and down the road.

"Pavel!" she called, running up to him as he was about to get into his jeep.

"Nora?"

"I ... I just wanted to apologise," she said, pushing a loose strand of hair back over her ear. "I wasn't very friendly back there. It's just been a long day."

He tilted his head. "No need to apologise. I think we got off on the wrong feet."

Nora laughed.

He smiled. "I mean wrong *foot*."

His face completely changes when he smiles, thought Nora, looking up at him.

"Fresh start tomorrow?" he asked.

"Yes, tomorrow."

"Okay," he said, opening his jeep door and sitting in.

Nora nodded and then gave a half-wave as he drove off before making her way back into the pub to her table.

Her friends were staring up at two people standing in front of them. They all looked shocked, like they had seen a ghost.

"Hello, Nora."

The familiar voice sent a shiver through her.

"K–Kevin?"

CHAPTER 19

"Oh my goodness, Kevin! Hi!" Nora leaned in to hug him but he remained stiff and didn't respond.

He hadn't changed much. He always looked like a young Keanu Reeves and now he looked like an older Keanu Reeves. He was dressed in black jeans and a black T-shirt. His black hair was shoulder-length now and his short beard was speckled with some grey hair. His skin was tanned from his years in Australia. He looked well, very well, but his blue eyes held no emotion.

"I was wondering if you'd make it back," she said. "Are you still living in Australia?"

"Yes," he said, looking down at her. "As far away from here as possible."

"Oh ..."

An awkwardness hung in the air between them.

"Hi, Nora."

Nora leaned forward to see the woman standing beside Kevin.

"It's Audrey," the tall, thin, blonde woman said as she leaned forward and put her hand out. She looked tanned too and very polished in black trousers and a black silk blouse.

"Oh god, I'm sorry, Audrey ... I would never have recognised you ... and I'm so sorry for your loss," Nora said, shaking her hand. "Did you travel together from Australia?"

"Yes, we did," Audrey leaned in to Kevin, slipping her arm through his.

He turned, smiled and kissed her on her forehead.

It was only then that the penny dropped. "Oh sorry," mumbled Nora. "I'm so out of the loop I had no idea ..."

Fern looked shocked and Rory looked down at his pint.

"Well, nobody had any idea," said Kevin. "We kept it quiet. We'd planned on coming back and surprising Danny. I would have loved to see the look on his face ... but ... we can't do that now, can we?"

What a strange thing to say, thought Fern.

"It must have been a terrible shock," Clo said to Audrey.

Audrey nodded and then pulled at Kevin's arm. "Can we leave?"

"Yes, of course," Kevin said, patting her arm.

"Good to see you," Nora said.

"Really?" Kevin said, turning to look at Nora and then at the rest of the gang. "No contact from any of you for nearly thirty years and it's good to see me?"

Nora opened her mouth to reply but he just turned around and left.

"*Well, well, well*," said Clo, staring after them.

"I need another drink after that," said Fern, "but not here. How about we go back to mine and open a bottle?"

"Good idea – it's getting very packed in here now," Nora said. She was exhausted from all the drama tonight.

"I can drive," Rory said. "I've only been drinking Guinness Zero as I'm up early tomorrow for a run."

"Oh, that would be great, thanks," said Fern.

They all stood up and hurriedly left the pub together.

"I'm trying to get my head around Kevin and Audrey," Clo said on the drive back to Fern's house. "I mean, it just doesn't add up. He despised Danny, so why on earth would he date his sister?"

"And the way he said they wanted to surprise Danny. It's almost as if he wanted to rub his face in it," said Fern.

"Yes, that's exactly what I thought," Rory said. "Something off about his whole vibe."

"But why?" said Nora from the backseat. "I know he hated Danny when we were in school but that was 30 years ago."

"Well, we never knew the full story there, did we?" Clo said. "Why Kevin hated him so much? But it seems very strange that he would have anything to do with the O'Connor family. Unless he has some other agenda."

They were still speculating about the matter when they reached the house.

"Okay, I'll leave you ladies to figure it all out," Rory said as he parked. "I'll walk home from here and I'll see you all tomorrow."

"And I'm shattered, girls, I'm going to have a shower and go to bed," said Nora, stepping out from the back seat.

"I'm going for a short walk. I need to clear my head," Clo said. "I'll be back in twenty minutes," she said over her shoulder to Fern.

"Sure," Fern replied, putting the key in the door.

"It's nice to see that they're still friends after all these years, isn't it?" Nora said.

"Yes, it is," Fern answered as she watched Clo walk down the driveway with Rory. "They seem very close indeed."

CHAPTER 20

Wednesday

Nora woke at three. She had tossed and turned all night, images of Danny rushing through her mind.

They don't know, she said to herself as she lay looking at the ceiling. Nobody knows that Danny and I were meant for each other – soul mates, destined to be together.

Lying back in bed, she remembered the first time she felt that special connection. It was at his 7th birthday party at his house. Even though their mams weren't close, they lived on the same road, Tallagh Hill. Danny's house was much bigger than anyone else's and they had a separate double garage out the back that her dad was very envious of.

Back then birthdays were celebrated within your family. Your grandparents and maybe a cousin if they lived nearby might come over for a birthday tea with homemade fairy cakes and a homemade birthday cake. But Danny's mam invited all the neighbours' kids around the same age in for a party tea.

Nora remembered thinking his house was enormous and she got lost once or twice looking for the bathroom. And the birthday spread! She had never seen so many cakes in her life for one birthday.

They had been playing a game of What Time Is It, Mr. Wolf? and when Nora fell and cut her knee it was Danny who had sat with her while his mother went off to get a plaster. He held her hand because she was crying and stayed with her until she felt better. Nora knew from that moment that she was his special friend.

But it was hard growing up having a crush on Danny O'Connor. So many other girls wanted to be his girlfriend and Nora spent many a football club disco watching him asking other girls up to dance and kissing them during the slow set. After a while, she stopped going to the dances every month as she was too upset afterwards.

Although she had been asked up to dance by other boys and had kissed her fair share of them, she wasn't interested in them and told herself that she was just practising for Danny.

Even though he never noticed her at those dances, they often walked home together after school and that's where she got to know the real Danny. And she knew he liked her. He laughed at her jokes and there was never a lull in conversation. She decided, in her own head, to let him have his fun with the other girls so he could get it out of his system.

Later, she used to come home from college in Dublin twice a month, knowing that she'd bump into him around the town or in the pub. He always stopped to talk to her or buy her a drink.

She heard on the grapevine that he was dating a girl called Rossa but didn't think it was serious since he never mentioned her in conversation.

All she knew was that Rossa was from Wexford but nobody knew much about her or her people. Apparently Danny met her while in college in Galway and didn't bring her home to Belmullet too often.

So it was a huge shock to Nora when he told her casually on the street that they had got engaged. She was devastated and, much to her embarrassment, she burst into tears in front of him. He looked so shocked by her reaction that it was clear to her in that moment that he had never felt about her like she felt about him. She stopped going home after that.

Oh god, I have to stop torturing myself, she said to herself now, pulling the quilt up over her head to try and get back to sleep.

When Nora next woke up it was bright outside. She leaned over to check her phone then sat straight up and jumped out of bed.

"*Shit! Shit! Shit!*"

It was 6: 45. She had arranged to meet Pavel at the school at 6.

"Oh crap, how did this happen?" One look at her phone told her that she had set the alarm time for 5 but forgot to switch the alarm on.

Pulling on her gardening trousers and a fresh T-shirt, she rushed out of the house, grabbing everything she needed on the way.

Oh, he's going to love this, she thought as she pulled out of the driveway.

Arriving at the school, she could see his jeep. She pulled down the visor, fixed her hair in a high ponytail and popped two Polo mints in her mouth as she didn't have time to brush her teeth.

Walking around the back of the school, she could see that Pavel had started digging out the marks she had made the day before. He stopped when he heard her approach and smiled, leaning on his shovel. He looked good today, she noticed, standing there in navy gardening trousers tucked into work boots, and a navy-and-white check shirt with a white vest top underneath. His sleeves were rolled up, revealing his tanned arms.

"I'm late," Nora said with a shrug.

"I can see that," he said with a big grin on his face.

Nora smiled back and shook her head. "You're enjoying this, aren't you?"

"Maybe a little," he grinned. "But, come on, we are a team so I won't say anything to anyone."

Nora laughed. "Fair enough."

"Have you had a coffee?"

"No," said Nora, picking up a shovel, "but don't worry about me."

Pavel put down his shovel and walked over to one of the school benches where his backpack and jacket were. Opening his backpack he took out a big flask and started to open it.

"Come!" He gestured to her with a nod.

"No, I'm fine."

"Come," he said again.

She realised that he would not be taking no for an answer, so she just did what he said.

"It's black, okay?" Pavel twisted the lid off and took two mugs wrapped in a tea towel from his bag. He poured a mug-full for Nora and handed it to her.

"You like your coffee strong," she said. "Thank you – it's just what I need."

She wrapped her hands around the mug and inhaled the coffee scent before taking a sip.

"Lovely," she said.

Pavel poured himself a cup and sat down.

"Sit," he said, patting the space beside him.

She wanted to say 'I'm not a bloody dog' but as she was the one who was late, she kept her mouth shut and sat beside him.

They sat and sipped, taking in the quiet of the early morning.

The town was still asleep. There was a distant sound of a tractor and cows somewhere in a field. Nora turned to Pavel to say something but he was sitting with his eyes closed, his face turned to the sun, so she did the same. Taking a sip of her coffee, she closed her eyes, feeling the sun on her eyelids and felt at peace.

The sound of a dog barking made her open her eyes and, when she did, she turned to see Pavel looking at her. She was mortified to feel herself blushing. She blushed so easily and hated herself for it. Turning away, she drank the rest of her coffee quickly.

"Okay, well, thank you for this," she said, standing up, shaking the excess drops from her mug. "We better get a move on. I see you've started on the digging. I put the heather plants in the shed so I'll get them out. I'd love to get that bed finished first as it's the biggest job. I have a delivery coming tomorrow with the rest of the plants and the garden seat. So, let's try and get the heather plants in today, yeah?"

"Yes, boss," he said as he stood up.

She held out her mug to him and, as he took it from her, their hands touched. Nora pulled her hand away immediately as if she'd had an electric shock. She looked up at Pavel whose surprised face told her he felt something too.

CHAPTER 21

The sound of a door slamming woke Fern with a start.

That must be Nora, she thought. Pushing herself up in the bed to sit, she put the spare pillow beside her behind her head. She felt terrible.

Oh god, I feel so groggy, she thought, rubbing her temples with her middle fingers. You'd swear I'd had loads to drink last night. Then she remembered the wine. She had ended up drinking the whole bottle of wine herself last night as everyone else had gone to bed.

"*Oh crap!*" She let out a long sigh before leaning over to grab the bottle of sparkling water on the side locker.

God, I need this, she said to herself as she twisted the cap open and gulped it down.

Nora had gone straight to her room when they got home.

Clo walked Rory part of the way home and returned flushed, saying she ran back. Fern had opened a nice bottle of red but Clo cried off saying she was getting up for a run in the morning.

She's fooling no one, thought Fern. There is definitely something going on between those two. Maybe they are reliving their youth? What do I care anyway? It's none of my business. Rory is a free agent and Clo ... well, who knows?

Although Clo and Pierre were together for about twenty years now, Fern had only met him a handful of times: at her own wedding in London, Nora's wedding, and once when they came to London with Sophia. Fern had invited them for dinner. Max and Pierre got on very well and Sophia must have been eight and Otto ten, so still young enough to play with each other without being embarrassed.

Clo and Pierre had never married. She was scarred by her parent's loveless marriage and swore from a young age that she would never get married and be tied to someone like her mother was. Even when she went out with Rory in their teens, she kissed other boys. If Rory didn't go to the local disco with her, she'd find someone else to snog. She had no interest in those other boys – she just did it because she could. She always went back to Rory and he always forgave her.

And yet when he asked her to follow him to America, she refused. She had already made plans to move to Paris without him. She could be so cold sometimes. He wanted her with him but she wanted something else, something more exciting. Clo always did what she wanted and Fern loved and admired her for that, but there was no doubt that some people got hurt along the way.

Fern was delighted when she heard that Rory had met a lovely American girl and got married. He was so sweet and deserved to be loved unconditionally by someone. But now, he was divorced, and Clo seemed to be closer to him than she was letting on. She definitely had commitment issues and kept her private life private.

But who knows what goes on in other people's marriages, anyway, thought Fern. And maybe even the best marriages have secrets. But we could have had that conversation last night, if Clo hadn't gone to bed. Not wanting to waste the wine, Fern had taken the bottle and one of her mother's Celtic ceramic goblets outside to the egg chair. As the sun set late in the west, it was still bright but a little chilly, so she had fetched a colourful blanket to wrap up in. Curling her feet under her, she sat back in the chair and poured herself a drink.

Didn't anyone want to stay up and talk about Kevin showing up like that, she wondered. He hasn't returned to Belmullet in thirty years and then shows up with Audrey. How long had they been a couple?

She understood that Kevin hated the football team in school. Some of them were idiots – but they were teenagers. He could have just ignored them – after all, he had no plans on staying in the area, so why care so much?

But his hatred of Danny was irrational. It was like an obsession. She had grown tired of his whinging any time Danny's name came up and was relieved when their relationship, if you could even call it that, fizzled out.

At first, his moody ways made him seem exotic but it could also be exhausting. He was interesting and clever but eventually Fern realised that he wasn't much fun. She'd thought he was the boy she would give her virginity to before going to college but he ruled himself out of that with his attitude to Danny joining the drama group and she was relieved not to date him anymore.

But could he really hold a grudge for thirty years? Did he really have feelings for Audrey or was it some weird, twisted revenge on Danny, and if so revenge for what? As these questions ran through Fern's head she refilled her wine goblet until the bottle was empty.

I'm paying for finishing that whole bottle, she thought now, as a headache began to creep in. But I wish I could have discussed all these questions with the girls instead of them sloping off to bed.

But more than all of this, she needed to talk to Clo and Nora about what happened that summer. The whole reason she asked them to stay here was to have the time to confide in them. She had kept a huge secret from them, all through their adult lives, and was desperate to tell them now.

But here we are, she thought, the day of the funeral. and I still haven't found the right time to have that conversation.

And what the hell is going to come up today, she wondered. A feeling of dread came over her as she lay back down for another hour's sleep.

CHAPTER 22

Clo tapped her phone immediately when the alarm went off. It was seven thirty and she was meeting Rory at the lighthouse in an hour. He was so fit he would probably run the whole way. She was certainly not doing that. She planned to drive there and then go for a walk before meeting him.

I'm playing with fire here, she thought as she stepped into the shower. I know Fern picked up on something last night. We should probably back off a bit but ... the adrenaline that came with sneaking around was such a turn-on. Also, there was always a sense that any time could be the last time with Rory.

He had already asked her to move to New York. She'd used Sophia as an excuse to put off making that decision. She didn't want to string him along but her business in Dublin was very successful which meant she had to stay in Dublin. 'Uptown Girl,' which she ran with Pierre, was a designer-clothes rental shop.

Having graduated from the College of Art and Design in Dublin, Clo worked in fashion houses in London, Milan, eventually settling in Paris. She adored Paris and it became her home for eleven years.

It was while working for a fashion house in Paris and doing fashion consulting for a list of wealthy clients that she met Pierre. He ran a string of boutiques across Paris and she regularly purchased items from his shops for her clients. As she had a big account with his stores, he invited her out to dinner to thank her and was enchanted by her quick wit and her confidence.

Clo continued to date a variety of men as well as Pierre but, after a few months, when he asked her to date him exclusively, she agreed and moved into his beautiful apartment in the 7th arrondissement, one of the most prestigious areas of Paris, and within walking distance from the Eiffel Tower.

Through Pierre, Clo landed a job as a buyer for a top-end designer store. She loved the job and the lifestyle that went with it. Fashion parties every week, restaurant openings, access to the best of clothes – she loved it all. She also loved Pierre.

Of all the men she had dated he understood the lifestyle in the fashion business and liked a luxury lifestyle as she did. He grew up with money, so expected to have a nice lifestyle with luxury items. His upbringing was in stark contrast to the house she grew up in, so even though he asked to go to Mayo and meet her parents and see where she was from, she put him off for years, too embarrassed by her parents and their miserable existence.

She spoke little of her family but had to tell him everything when he surprised her with a proposal while on holiday in Capri. The ring he chose was exquisite. However, she had to explain that while she loved him, and only him, she could not marry him or anyone else. Her biggest fear was getting stuck in a loveless marriage and, having witnessed her parents' marriage, had decided that the best way to avoid that was never to marry. Pierre was naturally disappointed but understood, so they agreed to become engaged with no plans to ever marry, and Clo agreed to take him to Belmullet to meet her parents.

She did love Pierre but, besides having an aversion to the whole idea of marriage, history had taught her not to make promises she might not keep. Nor was she convinced he'd been entirely faithful to her. Still, in every other way they worked beautifully together, and so they let the matter lie—an unspoken agreement never to probe too deeply into each other's wanderings.

When Sophia came along they were both delighted and she really believed her world was complete.

After a good friend of Pierre's opened a restaurant in Dublin, they began to visit him there quite regularly. He lived in the wealthy suburb of Dalkey in an Italian villa-style house overlooking the Irish Sea. Despite living and studying in Dublin for three years, Clo had never visited Dalkey and fell completely in love with the seaside village.

With Sophia about to start school, they discussed moving from their central Parisian apartment to the suburbs but couldn't decide where to buy. For the sale price of their Parisian apartment, they realised that they could buy a house with beautiful sea views in Dalkey. They moved to Dalkey and never regretted it.

When they first moved and were looking for a business to start up, Clo noticed that there were no designer-clothes rental shops in Dublin like there were in Paris, so she and Pierre started looking for retail shop leases in Dublin. With help from their friends and a little research, they took the plunge and opened their first business together.

That was twelve years ago. It was an exciting time, decorating their new home, their first house together, and fitting out their new shop 'Uptown Girl' just off Dublin's fashionable Grafton Street. They worked day and night to get it ready for its grand opening and it was an instant success.

That first year exceeded their expectations. Clo struggled to keep stock in the shop such was the demand. There was an option to buy the rental items too which meant that Dublin women could get top-end previously owned designer items at much reduced prices.

Sophia settled into a local school and Clo hired a French au pair to look after her and keep her French fluent. Both Pierre and Clo worked long hours for about two years, when they made enough profit to relax a bit and hire more shop staff. This also allowed Clo to travel more.

She adored Sophia but motherhood didn't come naturally to her. She never experienced that bonding glow other mothers spoke about. Pierre, on the other hand, was besotted with Sophia from day one and the two of them were thick as thieves.

Clo loved working and having more opportunities to travel, sourcing new stock for the shop. Pierre preferred to stay in Dublin and regularly did the school run and attended school events that Clo found unbearably boring. The arrangement suited everyone.

It was on one of her trips to New York, two years after returning to Ireland, that she bumped into Rory on the street in Manhattan. They hadn't seen each other in years and caught up on old times over dinner. He had just come through an amicable divorce and, when he invited her back to his place for a nightcap, she agreed.

She felt so relaxed in Rory's company. Having spent two years working long hours, consumed by the new business, always on the go, she could just stop and be herself with him. It was the first time in two years that she had been out with someone and never once mentioned work. So when a few drinks became a bottle, she let her guard down and fell into the familiar arms of her first love and didn't leave his bed for two days.

Stepping out of the shower now, she dried herself and rubbed in some Rituals body cream before dressing casually in a pair of leggings, a bright-purple fitted T-shirt showing off her shape, and a matching pair of bright-purple walking trainers.

She was excited at the thought of seeing Rory. How long would they feel this way, she wondered. He wanted her to move to New York but she couldn't see that happening. Sometimes she felt a sense of doom about the whole thing.

She didn't want to stop seeing him – the sex was amazing every single time – but she hadn't told him that she and Pierre were opening another branch of 'Uptown Girl' which would keep her in Dublin for years to come. She had a good working relationship with Pierre and a good personal life and this was not the time to disrupt Sophia's life. She couldn't see herself moving to New York in the next two years anyway. She didn't know whether to tell Rory this. Would it change things? Could they just go on like this indefinitely? She didn't see why not, as long as both their needs were met, but not everybody saw the world as black and white as she did.

CHAPTER 23

Clo parked her car near the lighthouse in Blacksod Harbour and looked out to sea. A mist hung over the horizon, completely blocking the view of Slievemore, the second-highest mountain on neighbouring Achill Island. The tide was in and the waves crashed noisily against the harbour wall, whipping up a wind. Clo shivered, regretting not bringing a hoody.

A couple of other cars were parked on the pier. Fishermen or walkers' cars, she reckoned. Also the Blacksod Sea Safari company operated from the end of the pier, running trips over to the nearby Inishkea islands. It was very popular with tourists so some of the cars were probably there for that.

There was no such thing as a sea safari when I was growing up, thought Clo, but she had wonderful memories of herself and the gang getting a lift in a fisherman's boat to Inishkea Island and spending many a day there in the summer swimming in the freezing cold Atlantic, followed by tea from a flask and homemade sandwiches, usually cheese or ham.

They were fantastic summers, hanging out with the gang. If the weather was good they disappeared for the day, visiting different beaches in the area, swimming in the sea, and playing football on the beach. If the weather was bad, as it often was, they might take a bus to a bigger town like Ballina or Westport and hang out there for the day.

They always managed to create their own fun and plan adventures. The highlight of the week would be the Friday night céilí dances where you might get to kiss a boy down from Dublin or up from Cork on their holidays. That felt like the most exciting and exotic thing to do, well, to Clo anyway. Even though technically she was going out with Rory, if he wasn't at the dance she took her chance to kiss a new boy if she could. She always needed to feel wanted.

Clo turned around when she heard the sound of running footsteps behind her. Rory stopped beside her, his hands resting on his thighs as he slowed his breath.

"My god, you must have run fast!" she said, checking out his fit-toned body in his singlet and shorts. "You're covered in sweat. Maybe we should have met for a skinny dip instead?" She suggestively bit her lower lip while looking him up and down slowly.

"Stop it, will you!" Rory looked away from her as he stood up straight, wiping the sweat off his forehead with his arm.

"What's wrong?"

Rory put his hands on his hips and took a deep breath.

"It's you."

"Me? What do you mean?"

"How you behaved in the pub last night."

"I don't know what –"

"With the gardener," Rory interrupted her. "I didn't say anything last night but ... it's been bugging me ever since so I have to say it."

"Say what?"

"You were an embarrassment, fawning over him."

"*Excuse me?*" Clo could feel her temper rising.

"As soon as you saw him you were practically salivating over him. 'What a ride!' you said, and then moved over to offer him a seat beside you. It was as if I wasn't there. You made everything awkward for everyone."

Clo's mouth dropped open. "*I don't fucking believe this!* Are you serious?"

"Yes, I am," he said, looking directly at her. "Even if you and I weren't together, it was embarrassing for everyone, including that guy."

"That's ridiculous!"

"Really? I was sitting beside you, Clo. Even Nora told you to stop it."

"It was ... it was just banter ..." Clo was lost for words. She knew she was a flirt but he was being ridiculous.

She looked around. Cars were pulling up and parking behind them as people got out to walk down the pier. The pier was getting busy as fisherman were unloading their catch, tying up the lobster pots and packing up their vans.

"I think you are way out of order," she said, leaning in and lowering her voice so people couldn't hear their row. "I'm sorry if you felt uncomfortable but I was just being polite."

"Polite? Well, it got me thinking – are you this 'polite' with other guys when I'm not around?"

"Oh Jesus!" Clo laughed. "Are you for real?"

Rory's jaw tightened. "Are *you* for real, Clo? Is what we have something real or am I just a distraction for you, a plaything who comes running when you click your fingers?"

"Don't be ridiculous!" Clo wanted to slap his face. "What you and I have is so important to me."

Rory turned to look at her. "Well, after last night you have put doubts in my mind. You have made me question everything. Have there been other guys?"

Clo shook her head. She clenched her fists by her sides to stop herself from losing her temper.

"*Jesus Christ, Rory!*"

Another car parked up on the pier and a chattering group of tourists got out.

"Are you still sleeping with him?"

"I don't want to do this here – there are too many people around. Can we go for a drive?" Clo said, reaching out to touch his arm.

He shook her hand off his arm.

"*Are you still sleeping with him?*" he asked again.

Clo shifted from one foot to another uncomfortably. "Why are you asking these questions now? We live together for fuck sake! So, yes, we sleep together – but you knew this! You've always known this but you never asked me because you didn't want to know!" Clo could feel her blood boil. "You've been happy to ignore that fact for five years, so why now?"

"I don't know." Rory looked away out over the sea wall and then back at her. "Last night seeing you flirt and drool over that bloke ... it triggered something in me. And I can't continue with this."

"*What?*"

"You need to make a decision, Clo."

Another car pulled into the car park and Clo heard the doors open and close behind her so she lowered her voice.

"No, don't do this, Rory."

"I can't go on being your dirty secret. You need to figure out what you want."

Rory took his car keys out of his pocket and walked away.

"*Wait!*"

Rory ignored her and kept walking to his car.

"*Rory, wait!*" Clo ran after him but he sat into the driver's seat and shut the door.

She was shocked.

"*I love you! For fuck sake!*" she shouted as the tears came.

He turned on the engine and slowly drove away.

"*Rory!*" Clo shouted.

"*Mum!*"

Clo spun around.

"What the ...?"

The blood drained from her face as she saw Sophia and Pierre standing beside their family car. Their shocked faces turned from Clo to Rory's car as he drove past them out of the car park.

"Who is that?" Sophia said, her face contorted with shock as tears ran down her face. "Who was that man?"

"I ... I ..." Clo felt her throat choke up.

"Dad ..." Sophia turned to Pierre.

His stoney face stared at Clo in disgust.

"Get in the car, love," he said to Sophia.

"But, Dad!"

"Get in the car," he said, turning and placing a hand on her shoulder.

"Sophia ... I ..." Clo moved forward towards Sophia.

"Leave her!" Pierre said, his face full of anger.

Sophia sat into the passenger seat and slammed the door. Covering her face with her hands, she started sobbing.

"Pierre ..." Clo's legs felt weak, she couldn't move.

"Who was that?"

"Pierre, I need to ..."

"*A name!*"

Clo let out a deep breath. She felt dizzy.

"Rory," she whispered.

"And are you shagging him?"

"Pierre, please ..."

Pierre shook his head and took a deep breath. "We drove all the way down here late last night to surprise you and support you for your friend's funeral. Sophia was worried that you might feel alone and wanted to surprise you this morning. But it is we who have had the biggest surprise."

He turned and opened the driver's door

"Pierre, wait ... we need to talk. I need to talk to Sophia."

"No. We are leaving now. We are staying in a hotel in town. Do not show up unless you ring me first. I will take care of our daughter." And with that, he got into the car, slammed the door, and sped out of the car park.

Clo's legs went from under her and she stumbled backward to the harbour wall to support herself. Her chest tightened as images of Sophia's face flashed in front of her.

"Oh Jesus!" she said, clutching her chest.

The mist had rolled in from the sea. Clo leaned over the sea wall as the wind whipped sea water up into her face. She gasped for air, gripped the wall and then threw up.

CHAPTER 24

"That's probably enough for today," Nora said, looking at her watch.

"We did well," Pavel said, leaning one arm on a shovel while he ran his other hand through his loose curly hair, "and it looks like the weather is on the turn."

Nora looked up at the gathering clouds and then down at her mucky hands before pushing a loose strand of hair behind her ear.

"How did you manage to keep your T-shirt so white when I'm a mess?"

"You are definitely not a mess," said Pavel, smiling, as he held her gaze.

She felt her cheeks flush when he looked at her.

Turning away, she bent down to pick up her tools. "Okay, I guess we should pack up. Are you going to the funeral?"

"*Em* ... yes. As I said, I knew Danny from the football. My boy Alek was on one of the teams he coached. He liked him very much."

Nora felt lightheaded and sat down on the bench. Her stomach felt sick.

"Are you okay, you look a bit pale?" Pavel walked over to her, a look of genuine concern on his face.

"I'm okay – I just need a minute. I ... can I tell you something ... in confidence?"

"Of course." Pavel sat down beside her.

"Please don't say anything to anyone, but I feel sick about the funeral. I really don't want to go," she said, clutching her stomach as she took a few deep breaths.

"Oh?"

"I fell apart at the open casket last night and made a show of myself and I don't want to do that again. I'm afraid that when I see the coffin I'll get upset again."

"You were close, you and Danny?"

"Yes. We grew up beside each other and ... this is embarrassing but I had a crush on him, for most of my life actually."

"I see."

"So I wish I could be anywhere else but at that funeral, but I have to go."

"*Hmm.*"

"I'm sorry, I'm keeping you."

"No, no, you are not. I have an idea." Pavel rubbed his chin. He looked at his watch. "The funeral is at eleven, yes?"

"Yes."

"Well, everyone knows we are working here at the school, so how about we arrive after the coffin goes in and the family have gone into the church. And we go in our working clothes."

"Like this?" Nora said, pulling at her T-shirt marked with soil.

"Yes. Then we sign the book, people see us and then we leave early to get back to work."

"I don't know," Nora said, shaking her head. "Will it not look rude?"

"No. It will look like we are so dedicated to preparing the place for the memorial event that we came from working here and went straight back to working."

Nora took a deep breath, thinking about what he just said. "I need to go to the funeral reception afterward in the Broadhaven Hotel but that part is okay. My mother is meeting me there with Millie and that part should be fine ... it's just the coffin ... I can't bear to think of him ..."

"Hey," Pavel put his arm around her shoulder.

He smelt amazing, a mix of earthy soil and a musky shower gel.

"This is a good plan, I promise you. We will go to the church and then come back here and do a little more work, and I will stay with you."

"Really? You'd do that?" She looked up into his hazel eyes. Their heads were so close they were almost touching.

"Yes." He nodded and then smiled. "You are my boss."

Nora laughed. "Thank you."

"And now, breakfast."

"Oh, okay," Nora said, straightening up "I am hungry, starving actually. Is there somewhere open in town?"

"Yes I know a place that does great Mexican eggs," he said, standing up and picking up the shovels.

"Really? Around here?"

Pavel smiled. "Yes, my place."

"Oh. I see." Nora felt a bit flustered.

"Is that okay with you?"

"Yes," she replied, "that's perfect, thank you so much."

"Okay, let's pack up."

Nora gathered up some tools and brought them to the school shed. She had been dreading the church bit, terrified that she'd make a fool of herself in front of Rossa and the kids and the rest of Danny's family. This idea could actually work. She just needed to message Fern and tell her she wouldn't be going with her.

I can't believe I'm about to go to the house of the man who made me so mad yesterday and he is going to make me Mexican eggs for breakfast. She shook her head and smiled to herself as she followed him into the shed.

CHAPTER 25

Fern heard a car drive up the driveway and stop outside the house as she buttered some toast in the kitchen.

"That's strange," she muttered, expecting to hear a car door open and shut. Putting down her knife she went to the front door to see Clo sitting in her car. Her hands were clutching the steering wheel and she was staring straight ahead.

Something was wrong.

Fern walked slowly to the driver's window and looked in.

"Clo?"

Clo didn't move.

"Clo, are you okay?"

Clo snapped out of the trance she was in and slowly opened her door.

"No, I'm not okay," she said, slowly stepping out of the car.

"You're white as a sheet! Has something happened?"

Clo sighed. "Yes, something has happened and it's a disaster."

"Let's get you inside." Fern took her arm and led her into the house.

In the kitchen, she pulled out a chair and said, "Sit down there."

Clo let out a long sigh. "I have fucked everything up," she said, throwing her hands up in the air.

Fern sat down beside her. "Is this to do with Pierre and Sophia?"

"Yes ..." Clo said, turning to look at Fern with a confused look on her face. "How did you know?"

"They called here to the house and I said you were out. I invited them in to wait but Pierre said that they'd try down the road to the lighthouse because they hadn't passed you on the road from the town."

"Oh, how I wish they had come in and waited here!" Clo said, shaking her head.

"Why? What happened?"

"It's complicated," Clo said, avoiding Fern's eyes. "It's hard to explain."

"I see. Is it anything to do with Rory?"

"*Rory?*" Clo snapped, slapping her hand down on the table. "*Why would you say that?*"

"Look, it's none of my business but you and Rory seem ... close."

"Oh God, I feel sick. Was it that obvious?"

"Well, it was to me but maybe not to anyone else."

"Well, it's a shit-show now."

"Do you want to talk about what happened?"

"No, not right now. But I have a lot of explaining and sorting out to do. Is Nora here?"

"No. I don't know where she is and we need to get ready for the funeral."

"Oh fuck!"

"We have an hour before we have to get going but I was hoping to talk to you and Nora before that ... I ..."

Just then both their phones buzzed.

"It's Nora," said Clo, opening hers first.

Still working here, will not be back before the funeral. I'll be in work gear so I'll stand at the back of the church for a bit and then go back to the school. I'll see you both at the reception later.

"Oh, I thought we could all go together," Fern said, looking at her phone.

"I'm sorry," said Clo. "I'm not sure I can do this today."

"What? Not go at all?"

"Yes. I need to get my head together and get my story straight."

"But it's Danny's funeral, it's what we came for!"

"That was an hour ago and so much shit has hit the fan since then." Clo stood up, pushing her chair back. "Look, I'm sorry, Fern, I don't know what I'm doing. I need to sort myself out."

"Can't you even tell me what happened?"

"No, I can't until I fix everything, if that's even possible now."

"Well, that's just great!" Fern said, folding her arms, annoyed at her two friends leaving her on her own to face the funeral. "*Everybody will be there!*" she said, raising her voice.

"That's the point! Look, I can't do this now," Clo said, walking towards the bedroom.

When she reached the door she sighed loudly and turned to look back at Fern. "I'm sorry, you're right. It is what we came here for. I'll go to the funeral with you but I just need some space first. I'm going to lie down." And with that she walked into the bedroom, closing the door behind her.

"What the hell!" Fern said. She pushed her chair back and paced the kitchen.

I really wanted to talk to both of them before the funeral but now Nora is going to be late and Clo doesn't even want to go. What the hell is going on with those two?

She had asked them to stay so that they could get that old best-friends feeling back again. Only then could she confide in them the secret she had been keeping from them for thirty years.

CHAPTER 26

Fern turned into the ALDI car park in the centre of town and parked the car.

"We won't get any closer than this. Every spot will be taken."

Clo just stared out the window ahead of her. They had driven in silence.

"Are you okay?" Fern asked.

Clo snapped out of her trance. "Yes. Let's get this over with," she said, opening the door and getting out of the car.

Clo didn't want to go in. She needed to sort her life out. Back in the house she had sat on her bed, looking at her reflection in the full-length mirror. Images of Rory's accusing face, Sophia's tears, and Pierre's disgust had flashed through her mind. She had taken out her phone but her finger hovered over the call button. Which man should she call? Did Rory see Sophia and Pierre or was he too angry when he drove away? Would he even know who they were?

Pierre had asked for his name. He knew Rory was her ex, although they had never met. What was going through his mind now, after hearing her shout out that she loved Rory? She needed to ring them both but she also needed to choose which relationship meant the most to her.

Someone she loved was going to be hurt because of her decision, no matter which man she chose. In the end, she took a deep breath and pressed call, hoping he would answer her.

The morning's mist had turned into a heavy fog which had rolled in from the sea, causing a drizzle to hang over everything.

"Do you want an umbrella?" Fern asked as she pulled up the hood of her long black coat.

Clo was only wearing a light black box jacket over tailored black trousers and black flats.

"No, I'm fine, thanks." She didn't give a hoot whether it was raining or not, she just wanted to get this over with. "Let's go."

A steady flow of people walked ahead of them and they all turned down Chapel Street towards the church. Part of Clo wanted to keep walking to the Talbot Hotel and talk to Sophia, but she knew she couldn't do that yet.

"Big crowd. It looks like the whole town will be here," Fern said, looking around at the stream of people heading towards the church.

"All hail the golden boy!" Clo said snidely.

Fern opened her mouth to say something but stopped. Clo was grating on her nerves today.

Fern nodded to a few people she knew as they reached the church gate and halted as an old friend of her mother approached her.

"I'm going inside," Clo said, walking on, not waiting for a response.

"I heard you were back, Fern. How's your mother?"

"She's great, thanks."

"Isn't it well for her, soaking up the sun?"

"Yes, indeed, Mrs O'Brien," Fern said, pulling her hood forward to avoid the wind and drizzly rain. "You should get in out of this rain."

But the old woman just shrugged and turned to talk to her husband. People of her age were well used to this weather, Fern reckoned. Thirty years of living in London must be making me soft, she thought, as she felt the drizzle on her face. She moved around the crowd outside the church, saying hello to people she knew. It was customary to wait until the hearse arrived before entering the church, except for older people who usually went in to get a seat.

Out of the corner of her eye, she saw Rory arrive. She put up her hand to wave to him but he turned away quickly. How odd, she thought, he definitely saw me. He must be avoiding Clo. What the hell is going on? She always had a hold over him but surely they're not ...

Her train of thought was halted as the hearse turned into the church driveway, followed by the funeral cars.

The first car came to a halt and Rossa and the children got out. The eldest boy linked his mother while Rossa held her daughter's hand and her other son stood beside his sister. The second car door opened and Danny's parents, his sister Audrey and Kevin stepped out. They stood in a line as the hearse eased forward and came to a stop before them.

Fern stood at the side by the big crucifix on the grounds and watched Kevin as he held Audrey's hand. How did those two end up together, she wondered. It's so strange. Apart from the fact that Australia is a huge country, Kevin hated Danny so why on earth would he date his sister?

She tried to remember the brief conversation in the pub but she couldn't. All she could remember was his cold attitude to everyone who used to be his friend.

As if reading her thoughts, he turned and looked directly at her. She nodded at him and he nodded back He then stared at her for about twenty seconds, before turning his attention back to Audrey. What was going on in his head?

He hadn't changed much – a little older, like the rest of them, but he had a healthy glow from his Australian tan. He looked well but something about him made Fern feel uncomfortable. It was clear when they met him in the pub that he wasn't about to put the past behind him. But could he still hold a grudge thirty years later because the gang chose Danny over him? Surely not?

The parish priest came out to shake the hands of the family while the undertakers took the coffin from the hearse, placing it on the gurney. The priest then said a prayer over the coffin before leading everyone into the church. Fern looked around the crowd for Nora, but she couldn't see her so she followed the crowd in and found a seat beside Clo.

The service was awfully sad. People from every area of Danny's life got up and said a few words about him. A beautiful smiling photo was on top of the coffin and it was hard to believe that he was gone. His father broke down when he spoke and Danny's daughter cried throughout the ceremony.

Once or twice Fern looked around for Nora but couldn't see her. She noticed Rory sitting with his mother but he didn't look her way. Clo sat staring forward as if in a daze. Fern didn't think she heard a word that was spoken.

When it came to the Communion time, Clo leaned over and said, "I'm going. I have to meet someone."

"You're leaving now?" asked Fern, astonished. "Are you not going to the reception in the Broadhaven Bay?"

"I have no idea, I'm sorry," she said, standing up quickly and exiting the church.

Fern sighed. I never thought I'd be sitting here on my own today, she thought. We came here for Danny's funeral and neither Clo nor Nora want to be here now. This is not how I imagined things at all.

"Excuse me. Excuse me."

Clo pushed through the crowd of mourners. As she exited the church, it seemed everyone else was trying to get in. Because the church was full, people who had stood outside for the service were now trying to make their way in for Holy Communion. Walking up the aisle for Communion was important as it showed the family and the community that you had showed up to pay your respects.

Once outside the church, Clo nervously scanned the road.

Where was he?

She turned her head when she heard an engine start, to see Pierre's car pull out of a parking spot outside the Hospice Charity Shop. He slowly pulled up beside her.

Normally he would hop out and open the passenger door for her but not today. He kept his eyes firmly ahead of him so she walked around the car and let herself in.

"Where to?" he asked, without looking at her.

"If you drive to Erris Head we can do the walk and we won't be disturbed. If you turn right at the corner –"

"I know where it is." Pierre cut her off without looking at her.

"Fine," she said and decided to keep her mouth shut until they got there.

CHAPTER 27

"Your house is beautiful."

Nora stepped into the one-storey whitewashed cottage just four doors down from her family home. It was only a five-minute drive from the town but was so peaceful.

"You are very kind, but it is tiny," Pavel said, pulling out a kitchen chair for Nora. "Sit, please."

Nora sat down as Pavel continued.

"There is just this kitchen, a small sitting room, two bedrooms, and a bathroom but the views from the side of the house are beautiful – I never get tired of that view over the bay. And every room has an open fire and this I like."

Turning his back to her, he pulled out a large frying pan from under the worktop and put it on a gas cooker ring. He added some oil and lit the gas under it, then took two steps to the fridge and took out eggs, tomatoes, scallions, sour cream and an avocado. Reaching up to a shelf overhead, he took down two plates.

"Tea or coffee?" he asked, looking over his shoulder at her.

"Oh, tea, please. Can I help with anything?"

"No, you are my guest."

He smiled at her and she was mortified to feel her tummy flip. What is happening here, she asked herself. She turned away to look at the paintings on the walls.

The cottage had an old Irish feel to it and it reminded her of visits to her grandad's house when she was a child. Her Granda Michael had only a turf fire for heat and every time she smelled a real turf fire it immediately brought her back to Sunday afternoons spent in his cottage.

Pavel obviously liked colour as the walls were painted a vibrant bright green and the old cottage chairs were painted orange.

"I can see you like colour or was it like this when you got it?"

"The cottage was wallpapered when we moved in and it was very dark from years of smoky fires," he said, turning to answer her, "so I asked the landlord if I could paint it and he said yes. And, yes, I love colour."

Pavel turned back to the cooker, adding the chopped spring onions and tomatoes to the pan. He made a space in the mixture with the back of a spoon and cracked six eggs into the well. Nora's tummy rumbled as the delicious smell from the pan filled the kitchen.

"I love colour too," Nora said, looking around. "I live in a two-bedroomed cottage in Dublin and colour really lifts the place, I think. Have you lived here long?"

"About five years. We lived in the town when we first came here but after my wife left I didn't want to stay in that house. We are divorced now and I wanted a fresh start."

"*Snap!*"

"Snap?" Pavel crinkled his forehead.

"I mean ... I'm the same," Nora explained. "My husband left, we got divorced and I had to move to a smaller house."

"We have a lot in common," he said, plating up the food.

The eggs and vegetable mixture were on one side of the plate and Pavel placed sliced avocado and sour cream on the other side. He dressed the food with chopped coriander and a pinch of paprika and brought the plates to the table.

"This looks and smells delicious," Nora said, seriously impressed by what he threw together and how he presented it.

"Here is some sourdough," he said, placing a breadboard with a loaf and a bread knife on the table, "and your tea."

Pavel put the teapot on the table and beside that a jug of milk. Then he sat and poured them each a mug of tea.

Just then a sheepdog appeared at the door.

"Who is this?" Nora said, smiling at the shy dog who eyed her nervously.

"This is Milis. Come here, girl!"

Milis went straight to Pavel's side, resting her head on his knee.

"Milis? The Irish word for 'sweet'?"

"Yes, she was so shy and nervous when I got her from the dog pound but so sweet. Alek was learning Irish in school at the time and he said we should call her Milis, so we did. She is a sweet girl but still very nervous." He gently rubbed her head with one hand while eating with the other.

"She's got a beautiful coat," Nora said, looking at Millis's shiny black-and-white markings.

"She doesn't seem nervous around you, which is a good sign. She is a good judge of character."

Nora flushed a little when he said this.

"This is amazing, thank you so much," she said. "You have made a very bad day so much better."

When she said those words their eyes met and this time she didn't look away.

CHAPTER 28

Following the sign straight ahead saying *Ceann Iorrais/Eris Head*, Pierre and Clo drove past clusters of dormer bungalows on the left-hand side and wide-open fields on the right dotted with individual houses. Beyond that, bare hills for as far as the eye could see.

The fields and hills were a light-brown colour. She could hear her father's words in her head – "We could do with a drop of rain" – but she didn't say them aloud.

A few days of rain would turn these hills back to the green, Clo remembered from her youth. How can this land look so bare and barren now, she wondered as she watched the fields go by.

The road up ahead looked damp from the fog hanging on the hills in the distance. The sun peeked out, creating a beautiful rainbow. Clo turned to Pierre, about to point it out, but his jaw was tense and his eyes were firmly fixed on the road, so she said nothing.

I hope that rainbow is a good omen, she thought as they drove forward.

They pulled over to let a yellow school bus pass. The Bus Scoile as they called it. Clo had taken the school bus every day of her school life. It seemed that the tension of the situation was making the familiar enhanced, as if she was seeing things through a visitor's eyes. Was it because everything was about to change? She didn't know.

The old wooden telegraph poles with the thick, black, looped cable seemed hypnotic as they turned left following the signs for the Wild Atlantic Way route to Erris Head. Houses became more sparse as they drove in silence.

Pierre slowed down as they climbed a small hill – some sheep had escaped and were wandering along the road. And then the sea came into sight. They had arrived.

Clo always drove out to Erris and did the loop walk when she was home for a visit. Although she couldn't wait to leave home and get away from this small town quickly enough when she was a teenager, she could see the attraction of the landscape here. Something about the untouched wildness of it, the expansive space, and the familiarity of it soothed her nervous system.

Although she had holidayed in some beautiful places in the world there was nothing like the wildness of this place. Summer or winter, the weather was unpredictable. It could be calm and sunny one minute the sun catching the golden furze and delicate yellow cowslips and then the fog could roll in from the sea, bringing drizzle blocking the sun, casting shadows, changing the bright-green grasses to dark, whipping up a wind from nowhere.

This place is wild and unpredictable, like me, thought Clo. Just when things were calm and smooth, I whipped up a storm of my own making. I ran away from this environment but it's part of my DNA, it's who I am.

The car park was empty. The coffee hut was there but not open yet.

This walk was very popular with locals, hikers, and tourists as the headland's steep cliffs gave some of the finest views of the Mayo coastline. Atlantic seals, porpoises, and bottlenose dolphins could occasionally be seen popping their heads up from the cold North Atlantic waters. Visitors often had to make their way past sheep on the route and it was not unusual for a wild hare to cross your path either.

But it looked like Clo and Pierre would be the only walkers out today.

Pierre turned off the engine and, without speaking, got out of the car. Walking around to the boot, he took out a jacket, put it on and zipped it up. It was a warm morning and there was no wind, but the sea fog was hanging heavy over the area, making everything feel damp.

Clo opened her door and stepped out. Pierre just stood staring out at the cliffs. Low-flying birds squealed overhead. The sound of the Atlantic Ocean crashing against the cliffs was interjected by the sound of sheep in the distance.

"Will we walk?" Clo asked, moving towards him.

Pierre didn't answer but headed for the steep metal stile that started the 5km loop walk. He didn't wait to help her climb over – he didn't even look back. She was well able to climb over it, but Pierre usually liked to be a gentleman about these things and would always offer his hand to help.

She followed him, his steps strong and determined. She could tell he was angry just by his pace.

I'll wait for him to speak first, she thought, walking a few feet behind him. He marched ahead on the grassy path that led to the highest point of the trail where the ruin of an old watchtower stood. Around them sheep looked on, disinterested, as they grazed along the cliff top. The fog was lifting but the ground was still damp, making it slippery to walk on in the Gucci flat pumps she was wearing.

He waited for her at the old ruin. When she reached it, he turned to her with his arms folded across his chest and looked at her for the first time. His eyes were cold, and his jaw was clenched.

"*Okay, speak*," he said.

Clo's mouth went dry.

"About today," she began, "I'm sorry you had to see that and Sophia –"

"So this Rory person," Pierre interrupted abruptly. "Is he an ex-boyfriend or a current lover?"

Clo swallowed hard. "Both."

Pierre closed his eyes and took a deep breath.

Pierre and Clo had an unconventional relationship. They were aware that they both had had encounters with other people. But as long as it was very discreet and didn't affect their core relationship they were happy to ignore it.

When Pierre had asked Clo to marry him she had argued that Pierre was too good for her and that she did not expect him to be faithful to her forever. But he loved her and wanted to be with her, saying that he would never tie her down or make her feel trapped like her parents were. They agreed to get engaged. In the early days, they remained faithful to each other, and they were so delighted when Clo became pregnant with Sophia, so infidelity was of no interest to either of them.

After they moved to Dublin things became quite stressful. They worked all hours to get the shop up and running. About six months after the shop opened Clo noticed some slight changes in Pierre. Their sex life was still good, but she sensed something was up. An unannounced visit to the shop confirmed her suspicion when she saw how their new assistant looked at him.

They had an open and honest discussion about it that evening. Pierre promised that he would never do anything to hurt Clo or embarrass her, so they agreed that if either of them had an encounter it could not be with anyone they knew, or anyone associated with the business.

The assistant was let go with an extra month's pay and they carried on supporting each other, working in the business and sharing parenting roles.

Three months later Clo had a fling with a buyer while on a business trip to Milan and felt neither guilty nor ashamed of it. She felt alive and free and desirable again.

Their agreement had suited them both until now.

"How long has this been going on?"

"I don't think that matters. He lives in New York; that's where it started. He only came home for the funeral, like me."

"Ah ... all those trips to New York. I had my suspicions."

"You did?"

"I'm not a fool. Nobody needs to make so many in-person visits. You could do half of them online, you know that."

"But you never said anything."

"I love you, Clo, and I love our life, and our business life works really well. Also, I would never do anything to disrupt Sophia's life. I wouldn't do that to her."

Clo always knew that Sophia's bond with Pierre was stronger than it was with her. Ever since she was a little girl Sophia favoured him. He was a natural parent, and she was not. She also knew that if they ever broke up Sophia would stay with Pierre, and she would be left out of their lives.

"Do your friends know about this affair?"

"No! God, no. I ... we ... have been very discreet."

Pierre tilted his head to one side. "But ... you said you loved him. You shouted it."

"I know, I know. We were having an argument, and he wouldn't listen, and he was walking away so ..."

"You can't stand it when you don't have everyone's full attention, can you?"

Clo squeezed her hands into fists by her sides. She had no right to disagree with him or answer back. She had been caught wide open.

"So ... you love him?"

"I ... I don't know."

"*Don't lie to me!*"

"I'm not lying ... I don't know how to answer that."

"We heard you! Sophia and I heard you shout 'I love you'!"

Clo shifted uncomfortably from foot to foot, feeling chilly now standing in the damp ruin.

"I've known him all of my life," she said, looking down at her feet, "so, yes, I do love him, but I love you too and I don't want things to change between us."

"Are you in love with him?"

"I avoid thinking too deeply about these things."

"Right now," Pierre said, looking directly at her, "I don't know what to believe. I find it hard to believe you."

"I know." Clo felt like crying. "I feel terrible. And Sophia, how is she? What did you tell her?"

"She is very upset. What do you expect? We came here to surprise you, to support you and this happens?"

"Oh god!" Clo paced up and down, clutching her stomach, feeling sick at the memory of Sophia's horrified face.

"I told her that there would be an explanation. That he was probably an old friend and it could be completely innocent but ... she's not a child anymore and she is no fool. She knows I am meeting you now."

The clouds had come over and blocked out the sun. The breeze from the sea was getting stronger and Clo shivered.

"I need to see her."

"And tell her what?"

"That I'm sorry, for starters."

"But what do you want, Clo?"

Clo could feel her heart beating in her chest and her head throbbed, giving her a piercing pain across her eyes.

"Don't you think it hurt me too, Clo, to see you call out like that after another man? It did. I can't think of anything else since. But ... if you want us to put this behind us, I am willing to do that for our family and our businesses. But one thing is for sure: you cannot see him again either here or in New York. That all stops."

Clo nodded but her heart was completely torn.

"It looked more than a fling to me, Clo."

Clo swallowed hard as tears welled up in her eyes.

"I know you," Pierre said, looking directly at her. "You need to decide if you want to stay with me and Sophia or go with him."

Clo's head was thumping now. Could she really never see Rory again? Could she lose Pierre and Sophia? Pierre stood with his arms crossed. He looked drained. She did love him, they had built a life together and a business together that was expanding, but if that was enough why did she go back to Rory over and over?

"You need to choose, and you need to tell me now before I go back to our daughter."

CHAPTER 29

The smell of the burning incense the priest had swung over the coffin was making Fern nauseous, and its thick smoke hung in the air as people shuffled down the aisle following the coffin and the family out of the church. It was going to take a while before the church emptied so there was no rush. She would sit until it did. It had been such a sad ceremony, and she felt heartbroken for all involved. She didn't feel like going outside and having to talk to people. And she certainly didn't want to speak to Rossa and the kids as they were so upset.

Placing the heel of her right hand on her heart, she tried to massage the tightness out of her chest. She remembered the lines of a John Grant song about pain feeling 'like a glacier running through you,' and that was exactly what this pain felt like, a big iceberg cutting through her chest. She closed her eyes, taking deep, steady breaths. She hadn't thought she'd be sitting here alone. She had hoped that Clo and Nora would be a support to her today but no – they had both disappeared. She had hoped that this would be a time the three of them could support each other through. And she had hoped to confide in them before today but that didn't happen either. Where are they now, she wondered? Nora was nowhere to be seen, and Clo couldn't wait to rush out of the church as soon as the Communion started. This was not how she imagined things when she had invited them to stay.

The service had been so moving. The priest had known Danny all his life and clearly struggled to come up with words of explanation for his untimely death. But, through it all, Clo sat staring into space. She was miles away and then couldn't wait to leave.

Watching the kids crying through the service was hard enough, but what hit most was when Danny's eldest son Ed got up and spoke to the congregation about his father. That hit hard. He spoke about how his dad was his best friend, how they travelled the country for the club's Gaelic football matches, and how they supported the Mayo County team. His comment about how his dad always believed that every year would be Mayo's year to win the All-Ireland brought a smile and nods of understanding amongst the congregation.

The priest announced from the pulpit that the funeral reception at the Broadhaven Bay Hotel would take place at half past one, following the burial in the local graveyard.

Fern looked at her watch. She would have to turn up to the funeral reception, the whole town would be there, but right now she needed to get out of this church and walk somewhere. Her head felt like it was going to explode. All these secrets. She shook her head. Looking around she could see that people were still making their way down the aisle towards the front door.

Two altar boys sharing a joke left by an open side door. Fern got up from her pew and followed them. This door led out to the car park where there was a gate out onto the street. Pushing on her big black sunglasses, she slipped out through the gate and walked back to her car, avoiding eye contact with anyone. I need to clear my head, she thought, her mind racing.

Driving out of town, she turned towards home. Her mind was blank as she drove by the familiar houses along the route. So many times she had walked this road in her mind when she was homesick in London. When the big city felt overwhelming she closed her eyes and followed this road.

When, as an eighteen-year-old, she lay in bed feeling scared and alone, she closed her eyes and thought of this route, imagining the colours of the wildflowers and the smell of the sea in the air. Later, when she started yoga and meditation, she always came back to this place in her visualisations. It was wild and beautiful and calmed her nervous system whenever she let her mind wander back here, back home.

Pulling into her driveway, she got out, opened the door to the porch and changed into her trainers. It was a warm day but the Atlantic breeze could be chilly so, hanging up her long black coat, she picked up a hoody and pulled it over her black funeral dress. Popping her sunglasses back on, she headed straight back out for a walk.

Going towards Elly Bay beach, she passed Uisce Irish College and Watersports Centre. The laughter of the kids rang out as they played a game of basketball in front of the college. Many times she and Danny had to referee those matches and there was always lighthearted banter thrown at them in broken Irish from the students. It was a bittersweet memory now.

Walking on, she passed Elly Bay beach. The earlier fog had lifted, and it looked like it was going to be a nice day after all. Walking across the road, she turned right up a smaller road that led directly to the other side of the peninsula. Inhaling the scent of the gorse and the salty air, she lifted her shoulders to her ears and then dropped them to ease the tension that had been there for days. Her whole body felt tense.

Nothing was turning out as she planned. She had asked Nora and Clo to stay with her for a reason. They shared so many good memories of the three of them hanging out there. She just wanted to feel that connection again. She had imagined long nights sitting in the house together chatting and looking back on their lives since leaving this place. She wanted that connection so that at last she could open up to them.

Reaching the top of the road she stopped to take in the view of the whole bay. This was the narrowest part of the peninsula so you could see Blacksod Bay on one side and hear the roar of the Atlantic on the other. In the distance, Slievemore could be seen clearly, now that the fog had lifted. It wasn't unusual for it to be hidden by sea fog for days on end but right now it was clear, its dark outline like a painting against the blue sky.

Looking left, the Bay of Blacksod sparkled in the sunlight. A few small boats sat still on the sea. To the right was the Atlantic Ocean. It was a calm day today but there were times, especially in winter when she could hear the power of the sea and the crashing waves from her house. A few cows turned to look at her as if to ask 'What do you want?' So she moved on.

By the time she reached the stoney beach the wind had whipped up a bit. Turning left, she walked to her rock and sat down. *Her rock*. She ran her hand over the huge smooth surface. She had come to her rock many times in her life. This entrance onto the beach was the quickest route to this side of the peninsula from her house.

As a child, she brought her dolls along and played with them on this rock while her mother swam. As a teen, she placed her towel and clothes on it when she went for a swim and needed space to figure things out. This is where she came for comfort and familiarity.

Looking out to sea now, she took a deep breath and let it out slowly.

That funeral was hard, she thought, so much harder than I expected. Her heart was breaking, and she felt drained with sadness. She felt like she had been hit by a spear in her chest.

It was clear that Danny was a great father to his three children. But what about his firstborn? What about their son, the one that she desperately wanted to tell the girls about, the one that nobody in this town or the packed church knew about except Danny, Rossa and herself?

CHAPTER 30

"*Mummy!*"

Nora stood at the function-room door of the Broadhaven Bay Hotel, looking around to see where her mother and Millie were sitting. There was a line of people at the bar and another line at the buffet tables along the side of the big function room. The rest of the space was taken up with tables and chairs.

"Oh, there you are!" Nora said as Millie ran to her and put her little hand in hers. "Show me where Granny is, sweety."

Millie pulled her through the crowd until Nora could see her mother waving.

"Hi, Mam," she said, bending down to kiss her mother's cheek. "Hi, Ralf."

Ralf nodded and went back to eating his heavily laden plate of food.

"You took your time, girl," her mother said.

"We just lost track of time – there is always more to do," answered Nora.

"Can I get a dessert now?" Millie asked her granny.

"I told her she'd have to wait until you got here," Margaret said to Nora. "I saved you a place, so why don't you get some food while there's still some left." She nodded towards the buffet. "There's a huge spread. I haven't seen a funeral like this in god knows when. The whole town must be here."

Nora looked around. It was a huge crowd alright.

"Have you seen Clo or Fern?"

"No, love," her mam said, going back to her food.

"That's strange, Fern's car was outside the door when I went back to the house to get changed but she wasn't there. I presumed she must have got a lift here."

When Nora had returned to the house she'd called out Fern and Clo's names, but there was no answer. So she went ahead and had a shower and pulled on a black cotton sundress she had brought to wear to the funeral. It was calf-length, not too tight, but flattering at her waist which was her smallest part. The thick straps on the shoulders gave her support where she needed it. She then applied some mascara, eyeliner and a light-coloured lipstick. She didn't have time to ring either Clo or Fern, so she put on some black flat sandals, tied her hair up in a high ponytail and rushed out the door.

"I did see both of them in the church," Margaret said.

"*Hmm*, I'll give them a ring." Nora took out her phone from her black clutch bag.

"Mummy, please! Can we go get dessert?" Millie said, pulling her hand.

"Oh, okay," she said, putting the phone down. "Yes, yes, let's go."

Millie led her over to the carvery buffet. They really had pushed the boat out for Danny, she thought, looking at the food available.

"I think I'll just have dessert too, Millie," she said, still quite full after Pavel's breakfast. "Show me what they have."

They chose desserts and returned to the table with their tray.

"Mummy let me have a chocolate brownie!" Millie said excitedly.

"Oh, lucky you!" Ralf said as Millie sat beside him.

Nora had just set her pavlova dessert down when her mother started waving at someone.

"*Pavel! Pavel!*"

"*Mam! Shhh* – will you leave the man alone? People are looking."

"Not at all," she replied, continuing to wave him over.

Pavel, wearing a black suit now, was making his way through the crowd. He scrubs up well, Nora thought, and he really helped me out today.

She noticed one or two women turn to look at him as he crossed the room. His dark wavy hair was still damp, and she shocked herself by imagining him standing naked in his shower.

Earlier, after breakfast at his place, they drove back to the school and walked over to the church after the service had begun. The church was packed to capacity, but they managed to squeeze their way in to sign the condolences book. They stood at the back but Nora couldn't see anything over the heads of the people standing in front of her, so after ten minutes she motioned to Pavel that she was leaving, and he left with her.

"You can stay if you like, Pavel," she said.

"No, it is okay. My boss is very strict," he said with a grin.

He placed his hand on her lower back as he directed her through the crowd standing outside the church, sending a shiver up her spine. He took his hand back when they reached the church gates, although she would have been happy if he hadn't, and they walked side by side back to the school.

Now, as he arrived at the table, her mother said, "We have space here."

Nora smiled at him. "Sorry about my bossy mother."

"Here is just fine," he said, pulling out a chair between Nora and Margaret. He smiled over at Millie as he sat down. "That looks nice."

"Mummy let me have it," Millie said before taking another bite from her brownie.

"So how is it going over there at the school?" Ralf asked.

As Pavel filled Margaret and Ralf in on their morning's work, Nora looked around again for Clo and Fern. Still no sign of them.

Then Danny's wife Rossa caught her eye and approached the table.

Nora's chest tightened.

"Hello, Nora."

Pavel followed Nora's eyes.

"I'm so sorry for your loss," he said, standing up and offering his hand to Rossa.

"Thank you, Pavel," she said as she forced a weary smile. "I wanted to come over and thank the two of you." She looked from Pavel to Nora. "I believe you are doing great work at the school."

Nora nodded. "Thank you. I hope you like the finished result."

"I'm sure it will be a lovely tribute, Nora." She looked at Millie. "And who is this beautiful girl?"

"Oh, this is Millie, my daughter."

"Hello, Millie, I don't think we've met," said Rossa, smiling.

"Hello. I'm Millie Cunningham and I'm six," Millie said proudly and then went back to eating her brownie.

"Well, nice to meet you, Millie Cunningham. She has your gorgeous hair, Nora. Did Fern O'Malley come here with you? I was hoping to speak to her."

"*Eh* no. I thought she'd be here by now but I'm sure she's on her way."

"Well, I'm going home now."

"You must be exhausted," said Margaret.

Rossa sighed. "I'm shattered and so are the kids. I just want to get them home. Danny's parents and Audrey are staying, to hold the fort so to speak. I ... I just can't."

Margaret reached out and squeezed Rossa's hand. "Of course, love, of course."

"So can you tell Fern I was looking for her?" Rossa said, turning to Nora. "Is she here for the week?"

"Yes, she is."

"I'll speak to her tomorrow or the next day so. Thanks again for coming and for the effort you're putting in." Rossa nodded and then slowly made her way to the door where her kids were waiting.

"God love her," Margaret said, shaking her head. "They were such a devoted couple, you know. He doted on her and the kids. A lovely family."

"Okay, Millie, I'm going to the bar," Nora said, standing up. "What would you like?"

"7Up, please."

"Let me get it," Pavel offered, pushing back his chair.

"Thanks but I'll go. I'm going to do a lap of the room to see if Fern or Clo are here somewhere and, if they're not, I'm going to ring them. Thanks, anyway. Can I get you something?"

"No thanks, I'm going to grab a plate of food first," he said, standing up.

"Mam, Ralf? Do you want anything from the bar?"

"No, love, we're grand," her mother answered. "We won't be spending much longer here."

Nora made her way through the different groups of people, saying hello to some familiar faces and old neighbours, but Fern and Clo were nowhere to be seen.

Where the hell are they, she wondered as she opened her phone to see if they had left any messages. And what on earth does Rossa want to talk to Fern about?

"Hey!"

Nora turned to see Fern beside her at the bar.

"There you are! I was just about to ring you. I've been looking for you. Is Clo with you?"

"No, and I've just got here." Fern put up her hand to get the barman's attention.

"Are you okay? You look a bit ..."

"No, I'm not okay really," Fern jumped in before Nora could finish her sentence.

Nora looked at her friend. Fern wasn't her usual relaxed self – she looked restless and anxious.

"Things haven't worked out quite how I'd hoped," Fern said, waving the barman over.

"What do you mean?" asked Nora.

"How are you, Jerry?" Fern said when the barman came over. "Can I have a Rum and Coke and a pint of Coors, please, for myself – and Nora?"

"A 7Up and a Diet Coke, please."

Jerry nodded and headed off to get the drinks.

"Are you not drinking?" Fern asked.

"Not yet anyway. I haven't decided what I'm doing. I have the jeep parked outside and I have Millie here too so ..."

"Well, I'm getting drunk."

"Maybe not such a good idea after such an emotional day?"

"Thanks, Jerry," Fern said as he placed the Rum and Coke in front of her. She picked it up and drank half of it in one go.

Nora's eyes widened. Fern was definitely not herself, and she certainly wasn't a big drinker.

"Where is Clo?" she asked.

"She was in the church with me and then ran out at Communion time. She's in a state about Pierre."

"Pierre?"

"Oh, I forgot, I haven't seen you. Pierre and Sophia called to the house when Clo was out. They came down as a surprise to support Clo."

"And? She's in a state about that?"

"Well, I told them she went out for a walk so they decided to go look for her on the road. They'd come from the town and didn't pass her, so they drove towards the lighthouse."

"Now, ladies, that'll be twenty-two euro," Jerry said, returning with the rest of the drinks.

"Here, I'll get it," Fern said, taking out her card and tapping the card reader. "Thanks, Jerry."

"You're welcome."

"Anyway," Fern said, turning back to Nora, "about twenty minutes later I hear Clo's car pull into to driveway, but she doesn't come in. So, I go out and open the front door and she's just sitting there clutching the steering wheel, white as a ghost, staring into space."

Nora gasped. "What happened?"

"She wouldn't say. She came into the house, and I asked her what was wrong, and she said the shit had hit the fan. And then, I don't know why I said it but ... I said, 'Is this about Rory?' Well ... if looks could kill ..."

"Oh dear, you don't think ..."

"I felt like something was going on there, but what exactly and for how long, who knows? And it's none of my business, and I wish I'd kept my mouth shut but it just came out."

"And what did she say?"

"She didn't deny it – in fact, she admitted that they were 'close'. She was upset, very upset, but I still don't know the whole story of what happened with Pierre."

"But where are Pierre and Sophia now?"

"They're staying in the Talbot Hotel, but I didn't see them at the church and Clo was with me, so I don't know what's after happening."

"And then she left?"

"*Yep*. We drove to the church together in silence and then she upped and left."

"Mummy! Where's my drink?" Millie appeared at Nora's side.

"Oh, sorry, baby, I'm coming now. I'll take her back to the table," she said to Fern. "Are you coming?"

"You go ahead. I'm going to order another one of these," she said, holding up her rum glass.

"Okay."

Millie led Nora back to the table and squeezed herself in between Margaret and Ralf who were talking to some neighbours at the next table. Pavel was on the phone. Sitting down, she looked back over at Fern who was talking to some old school pal at the bar.

"Everything okay?" Pavel said, closing his phone.

"Yes, well ... no. I don't know what's going on actually." She shrugged. "My friends seem to be going through their own drama today."

Pavel nodded. "It's an emotional day – a funeral like this where you all knew him so well."

"Yes, but it's not only that. Everyone seems out of sorts. I had planned on taking Millie back with me to stay the night but Fern plans on getting drunk and Clo has gone AWOL so I think I might have her stay at my mam's."

Just then Margaret turned around.

"Nora, love, we're going to go now. We're getting a lift from Paddy and Mary. Do you want us to take Millie?"

"Oh, could you? And can you keep her tonight?"

"Of course."

"*Yay! I'm staying in Granny's again!*" Millie cheered.

Nora laughed. "Well, I'll try not to be insulted."

"What does *insult* mean?" Millie asked, crinkling up her nose.

"It doesn't matter. Mummy is just making a joke. How about I pick you up in the morning and we'll have breakfast in town?"

"Yes! And we can see Donald."

"Donald?"

"Donald the Cat, silly," Millie said, giggling.

"Donald the Cat is a celebrity around here," Pavel said.

"Oh, I know all about him but we haven't been formally introduced," said Nora, smiling. "You can introduce me tomorrow, how's that?"

"*Hooray!*" Millie jumped down from her seat and gave Nora a big kiss.

"Right, Millie," Ralf said, standing up and helping Margaret with her jacket, "let's get you home."

"Goodnight, love," Margaret said, leaning down to kiss Nora on the cheek. "And goodnight to you too, Pavel."

"Goodnight," he said, standing up and pulling her chair out of her way.

"Bye, Mummy!" waved Millie, then took Margaret's hand as they left.

"So Donald the Cat is a celebrity around here now?" Nora said, turning to Pavel.

"He sure is," answered Pavel. "I can't believe you haven't been formally introduced."

Nora slapped his arm playfully.

"Listen, I might be a little late tomorrow if that's okay. The delivery from the garden centre isn't arriving until ten so I was going to take Millie for breakfast as a treat. I'll be in time for the delivery though. Is that okay with you?"

"No problem. I'm sure Millie will enjoy it."

"I think she saw pancakes on a menu somewhere, when she was out with my mam, so she'll be very happy," said Nora. "You must miss your son when he's in Poland."

"Yes, but we talk every day. That was him on the phone, wanting to know about the funeral. He really liked Danny."

"*Aw*, that's nice of him to call."

"Yes. He is a good boy." Pavel's face softened when he spoke about Alek and Nora couldn't help looking into his eyes.

"Free seats?" Fern arrived, carrying a full pint and a shot of something.

"Yes, please sit," Pavel said, standing up.

"You're leaving?" Nora asked.

"Yes, I will leave you to your friends."

"Don't go on my account," Fern said as she sat down and put her jacket on the back of the chair.

"We didn't talk about the plan for tomorrow," Nora said, realising that she didn't want Pavel to leave.

"I will go up to the school in the morning and you come after breakfast. We'll take it from there."

"Sure."

Pavel said his goodbyes and Nora watched him as he left.

"*Eh, hello?*" Fern said, waving her hand in front of Nora's face. "There's some serious chemistry between you two."

"Don't be silly!" Nora said but she felt it too.

"You never could lie," Fern said, shaking her head.

If only you knew, thought Nora as she took a sip from her Diet Coke, if only you knew.

"By the way, Rossa was looking for you," she said, changing the subject.

"Rossa?" Fern's smile dropped, and she looked taken aback.

"Yes. She came over to me before she left asking if I'd seen you and to pass on the message that she wants to talk to you."

"Oh," Fern said, looking concerned.

"Is everything okay?"

"Yes, yes, of course," Fern said as she smiled and took a gulp of her drink.

Fern reckoned that Rossa might want to speak to her at some stage throughout the week but not at Danny's actual funeral. She pushed her concerns away and finished off her Rum and Coke. She didn't want to think about that now.

"So, are you going to leave me drinking on my own or what?" she said, winking at Nora.

CHAPTER 31

It was after seven when Nora and Fern decided to leave. Nora was sick of drinking Diet Coke and Fern was drinking fast which would only end in disaster if she kept going. A lot of people had left to go home or to move on to a pub. Others arrived from McDonnell's pub to replace them. There would be an ebb and flow of people all night.

It was nice for Nora to catch up with some old faces from school. She had also chatted with some neighbours and friends of her mam's who all asked after Millie. Some had met her around the town with her granny, and they all doted on her.

She'd even tried talking to Kevin, approaching him on her way back from the ladies'.

"You're looking well," she said, as she stood beside him at the bar. "Australia must suit you."

"It does," he said, looking straight ahead.

"Do you come back much?"

"No."

She got the feeling he didn't want to speak to her. She was about to move away but the barman came her way.

"A Rum and Coke and a fizzy water, thanks, Jerry."

"Fern drowning her sorrows," Kevin said with a smirk.

"Well, it's a sad day for everyone," Nora said, irritated by his tone.

He turned to face her now, leaning his right arm on the bar. "Oh yeah, that's right, you had a crush on Danny too," he said, a smile creeping across his face. "But you never had a chance with him, did you?"

"I beg your pardon?" Nora said, feeling her anger rise.

"Poor little Nora! You had to look on while he had his hands all over Fern – and others. In fact, half the women here have probably been with Danny O'Connor," he said, looking around.

"Don't be ridiculous. You're being rude now," Nora said, cursing herself for getting annoyed by him.

She looked down towards barman Jerry, wishing he would hurry up. Kevin had really pissed her off. The cheek of him!

"You've been away a long time, Kevin," she said, fiddling with a bar mat. "Do you not think it's time to get over yourself?"

"Me? Oh, I have moved on."

"Yes, I can see that, but with Danny's sister?"

"That was a happy coincidence," he said, looking over to where Audrey was sitting. "I have moved on from this hole of a place with its narrow-mindedness and secrets, but I don't forget. I won't forget the damage he did."

Kevin picked up his drinks and walked away, leaving Nora wondering what on earth he was talking about.

Jerry brought her drinks and she returned to the table.

"Well, that was just weird," she said as she sat down.

"What was?" Fern asked.

"Kevin. He was so rude and I don't know ... he just made me feel uncomfortable."

"I'm avoiding him," Fern said, taking a sip of her drink. "I was standing outside the church today and I felt him looking at me, so I nodded over, to be polite, and he nodded back but ... I don't know. It's like he wants to say something or get something off his chest. He always was difficult to figure out."

"Well, I tried to be nice, and he wasn't having it – so feck him!"

"Do you fancy getting out of here?" Fern said, looking around. "I think I've said hello to everyone and I'm starving now."

"Yes, I'm hungry too but you've just got your –"

Before Nora could say 'drink' Fern had lifted the glass to her lips and swallowed the lot of it.

"Okay then, let's go but can we go via the chipper?" said Fern.

"Oh god, yes! I'll stop at Cois Cuan, I love their chips," Nora said, standing up and pushing the strap of her bag up onto her shoulder. "But what about Clo? Have you heard from her at all?"

"She legged it out of the church and didn't bother her arse showing up here so ... oh, hang on, there she is at the bar."

Nora turned around to see Clo getting a drink from Jerry. Her shoulders were rounded, and she looked exhausted.

"Hey, we were looking for you," Nora said as she approached her.

"I'm sorry," Clo said, turning to the two of them. "I've had the day from hell. Is Rory here?"

"No, he left with his mother," Fern said.

"Creepy Kevin is over there staring us out of it," Nora said, nodding in his direction.

"Nothing new there," Clo said, taking a sip from her drink. "Are you guys leaving?"

"Yes," said Fern. "We're going to the chipper and then home to open a bottle of something."

"Sounds perfect. I'll come with you," Clo said, throwing back her Vodka and Coke.

"Jesus, you women are fierce fast drinkers!" said Nora with her hands on her hips.

"Okay, Mammy!" Fern laughed.

"Is everything okay with you now?" Nora asked Clo, looking closely at her friend who looked drained.

"No, everything is still a big mess but there is nothing more I can do tonight. To be honest, I am tired of talking. I want to forget about it now. I just don't have the energy."

"Of course," Nora nodded.

The three said goodnight to Jerry and left the bar.

Just as they left the function room Audrey came out of the toilets.

"Are you leaving, ladies?"

"Yes. It's been a long day. You must be exhausted yourself," said Nora.

"Yes, I think we're all shattered – it's been a terrible day – and of course all sorts of memories bubble to the surface," Audrey said, looking directly at Fern.

"Yes ... well," Nora said, "we'll be off then."

"I believe Rossa was looking for you, Fern?" Audrey said as they were about to move on.

Fern felt very uneasy. Something about the way Audrey was looking at her made her feel very uncomfortable.

"I'm sure you two have a lot to discuss," Audrey said.

"Well, goodnight," Clo said, pulling Fern away to the exit.

They stopped outside.

Clo said, "What the fuck was that about?"

But Fern couldn't answer. That encounter didn't feel right, didn't feel right at all.

CHAPTER 32

"Thank you for driving," Fern said as they entered the kitchen. "I'll get some plates out. Can someone put the kettle on?"

"Yeah, sure," said Clo, "Those chips smell divine!"

The smell of the freshly cooked chips covered in vinegar filled the kitchen.

"Will I get the bread out for some chip sandwiches?" Nora said, opening the press.

"Oh god, yes!" said Clo. "A double carb dose – my body won't know what happened it. I never eat bread anymore."

"Really?" said Fern. "But you haven't a pick on you."

"That's why! Bread bloats me like you wouldn't believe."

"And you're married to a Frenchman – surely that's a crime in France," added Nora.

Clo winced at the thought of Pierre but forced a smile on her face. "Yes, he cannot understand it at all."

Fern put the plates on the table and Nora took the bread and butter from the press.

"It can only be white sliced bread for a chip sandwich," Fern said, taking out the salt and vinegar as well.

"Will I make a pot of tea?"

"Yes, thanks, Clo."

The three friends sat at the table, buttered the bread, and made up their chip sandwiches.

Clo moaned as she took a bite. "Oh my god, this is heavenly," she said, eating with her eyes closed. "This is the best thing that's happened to me today."

She took another bite of her sandwich and a gulp of tea. Looking at her two friends, she decided to come clean.

"Everything is a disaster and surprise, surprise, it's all my fault. I am just as messed up as I ever was," she began.

Fern and Nora looked on as Clo lowered her head.

"I have been seeing Rory in New York."

The two friends said nothing.

"And when I say 'seeing' I mean sleeping with him."

Clo looked up at Fern and Nora.

Fern was the first to speak. "*Em* ... I could see that there was something between you two since we got here but I didn't know if it was old feelings or new."

Nora shrugged. "I didn't notice anything, to be honest, but you and Rory were together all through secondary school so it's natural that there would be some feelings there."

"Well, thank you both for being so polite and non-judgmental about it, but Pierre and I are as good as married and I have seen Rory every time I go to New York."

"And I take it you go there a lot?" Fern said, getting more of a picture now.

"Yes, about every six weeks and that was fine because I could just keep that in a box in my head, a New York box, Rory and New York. It never spilled over into my home life ... but it has now."

Clo put both her elbows on the table and rested her head in her hands.

"Today I met Rory at the lighthouse. He had parked his car there earlier and had gone off for a run to Faulmore Bay and back. We just met for a chat, but it turned into a row. A silly row." Clo turned to Nora. "He got jealous of me chatting to your gardener friend in the pub."

"Pavel?"

"Yes, something about how I looked at him. He said I was flirting and the row got heated. So much so, that I didn't hear Pierre's car arrive with Sophia in it."

"Oh god!" Fern's hand flew to her mouth.

"Yes," sighed Clo. "They got out of their car as Rory was storming off but just in time to hear me call after him, shouting that I loved him."

Nora's jaw dropped open. "So what happened then?"

"Sophia roared at me and then burst into tears. Pierre's face was like stone. He told her to get back in the car. He wouldn't let me talk to her and they drove off." She looked at Nora. "And for the record, I am not after the gardener, Nora. Maybe I was a bit flirty ... I don't know ... but that's who I am. I know what I'm like when it comes to men. I'm a mess-up."

"Don't say that!" pleaded Nora.

"No, it's true. I have always blamed my parents' shit marriage as an excuse to not commit, to play around, but I've been using that excuse for way too long now. I'm a bitch, I'm unfaithful and now it's come back to bite me. Rory won't answer my messages or calls, and Pierre has issued me with an ultimatum."

"Oh pet, I'm so sorry," Fern said, reaching across the table to squeeze Clo's hand.

"I have nobody but myself to blame for this. And the timing ... well, that's why I left the church early. Sorry about that."

Fern shook her head. "It doesn't matter now."

"So what's the situation now?"

"I went up to Erris Head with Pierre and he basically said it's either him and Sophia or Rory. He knows Sophia will take his side and he's right."

"Oh god, I'm so sorry this is happening to you, Clo," Nora said.

"You two are the only people who really know me. I couldn't stay faithful to anyone. Even when I was going out with Rory I was snogging other people at the dances. I don't know how he put up with me."

"He was always besotted with you, Clo," Fern said. "And this thing with Rory now, is it just a fling, for old time's sake, for nostalgia?"

Clo looked at her two friends and winced. "It's been going on since his divorce."

Clo looked at her friends' puzzled faces until the penny dropped.

"Wait ... that's ..." said Fern.

"Five years," Clo said, looking at their shocked faces. "Please don't judge me and please keep this to yourselves. Pierre said he doesn't want to know how long it's been going on, but he has no idea it has been that long. Now, he's no angel himself. Pierre and I have both had flings. We have an agreement that if we go offside, we don't tell each other, and it must be short-lived and never cross over into our home life as a unit with Sophia."

"And you're okay with him having flings?" Nora said wonderingly.

"Yes, I'm okay with that. We work so well together, and we do love each other, and have a great life together."

"And Rory? He knows about your life with Pierre?"

"Yes, I have never lied to Rory, ever. We just don't talk about it when I'm in New York. He did ask me to move there and move in with him, but I won't make any decisions until Sophia is finished school and settled in college."

"So are you planning on leaving Pierre for Rory then?"

"I planned on thinking about it then. That's all I have promised Rory. I have just enjoyed this double life as such and Rory is free to stop it at any stage. I'm a coward really and I didn't want to make any decision. But I can't carry on anymore. That all changed today."

"Oh my god, Clo!" Nora sighed. Clo was always the wild one and she didn't always agree with her behaviour, but she loved her and hated to see her in this position now.

"What are you going to do?"

"I've done it. I told Pierre that I wouldn't see Rory again and that I would stop travelling to New York. We'll send one of the managers from the shop instead."

Clo pulled nervously at her right ear and fidgeted with her hair.

Fern was looking at Clo, trying to read her. "And ... is that what you want?"

"No, not really. I love Rory and the thought of not seeing him again breaks my heart, but I have no choice. I have to be practical about this and think of other people besides myself. I've been selfish for too long. Sophia adores Pierre. He has been a more present parent to her than I ever was. They're like two peas in a pod. If I choose Rory, she will side with Pierre. She will hate me and maybe never speak to me again. I can't do that to her."

"And what about your business?" Fern asked. "What would happen with that if you chose Rory?"

"Business-wise, Pierre and I have acquired a property for a second shop. It will take a lot of work to get it up and running and we need to work side by side on that together to make it a success. If I choose Rory and move to New York I would be giving all that up. I can't do that."

"So how did things end with Pierre? You are obviously here and not at the Talbot with him and Sophia."

"Yes, we both agreed that I stay here to put a bit of space between us. I told Sophia that you guys needed me here."

"So you've spoken to her?"

"Yes, just before I met you tonight. Pierre told Sophia that it was all a misunderstanding and that Rory and I were old friends who met to talk as he was going through something and that when I said I loved him, I meant it as a friend, an old friend."

"And she's okay now?"

"He messaged me after he told her, and I called up to the hotel to confirm his story. She did ask why I hadn't come and explained sooner so I told her I was wrapped up in the funeral and supporting you two. I'm not sure if she buys the story – she's no fool – but she normally believes whatever Pierre tells her. We've made plans to go to Westport tomorrow. Apparently there are a few coffee shops that are cool on Instagram right now that Sophia wants to get photos in. Can you believe it?" Clo laughed. "A bloody happy family day out tomorrow as if nothing ever happened." She shook her head.

"And what about Rory?" Nora asked.

Clo's eyes filled up. "I need to speak to him but he's not answering my calls today. I don't blame him. I texted him to tell him Pierre and Sophia are here, so I hope he sees that message." Tears started to fall down her face. "When I think of telling him it's over, it breaks my heart. I feel so much pain when I think of not seeing him again but ... what can I do?"

Fern and Nora looked on helplessly as Clo put her head on the table and sobbed.

CHAPTER 33

Thursday

Nora rose early, at six, and decided to walk Penny. She had arranged to pick Millie up at half eight so she had plenty of time.

If I give Penny a big walk now she'll be happy until I get back later, she thought, pulling on a pair of black leggings and a cosy hoody.

Penny rose from her dog basket when she saw Nora enter the kitchen. She stretched before walking over to Nora, wagging her tail. Not wanting to wake anyone, Nora picked up the lead and some doggie bags and walked out to the porch with Penny at her heels. She shut the door gently behind her. Slipping her feet into her trainers, she grabbed a light rain jacket, opened the front door, and let herself and Penny out.

It was a chilly morning. The fog was well and truly down, making the air feel damp, meaning her clothes would probably get soaked. She didn't care; it was refreshing, good for the head. I'm so glad I didn't drink yesterday, she thought.

What a day! The funeral was bad enough but then Clo! She didn't know what to think. On the one hand, it was clear that she loved Rory but, on the other hand, she'd an affair for five years that Pierre knew nothing about. At least we can be here for her, I guess, she thought, as she stepped down onto the sand.

The beach was deserted. She took a tennis ball from her jacket pocket and threw it as far as she could for Penny. Just then her phone buzzed in her pocket.

A smile crossed her face: it was a WhatsApp message from Pavel.

Good morning, Boss. When you read this can you let me know what you want me to start on this morning? Pavel.

She started to type an answer but decided to call instead.

"Hi, it's me."

"Oh sorry, I hope my message didn't wake you"

"No, it didn't. I'm up and out on the beach with Penny."

"Oh? Which beach?"

"Elly Bay."

"I can see you."

"What? Where ...?"

Nora squinted and could just make out a figure with a dog through the fog, up ahead.

"Is that you?" she asked.

"Yes, I'm waving now."

"I'm waving back!"

She hung up the phone and continued to walk towards him.

Walking out of the fog Pavel looked like the dramatic hero in a movie. Her stomach did a little flip. Act cool, she told herself, instantly regretting not brushing her hair or washing her face.

The two dogs barked and ran to each other and then ran in circles around each other.

"I think Penny just made a friend," Nora said when she reached Pavel.

"Yes, they seem happy to see each other, and I am happy to see you out here too."

"It's beautiful, isn't it?" Nora said, standing looking out to sea as the fog was rising allowing for more visibility.

"Beautiful, yes," Pavel said softly, and when Nora turned to him he was looking right at her.

"*Em* ... *eh* ... you wanted to talk about today's work?" she said, dragging her eyes away from his. "Shall we walk and talk?"

They walked side by side, discussing what needed to be done at the school today, the garden-centre plants that needed to go in today and what was left to be done on the project.

Penny and Milis raced around, chasing each other in and out of the water.

"We are both soaked from the fog," said Pavel when they reached the end of the beach, "and so are the dogs. My jeep is just over there," he pointed towards the small carpark, "so let me give you a lift back."

"That would be great," answered Nora. "The time has flown, and I need to pick Millie up."

"Of course, you're going out for breakfast," he said, opening the back of the jeep for the dogs to jump in. "Take your time today, I can work away."

"Thanks, but I want to be there for the delivery and, besides, I enjoy the company." The words were out of her mouth before she realised it. She felt herself blush and turned her head away.

Pavel smiled, closing the back of the jeep. "Me too."

Nora hopped into the front seat and Pavel drove out of the car park.

She stared out the window, looking at the fog hanging like candy floss over the fields. The truth was that she did want to go and work beside him today. He calmed her. She felt relaxed and safe working alongside him. And, yes, she did find him attractive, and as soon as she woke up this morning her thoughts were only of him.

There was so much anguish going on in her own head these past few days ... and then Clo's revelation last night ... well, it was all quite unsettling. Spending time with Pavel was just what she needed right now and, more than that, it was what she wanted to do today.

"Thanks, I'll see you later," she said when he came to a stop.

"Nora, are you free tonight?"

"*Em*, I don't have any plans, but I do have Millie tonight – she's staying here with me."

"Well, if it's okay with you and with Millie, of course, I would like to invite you over for dinner."

"Oh."

"You don't have to tell me now."

"No, I would love that and I'm sure Millie would too, thank you."

Pavel's face lit up. "Great. I will see you later at the school and we can talk then."

Nora stepped out of the jeep, opened the back to let Penny out and then waved as he drove away.

What am I doing? She took a deep breath, looking out across the bay. My husband left me, and the love of my life was buried yesterday. Feck it ... I'm going with my gut on this one. Life is short, way too short.

She felt butterflies in her stomach, thinking about spending the day with him, and smiled as she let herself and Penny back into the house.

CHAPTER 34

Clo woke up in a sweat, tangled up in the covers. She had spent the night tossing and turning and her head was sore and stuffy from crying.

Today is a new day, she said to herself as she lay back staring at the ceiling. I have to move on from this.

"*Fake it till you make it, girl,*" she said out loud as she pulled herself up to sitting position and swung her legs out of the bed.

Glancing at her phone, she saw that she had missed a text from Pierre: **We'll pick you up at 10.30**.

Blunt and to the point, thought Clo.

Checking the secret phone she kept for Rory, she saw that he had left a message too. Her stomach flipped as she opened it.

I'm sorry. We need to talk. Is that possible now with your family here?

Family, thought Clo as she sighed. She needed to see him. It was going to hurt telling him it was over, but she needed to do it quickly or she might change her mind.

Can you meet me today about 3 o'clock? Belderra Strand?

Sure, he replied. **See you then. x**

She closed the phone. She couldn't reply with an X. Not today.

Clo pulled her best acting skills out of the bag for the trip to Westport. She dressed in a beautiful Stella McCartney poppy-print maxi dress, matched with a pair of pink-rimmed sunglasses and pink pump shoes. She was a little overdressed for a coffee outing, but she needed to feel confident and in control.

Clo always knew she wasn't a natural beauty, but she also knew that an expensive designer wardrobe could make up for that. When she made the effort and wore designer clothes, she felt more in control of her life and that's how she needed to feel today.

When she got back to Fern's from the Westport trip, she hung the dress back up on its hanger. She sat in her underwear at the small dressing table in her room, removing her make-up and thinking about the morning.

It had been a pleasant trip. There was tension between herself and Pierre, but Sophia was too busy posting reels and shopping to notice. Pierre didn't try to hold her hand as he usually would as he was always very tactile, but he did open the car door for her and was polite. I really hurt him this time, she thought, and now I have to hurt Rory too.

It was a beautiful still day. Looking out her bedroom window she could see the bay was calm and there were just a few clouds in the sky. The weather could change quickly but the forecast was good.

Belderra Strand was Clo's favourite spot. The beach was so beautiful and even though it was on the Atlantic side, the horseshoe shape of the cove provided shelter from strong waves and winds. In summer, the sea was a beautiful mix of blues and greens, and the sand was fine and soft. On a windy day, the surfers arrived to catch some of the strong waves of the Atlantic.

Hopefully it wouldn't be busy today.

Most people with children favoured Elly Bay because you could park your car right next to the beach. Belderra was more out of the way and only had a few parking spaces.

Clo threw a long chiffon paisley sun dress over a turquoise bikini and, after applying sunblock, put a towel, a bottle of water, and a sunhat in a matching turquoise beach bag.

Once I do this, I want to get into the cold sea and try to feel something other than dread, she thought, slipping her feet into her sequinned flip-flops before heading out the door.

Driving up the road she took her time. She felt numb. She didn't know what she was going to say to Rory or how the conversation would go. Turning off at Binghamstown, she felt incredibly sad. This day had been coming for a while. Sooner or later I was going to have to make a choice, she thought.

As she passed the odd car or person on the road she lifted her finger off the steering wheel and nodded. There was a lovely familiarity to it from her childhood. You would never pass someone around here without acknowledging them.

She passed Cross Cemetery where some old men were leaning against the wall of the small graveyard, having a chat. They waved and she waved back. She never saw her dad leaning against a wall having a chat. He was a loner. If he had friends in O'Raghallaigh's pub, his local, she never saw him with them or heard him talk about them.

Parking up her BMW, she got out, pushed her bag up on her shoulder and walked down to the strand. There were two surfers running in and out of the water with their boards but apart from them the beach was empty. Pulling her towel out from her bag, she placed it on the sand and sat down.

The sound of the waves was hypnotic. Sea birds squawked overhead. The smell of the sea and the warm sand soothed her. She spent almost every summer of her youth on the beaches around here. She had no choice. Her parents never went abroad so Clo and her sisters had to entertain themselves at home.

I was so glad to get away from this place but it's in my DNA. The wind, the sand, and the smell of the grasses; its sooths me like no other place can.

Clo turned to the left, almost sensing Rory's arrival, and there he was. Her heart leaped in her chest as she looked at him walking towards her. He was barefoot, wearing navy swim shorts and a white cotton shirt opened halfway down exposing his toned chest. She only had to look at him to want him.

"You picked a great spot," he said as he approached. *"Far from the madding crowd."*

He sat down beside her. She could smell his cologne on his warm skin.

Turning to look at her, he took off his sunglasses. "I presume you picked here for a reason," he said as he tilted his head and ran his finger down her arm.

A single tear ran down her face as she began to tell him what happened.

"So that's it," she said, having told him everything. "That's where I am right now."

"*Hmm* ..." Rory nodded and stared out to sea.

They sat in silence for a few moments before Rory gently reached for her hand and held it in his, sending an electric current through her.

"This was probably coming," he said, looking out to the sea. "I just didn't want to think about it, I suppose."

"I'm so sorry." Clo bit her lower lip. "I feel like all my life I've been messing you around and now I'm ending it."

"But all my life it's always been you and me," he said, turning to her. "It's always been Rory and Clo. I know you, with all your faults, better than I know most people in my life but I always wanted to be here, wherever you were."

"How are you not angry with me?"

"Because you are my Clo and you always will be. This is not the end of our story."

"Do you really believe that, after all the mistakes I've made?"

"The Clo I know doesn't do things in a straight line like other people. You zigzag your way through life but you lead with passion and sometimes, like now, you might feel like you are falling off a cliff but I'm always here to catch you. You are the love of my life, whether we are together or not doesn't change that."

Clo looked into his eyes, using her free hand to wipe away the tears that were flowing now.

"I love you so much," she whispered.

"And I love you and that's why we will always find our way back to each other."

Rory gently wiped the tears away and held her face in his hands. Leaning in, he kissed her tenderly. Her body responded instantly, craving him. She moaned as his kiss deepened. She was so hungry for him now.

Rory pulled back and smiled. "We'd better stop so we don't get carried away. We don't want to upset the locals but ..."

"But what?"

Rory nodded to the sea. "It's a beautiful day for a swim."

A slow smile crossed Clo's face. I really shouldn't, she thought, but what if this is our last time together? Looking around, the surfers were packing up their van and there was nobody else around.

"Let's do it," she said, pulling her sundress up over her head.

Rory stood up and held out his hand to help her up. She looked around again. They had the beach to themselves. Hand in hand, they headed for the sea.

The cold Atlantic water was a shock and Clo gasped for breath.

"It'll be fine in a minute," Rory said, leading her by the hand over to the left-hand side of the cove.

"We'll have more coverage over there," he said.

Stopping at a calm spot, Rory turned to look at Clo.

"You are fucking gorgeous, you know that?" he said, taking in her figure in her tiny bikini.

Clo didn't answer. She smiled and reached up to him, putting both her hands on his chest. He leaned in and kissed her. This time they didn't stop. Clo moaned as he pulled her to him, his strong arm around her tiny waist.

"*Oh god!*" Clo gasped as his free hand moved down the front of her bikini bottoms. Rory looked around, but the beach was still deserted. He hooked his thumb under the band of her bikini bottoms, pulling them down enough for Clo to squirm out of them. Once released, she wrapped the bottoms around her wrist and threw both her legs around his waist. Rory grabbed hold of her thighs as he carried her to a deeper section. Clo clung to him, her right arm looped around his neck while her free hand slid his swim shorts lower.

He released himself with one hand while caressing Clo's buttock with the other. He could wait no longer. Holding Clo up, he plunged deep into her waiting body. She arched her back as he kept rhythm with the waves. Clo felt like her body would explode.

"*Oh my god!*" she cried out, joined by Rory's deep moan, the sound of the gulls overhead and the Atlantic waves drowning out their cries.

CHAPTER 35

Fern messaged Nora and Clo to see if they could all have dinner together. She hadn't seen them all day. She had risen late, favouring a lie-in today, and by the time she got up the house was empty.

Hiya, Nora replied first. **Millie and I are out for dinner tonight, but we'll be home around seven as Millie is staying with me tonight**.

Clo replied with a thumbs-up emoji and **I'm in. I am meeting Sophia and Pierre in town later. Do you want me to pick something up?**

No, that's fine. I'll organise something, replied Fern.

Okay, Fern said to herself. Tonight is the night. I need to speak to the girls and get everything off my chest.

She busied herself by cleaning the house before popping into town for some food shopping. Grabbing a basket, she browsed the aisles in Aldi, picking up some bags of salad and some chicken wrapped in Parma ham for dinner and some more groceries to keep the kitchen stocked for a few more days.

"Hey, there!"

Fern recognised the voice without having to turn around.

"Kevin," she said, smiling. "I was hoping I'd bump into you."

Despite what had happened during the Leaving Cert year, she always liked him and felt people judged him too harshly. He looked well. He had traded his all-black attire for faded denim jeans, a white T-shirt and sandals, his Australian tan making him look healthy and relaxed.

"Well, I'm glad I bumped into you too," he said warmly. "I was actually going to call out to your house today. I was hoping we could talk?"

"Yes, of course, I'd like that. I won't be long here," she said, looking at her basket. "I just have to pay for these. Do you want to grab a coffee in town?"

Kevin ran his hand through his shoulder-length black hair, letting it fall back around his face. "I was hoping for somewhere more private, without the chance of bumping into people."

"Oh! Well ... I was going to head to the tidal pool for a dip after here. It should be quiet at this hour. Do you want to meet me there?"

Kevin nodded. "Yes, that's ideal actually. I'll just grab my swim things and meet you there in about fifteen minutes?"

"Lovely."

Kevin gave a little smile and then walked slowly down the aisle. He always walked slowly, remembered Fern, slow and steady. She was glad they were meeting up to get a chance to talk. He seemed more relaxed today. He was an introvert and a deep thinker and she never really knew what was going on in his head when they were dating. He could be so kind and gentle but there was a dark side there too, no doubt about it.

But today we are meeting as old friends, Fern thought as she made her way to the checkout.

Arriving at the tidal pool before Kevin, she parked beside the wooden log-shaped Sona Sauna which was a new addition since the last time she was home. There was also a cute horsebox converted into a tiny coffee shop, ideal for a warm-up after an icy swim.

Fern was just nine years of age when the tidal pool was built. She remembered the excitement at the time. Filled by each high tide it was a safe place for adults and children to swim and quickly became a tourist attraction bringing new visitors to the area.

She had put her swimsuit on before leaving the house, throwing a long denim sundress over it. Grabbing her swim bag with two towels, her sunblock and her book, she stepped out of the car and headed down the steps.

Two older women had been in for their swim and were sitting chatting in the sun on one of the benches. Fern said hello to them and then walked to the second empty bench just past them. Putting her belongings down, she took off her sunglasses, pulled her dress over her head and slipped her feet out of her flip-flops. Then she tied up her long curly hair in a loose bun.

She checked her watch. She was early, so taking her new book – *A Week To Remember* – out of her bag, she picked up where she had left off. The story followed three Irish women as they walked the Camino de Santiago and getting lost in their adventures was a great release from reality at the moment.

A child jumped into the tidal pool and the sound of the splash made Fern jump, triggering a memory.

"*Oh god!*" Fern's hand flew to her mouth. Why did I pick here? Memories of that horrible last day of school came flooding back. "*Oh shit, shit, shit!*" she said under her breath.

CHAPTER 36

It was the last day of the Leaving Cert – June 1994 – and all the sixth years headed straight from the school to the tidal pool to celebrate the end of two gruelling weeks of state exams. It was a local tradition to gather at the docks just off the main street with cans of beer but, since the weather was so good, a group of final-year students decided to meet at the tidal pool first.

It was the perfect way to wash off the last of the schooldays before a summer of freedom, and before everyone went their separate ways in the autumn to universities, colleges and elsewhere across Ireland.

Since the school play in April, Danny and Fern had been officially "going out" but with everyone locked indoors studying, they hadn't been seen together in public. They mostly spent time at Fern's place, which was often empty – her parents were frequently away at exhibitions or staying with fellow artists.

But today the whole year could see they were together. Danny had his arm around Fern as they sat on a towel by the pool with Clo, Rory, and Nora. Clo had brought a cassette player and was singing along to Oasis's latest album.

Fern noticed the surprised looks from some of the girls – girls who probably never imagined someone like Danny would go for someone like her. With her grungy clothes and wild, curly hair, Fern was far from the "cool girl" stereotype, but she didn't care. She could feel the stares and laughed when a few dirty looks came her way.

"The Barbie dolls aren't too happy you took their Ken," Clo said with a cheeky grin, waving in their direction.

Fern laughed.

"Clo, you're a nutter," said Nora, pulling a cardigan around her shoulders and adjusting her oversized sunhat to shield her pale skin.

Clo just shrugged, lying back in her skimpy bikini, soaking up the sun without a drop of sunscreen on her porcelain-white skin.

Danny leaned into Fern, resting his forehead gently against hers. "So I'm Ken now, am I?"

"Not to me," Fern said, looking into his brilliant blue eyes.

Danny smiled and leaned in for a kiss.

Nora looked away. It was hard enough that her best friend was dating the guy she believed was her soulmate – watching them fawn over each other only made it worse. She'd tried to distance herself from them after the play, but it was impossible. They still shared the same classrooms every day and, if she was honest with herself, she'd rather be near Danny – even if it hurt – than not see him at all.

After the kiss, Danny stood up. "Who's up for a swim?"

"Not me. It's freezing in there," Fern said, smiling up at him.

"Coward!" Danny teased, bending down to kiss her again before diving into the pool.

As Fern stood to rearrange the towels, she noticed a shadow fall over her. She raised her hand to block the sun.

"Oh, hi, Kevin."

Since Kevin pulled out of the school play and Danny replaced him, Kevin had barely spoken to Fern, though he still hung out with Rory from time to time. On the night of the play, after Fern and Danny kissed in the final scene, Fern looked out to see Kevin storming out of the school hall.

According to Rory, Kevin had been hoping Danny would drop out and go back to his rowdy football crowd. That never happened. Rory suspected Kevin still thought he and Fern had a chance – until that kiss on stage proved otherwise.

"So it's official then?" Kevin asked Fern, his eyes fixed on Danny, who was now splashing around with his football friends.

"If you mean with Danny – yes, it is," Fern said, her tone firm.

"I can't believe you'd let *his type* near you!"

"His *type*?" Fern replied, irritation rising as she put a hand on her hip.

"You know what I mean. You've seen the girls hanging off him. You really think he's going to be loyal to you?"

"*How dare you!*" Fern snapped, stepping closer to him. "Just because it didn't work out with us –"

"It's not that," Kevin interrupted, locking eyes with her. "You're better than the bimbos he usually goes for."

"Fuck off, Kevin!"

"Everything all right here?" Danny asked, appearing at Fern's side, dripping wet. He placed a protective arm around her shoulders and stared Kevin down.

"It's fine," Fern muttered, not breaking her glare at Kevin.

"I was just telling Fern I'm surprised, that's all," Kevin said.

"Surprised?" Danny asked. "At what?"

"That she'd let someone like you near her," Kevin said, giving Danny a slow once-over.

"*Someone like me?*" Danny stepped forward, dropping his arm from Fern.

A hush fell over the poolside as others turned to watch.

"You don't scare me," Kevin said, his jaw clenched.

"Fuck you! You had your chance. She wants *me*, not you!"

"She'll see through you soon enough," Kevin spat, squaring up to him.

"Oh really? Because right now I'm making her happy and giving her something you couldn't!"

Kevin's face twisted in fury. He suddenly drew back and punched Danny in the jaw, sending him stumbling backward into the pool with a splash.

"*Danny!*" Fern shouted, racing to the pool's edge.

A crowd of teens jumped to their feet and rushed over.

"*What the fuck did you do that for?*" Fern screamed at Kevin, who now looked shocked at his own strength.

Silence fell. All eyes were on the pool – but Danny didn't resurface.

"*Danny!*" Fern screamed again.

Kevin, now panicking, jumped in and pulled Danny up as he gasped for air. But Danny, dazed and furious, lunged at Kevin, grabbing him by the throat and shoving him under the water.

"*Oh my God, Danny, stop!*" Fern sobbed.

"*Leave him, Danny!*" someone shouted.

Then another splash – Rory had jumped in. He grabbed Danny and forced him off Kevin. He hauled Kevin to the pool's edge where two lads helped drag him out. Kevin lay coughing, gasping for air. Danny followed, climbing out slowly, panting. He walked straight to Fern's side.

"You ... you nearly killed me," Kevin wheezed.

"*You started it!*" Danny shouted, pointing at him.

A few boys helped Kevin to his feet and led him away toward his things. Kevin turned and looked back at Danny, who now had his arm around Fern.

"*Go on – fuck off, you fuckin' weirdo!*" Danny yelled after him.

Kevin looked at Fern, then at Rory and Clo. No one met his eyes. Nodding in disgust, he gathered up his clothes and towel and walked away. No one stopped him, and he never spoke to them again.

A few days later, Fern heard from her mother that Kevin had gone to stay with an aunt in Waterford for the summer. By the end of the holidays, his parents had decided to move there too. The last anyone heard, Kevin had secured a visa to work in Australia through a relative – and he was planning to leave for good.

CHAPTER 37

It's too late now, Fern winced, pushing the memory from her mind. She put her book back in her bag and headed for the water.

He'll be here any second and I don't have a number for him anyway to switch locations.

Carefully she lowered herself into the cold seawater just as Kevin arrived.

"*My stuff is over there!*" she called out to him, pointing at the bench. He had swapped his jeans for swim shorts. She watched him walk to the bench, take off his T-shirt and flick off his sliders. She couldn't help but notice how fit he was.

It made her wish Max was here. She missed him. They spoke every night on the phone and, since Otto arrived in Morocco, she was receiving WhatsApp updates and photos of the two men she loved most in the world having a great time. She longed to be there with them, but also knew that she could not leave this place until she dealt with the ghosts of the past.

"*Jesus!*" Kevin gasped as he lowered himself down the steps. "I had forgotten how cold the sea is here."

Fern laughed. "Has the Aussie heat softened you up?"

"I think it has," he said, taking short breaths and swinging his arms from side to side to warm up.

He looks so much nicer when he smiles, she thought as she watched him hop up and down.

"I don't spend long in. It's fabulously refreshing though," Fern said, swimming to the other side.

Kevin took a breath and ducked his head underwater and then jumped up, pushing his hair away from his face before swimming over to Fern at the other side of the pool.

"There's refreshing and there's Baltic," he said, laughing, as he reached her.

"Let's get out and get warmed up," Fern said as she swam back to the steps.

She dried herself off with a towel, placed it on the bench and then sat on it, letting the sun warm her up.

"Do you come down here often?" Kevin asked as he joined her.

"I try to come for a dip every time I come home."

"You still call it home?"

"Yes, but I call London home too. I've lived longer in London than I ever did in Ireland which seems so mad. But I love coming back to visit and luckily Max and Otto do too."

"How's the movie business going for him?" Kevin asked, sitting beside Fern on the bench now.

"Great, really busy. Hey, how did you know he was in the movie business?"

"Danny and Audrey were in touch every week," said Kevin. "He kept her up to date on everyone."

"Of course. Well, Max is shooting something in Morocco at the moment and Otto has gone out to work as an AD on set. They're having a great time. I was supposed to go there too until this happened."

"Yeah."

"But what about you? What do you do in Australia?"

"I am a forensic psychologist, so I work a lot with the government and the court system, assessing criminals and providing testimonies in court cases, but I also have my own clinic in Melbourne for regular clients. I have a team of mental-health experts there and it does very well. That's where I met Audrey actually."

"Really? I was wondering how that came about."

"She came to work temporarily as a clinic administrator. I didn't hire her. I was away in Perth for about three weeks working on a high-profile case and when I came back she was there. I didn't recognise her at all, and I wasn't happy when I discovered who she was. Let's face it, I don't have great memories of this place," he looked around, "but she proved herself invaluable to the team and my colleagues wanted to hire her. I travel a lot, so I didn't see much of her at first – in fact, I avoided her but ... I got over that and we got on and these things happen, I suppose."

"I see. It's incredible really," Fern said. "I mean, it's bizarre to be living in a place as big as Australia and to bump into Audrey and then date each other."

"Bizarre or fate, who knows," Kevin said, looking out to sea.

"Yeah, but ..."

"But what?" Kevin asked, turning to her.

"You hated Danny when we were in school, so to be dating his sister is just ... I don't know ... strange, I guess."

"Yes, you of all people knew how much I hated the guy. We planned this trip back before his accident. I was so looking forward to seeing his face when we walked in together."

"So he didn't know you guys were dating?" Fern asked, puzzled. "I thought Danny and Audrey were in touch?"

Kevin sighed, looked around and then turned to look at Fern. "That's what I wanted to talk to you about."

She looked at him. He held her gaze, but something made her feel uneasy.

"Fern, I don't want to make you feel ... uncomfortable or ..."

"Or what?"

"Audrey fell out with her parents years ago, well before she left for Australia. Basically, they idolised Danny, and they made her feel second-best to him. He could do no wrong in their eyes. And of course, she was the one with the business head – I mean she's brilliant at her job – but the quarry was always going to Danny. She worked so hard to impress her dad and she has brains to burn and Danny, well ..."

Fern was puzzled. What had this got to do with anything?

"Audrey has always been different to them. She's intelligent and quiet and very hardworking but they never appreciated her. So it was a relief for her when she came to Australia and people appreciated her talents."

Fern shifted on the bench. A gentle breeze came up from the sea, giving her goose pimples, so she pulled her other towel over her lap.

"So what I'm saying is that she has had very little contact with the parents over the years even though she and Danny always remained close."

"Okay." Fern had no idea where he was going with this conversation. Yes, it explained why Audrey wasn't staying in her parents' house but why was he telling her?

"My point is, Danny confided in Audrey ... a lot."

Fern felt her throat tighten and a shiver ran over her bare skin.

"And?"

"We know about DJ, Dan Junior," he said, looking into her eyes.

Fern started to breathe deeply, her heart racing in her chest. Her head spun and she put her hand on the bench to steady herself.

Kevin put his hand on her bare shoulder.

"Fern, we are on your side," he said. "Danny did you wrong. He should have insisted that his parents acknowledge DJ, their first grandchild ... he had all that time ... and they should have –"

"*No, no, no, no, stop!*" Fern swayed back and forth. "*Stop talking!*"

"I'm sorry. I know this is a shock but when Danny told Audrey that DJ had contacted you and that he was living in Australia, Audrey begged him to tell their parents."

"*This is absolutely none of your business,*" Fern hissed, pushing Kevin's hand from her shoulder.

"Fern, I would never do anything to upset you. It's just so wrong how they have treated you. And Danny should have had the balls to confront his parents."

"*Why the fuck do you care!*"

"Because I care about you, I always have. And now I care about Audrey, and she was so upset about it and ..." Kevin paused and seemed reluctant to go on.

"What?"

"We've met him."

Fern's jaw fell open. "You've *what*?"

"Just recently. I told him not to say anything until I told you because ..."

"Jesus Christ ... I don't believe this," Fern said, standing up.

"I know it's a crazy coincidence that I happened to be dating Audrey when she found out. She wanted to meet him for herself. If she wasn't with me she would have met him anyway."

"This doesn't add up. Danny would have rung me, he would have told me if he passed on Dan's details to Audrey."

"He didn't give any details, except the name of the team he played for in Sydney. He couldn't help but be proud of that. After that it wasn't too hard to find him – he's the spitting image of his dad."

"Jesus Christ," Fern said, bending over. "I think I'm going to be sick."

"I'm sorry. I know it's a shock but it's not right. Danny should have sorted this out."

Fern took a deep breath to steady herself. "But this has absolutely nothing to do with you. What do you hope to gain out of all this?"

"Gain? Audrey just wants her parents to acknowledge him, and I support Audrey."

"*No, no, no!* This is the wrong time to do this," Fern said, standing up and moving away from him. "Whatever is going on between Audrey and her parents has been going on for a long time. I don't want her using DJ to get back at them. It's not her place to come back here and tell them now when they have just lost Danny. That job was his dad's and now his dad is gone." She grabbed her bag and stuffed her towel in it. "You tell Audrey to say nothing, *do you hear me?*" Fern was trembling with rage. "Leave those people to mourn their son. And tell her to stay away from Rossa and those poor kids! Danny's kids know nothing of this and now is not the time. *They've just buried their father, for god's sake!*"

"Fern ... I ..."

"*I mean it, Kevin. This is not the time.*"

Rushing to her car, she almost threw up.

"*How fucking dare he!*" she shouted when she sat into her car, slamming her fists on the steering wheel.

Kevin ran up the steps after her and walked towards her car. She started the engine.

"*Fern, please!*" he said as he reached the driver's window.

"*You stay away from me, well away from me!*" she yelled as she put the car in drive and sped away.

CHAPTER 38

Fern raced back to the house, trembling with rage and shock. This was not the time for the whole town to know her secret. She had no time for Danny's parents but they had just lost their only son and, as for Rossa, she had no idea how much she knew.

She wanted to keep driving to get as far away as possible, but she was still in her wet swimsuit and everything else was shoved into a ball at the bottom of her bag.

As soon as she got in, she pulled out her phone and rang Max.

"*Sorry, I'm unable to come to the phone, please leave a –*"

She hung up. She desperately needed to speak to him to talk it out.

"Oh god, I just want to jump on a plane to Morocco just to hold them, to breathe them in!" she cried. But that was not possible.

Pulling on a pair of leggings and an oversized T-shirt, she put a baseball cap on, pulling her thick hair through the hole at the back, grabbed her sunglasses and keys, and marched out the door. She needed to walk and walk and walk.

She walked a bit and then ran a bit on the road until she was out of breath. After an hour, she turned around and did the same thing until she got home. She wanted to shake her anger off. She was exhausted and her legs were sore but that's what she wanted.

After a hot shower, she fell into bed and slept for an hour.

She felt calmer when she woke up but had a pain in the pit of her stomach, thinking about telling the girls her story tonight. It had to be done. After her encounter with Kevin today, she needed her friends around her more than ever.

Clo arrived home first, looking radiant.

"Well, you look a hundred times better than yesterday," Fern said as Clo wandered into the kitchen barefoot, wearing a short yellow sundress, towel-drying her hair.

"I feel much better," Clo said, stretching her arms over her head. "Sometimes when you are in the thick of it you can't see the woods from the trees."

"How did your trip to Westport go?"

"Very well under the circumstances. Pierre and I were civil to each other, and Sophia was so self-absorbed taking photos and making reels everywhere we went she was a great distraction. She wanted to check out all the best Instagram spots. Everything is 'content' apparently." Clo raised her eyes to heaven. "Honestly, we had to take so many photos of the same thing, never mind about three photos of our food, before she got the right shot."

"I know, it's nuts," Fern said, trying to keep her voice steady. "Every moment is documented. Kids are becoming amateur photographers and filmmakers, but the demand is there. This is what kids want to watch these days. I can't remember the last time Otto sat down to watch TV unless we were watching a movie together. And that can be a nightmare for me, having two filmmakers analyse every frame of a movie while I just want to eat popcorn and watch it all unfold." She smiled, thinking about the cozy movie nights she loved so much with her men. Her body ached, she missed them so much today. "So things are okay between you and Pierre?"

"They are bearable. We are putting up a happy-family front, and Sophia is too distracted making Instagram posts to notice anything. She is also learning to drive so I think both Pierre and I were focused on staying alive as she drove on those narrow roads."

"Oh god, Otto hasn't learned to drive yet but it's something they have to learn really."

"In fairness, she has had all her lessons and is waiting for her test date so it's all practice at the moment. Pierre has way more patience than I would ever have, so they have been driving all over the place down here, stopping at beauty spots for photos. So, yeah, we have lots to talk about when Sophia is around. The real test will be when she's not. But I just want to get through this week and see what happens when we return home. The new shop will be a great distraction for both of us."

"I really admire you, you know," Fern said, looking at her friend.

"Me?"

"Yes, you. You are so strong. You just made a huge life decision and, even though it hurts and you are not even sure it's the right decision, you dust yourself down and get on with it. You're amazing."

"Well, thank you for saying that but please do not use me as a role model. Everything is hanging on by a thread and that thread could snap at any moment. Now, something smells delicious – I'm starving, are you?"

She walked to the back door and looked out at the Bay, putting an end to that conversation. It was a warm evening and the sliding door at the back of the house was open. A gentle sea breeze swayed the egg chair outside.

"I'm no Master Chef, so it's salad with chicken wrapped in Parma ham in a tin tray, from the supermarket," Fern said. "I picked up some fresh bread and cakes from An Builín Blasta too. Millie might want some when she gets back."

"Is Millie back tonight?"

"Yes. Nora said they wouldn't be home for dinner so they must be eating in her mam's."

Clo unwrapped the towel from her head and shook her hair. "Nora's working very hard up at the school – she's always there."

"It's going to look great. It's a tough job. Sure it's hard to keep anything growing around here."

Only certain types of plants and trees could withstand the salty air of the area. The winters were hard too. Very few trees survived the environment of the Mullet peninsula. Any trees that did, grew sideways, battered by the horizontal winds.

"Yeah, well, it's not called the *Wild* Atlantic Way for nothing," Clo said, walking to the fridge. "Will I open a bottle?"

"Sure, why not? But there should be an open bottle of white in there. Will we sit outside for a bit? That chicken needs another ten minutes."

"Perfect." Clo grabbed the open bottle of white from the fridge and took down two glasses from the shelf while Fern put two sun-chairs together outside.

They sat down, facing the sun.

"Ah, this is bliss!" Clo said, closing her eyes. "As much as I was desperate to leave this place, I do miss it."

"I thought you hated coming home?" Fern asked, her face turned up to the sun too.

"I hated coming home to my own house. The atmosphere there is just so awful, and it frustrates me that they will just sit there in that house till the day they die. But I guess that that is just their way. I can't change that, so there is no point in me getting angry and frustrated at them. I need to let them live their life – it's the life they chose. And sorry if I'm boring you, but I've thought about this a lot – if my mother was that miserable, of course she could have left. Maybe she wasn't miserable. Maybe they found companionship and some sort of security in keeping their lives small. I spent most of my teenage years complaining about the house and the holidays we never had, and I was probably a nightmare to live with. I'm just so different from them. My sisters don't have the same hang-ups that I do, so we view things through a different lens. I need to cut them some slack. Just because they live a life I never could, doesn't mean they are wrong, and I am right. We're just different."

"*Wow!*" Fern said, looking at her friend.

"I know!" laughed Clo. "It must be old age making me tolerant, at last. But, seriously, look at this view."

Fern took a sip of her wine and looked out across the bay. The sun was still high in the sky as the sunset wasn't until after ten in summertime. "On an evening like this, it's better than the South of France."

"And this place is in our DNA. Wild and unpredictable," Clo said, staring out over the bay.

"You should get a T-shirt with that on it," smiled Fern "It describes you to a T!"

"Oh yeah, that's me all right."

"Speaking of which," Fern began, "did you see Rory today?"

Clo sighed. "Yes. I met him this afternoon and, as usual, he was amazing about everything."

"You've known him forever and it will be hard not seeing him or being in contact but what will be will be, I guess, and if you guys are meant to be together down the line, well ... so be it."

"*Hmm.*" Clo looked into her glass of wine. She didn't need to confide in the girls anymore. She didn't know what the future held but she and Rory had agreed to cool things for now. There would be no more trips to New York for the foreseeable, but the secret phone was staying.

He is as much a part of me as this place is, she said to herself. I couldn't cut him out of my life even if I wanted to. When she closed her eyes, she could still feel his hands on her body. *And I definitely don't want to,* she decided.

"Nora said they will be back around seven," Fern said, looking at her watch.

"Millie is such a dote, isn't she?"

"Yes, she's like a miniature Nora. What is the story with her ex – Greg?" asked Clo.

"I don't know," Fern said. "She never mentions him. Millie did say that her dad's friend made her lasagne in Italy, so I guess they visit him and – what's his name again?"

"I don't remember," said Clo, shaking her head. "It's one thing for your husband to run off with another woman, but a man!"

"I know. I think she was completely blindsided. I mean they were obviously still having sex if Millie was conceived."

"Poor Nora. Do you think she rushed into it?" Clo asked. "Marriage, I mean? I don't think they were dating long before they got married, were they?"

"No, but she knew him for years through work. He restored period houses and historic estates, and she designed the gardens. So she did know him, but they were only officially dating eight months, I think, before he popped the question."

"And with the old biological clock ticking ... "

"Yeah. I always did wonder though if she rushed into that marriage because Danny got married."

"Really?"

"Yes," said Fern. "She had a crush on Danny, like forever. And I did wonder over the years if she held out hope that they might be a couple."

"Ah god, I don't think so, Fern. I mean they were always only friends."

"Yes, but she wanted more. I don't think it's just a coincidence that Danny gets engaged to Rossa and a few weeks later Nora gets engaged to Greg after such a short time. I think she might have been holding a candle for him all those years and then Rossa blew it out, so to speak."

"Oh god, I hope not."

Just then the oven bell went off.

"Right – our dinner is ready," Fern said, getting up. "Will you grab some cutlery there? I think we'll eat outside."

"Great idea and I'll grab the wine too."

"Definitely." Fern didn't want to drink too much but she would need to have some courage to tell the girls her whole story tonight. After her meeting with Kevin today, it had to happen tonight.

CHAPTER 39

"*We're home!*" Nora called from the front door as Penny ran in and went straight over to sniff and say hello to Clo and Fern.

"Hello!" Millie came in, carrying her little backpack. "I'm sleeping here tonight."

"That's great news," Fern said. "Are you hungry? Do you want a snack?"

"*Nah*," Millie said, tilting her head and rubbing her tummy. "I'm full of my dinner from Pavel's house."

"Pavel's house?" Clo said, turning to Nora with a smile.

Nora smiled back. "Yes, Pavel invited us to dinner in his house."

Millie yawned.

"Okay, missy, let's get you to bed," said Nora. "Say goodnight to everyone."

"Nighty-night," Millie said, rubbing her eyes.

"Night, Millie," said Clo and Fern.

"Back in a while," Nora said, leading Millie to the bedroom.

"Pavel's house?" Clo said to Fern with a surprised expression on her face.

"I know. This is an interesting development."

Fern took down another wine glass for Nora and she soon joined them at the table outside in the back garden.

"Wine?" asked Fern.

"Oh yes, please."

Fern poured. "We need another bottle." She went to get it and check on the chicken.

"Millie will be asleep in a minute, she's exhausted," said Nora. "It's so nice to sit outside at this hour, isn't it?"

"Forget about that," said Clo. "Dinner with Pavel, let's talk about that."

Nora blushed. "It was just dinner with a friend – a work colleague and it was very nice. That's all there is to it."

"Whatever it is, Nora, if it feels good go for it," said Clo. "You could do with some luck in that area."

"Jeez, thanks," replied Nora mockingly.

"I'm sorry," Clo said. "I shouldn't have said that. I'm the last person you should take relationship advice from."

"It's okay. I do like him and the fact that we are spending all day together without annoying each other means that he likes me too, I hope. We'll see."

Fern, listening from the kitchen, took another bottle of wine from the fridge and paused to take a deep breath. It's time, she thought.

She opened the bottle and went back outside.

She bit her bottom lip nervously as she sat down. "Girls. I need to talk to you about something," she said.

"Is everything okay?" Clo asked.

Fern looked at her two friends.

"No, not really. I've been waiting for the right moment to tell you two something. I love having you here, but I also wanted you to stay here because I have to tell you something that I've kept a secret for so many years. And I had a very disturbing encounter today which means I have to tell you right now."

"Jesus, Fern, are you ... unwell?" Nora asked, alarmed.

"No. Nothing like that, but I think my news will come as a huge shock to you both." She heaved a huge sigh. "Thirty years ago I came home from my first term in London for the October mid-term break. I sat at that kitchen table with my mother," she said, pointing behind her. "Upset and terrified, I told her something."

Fern's chest tightened as she recalled that awful conversation she had with her mam. She took a deep breath and began.

CHAPTER 40

Thirty Years Earlier

October College Midterm Break

"Oh god, Mam, I'm in big trouble."

Fern crossed her arms on the kitchen table, laid her head down on them, and wept.

"Jesus, Fern, what is it?"

Her mother Angela pulled her chair nearer and put an arm around Fern's shoulders. "Let me call your dad."

"*No!*" Fern jerked her head up, her eyes red from crying. "Please don't tell Dad!"

"Okay, okay, just breathe, pet, and tell me what it is. You're in an awful state."

Fern pulled the sleeves of her sweatshirt over her hands and wiped a mixture of tears and snot from her face.

"Here," her mother reached into her smock-dress pocket and handed her a packet of tissues.

As Fern pulled out a tissue, she wondered where she should start.

"I ... I ... oh god!"

"Take your time, love," her mam said, gently rubbing her back.

"I'm so sorry, Mam ... but ... I'm pregnant."

"Oh Mother of God!" Angela clutched her chest.

"I'm so sorry, Mam!"

"Oh, you poor pet! How far?"

"Huh?"

"How far are you gone?"

"I did a test in London so I think it's seven weeks."

"So it's hardly a lad in London, is it?"

Fern shook her head.

"Right. Is it Danny O'Connor's?"

Fern nodded.

"Does he know?"

"No, not yet. I was going to tell him later. But, Mam, what am I going to do?" Fern's face was contorted with pain and anguish. "I can't do this. I can't have a baby. How would I look after it? I'd have to give up college and I couldn't have it here and have people gossiping about me and I couldn't raise a baby in London. What am I going to do?" She burst into tears again.

Angela pulled her close and kissed her on the side of her head. "Hush now, we'll sort this out. Let me think for a second."

"You and Dad are heading off on a tour so I can't ask you to ..."

"The tour dates are all booked for next year," sighed Angela. "And, anyway, the touring road is no place for a baby."

Fern could see her mam's eyes dart from place to place as her brain tried to process this.

"But what about your life and your dreams?"

"I love college, Mam, but I'm going to have to leave and ..."

"Who else knows about this?"

"Nobody."

"Have you told any of your friends?"

"No."

"Aunty Joan?"

"No, I didn't say a thing. She did ask if I was feeling okay because I was very quiet but I told her I was fine. She's busy getting ready for an exhibition in London so she's in her studio a lot."

Fern and her mam sat in silence, looking out ahead of them at the rain bashing against the window.

Angela turned her chair to face Fern. Putting her hands on her daughter's shoulders, she took a deep breath.

"Listen to me now. You don't have to do this."

Fern's jaw dropped open. "You mean ...?"

"Yes. You know exactly what I mean. Nobody knows about this and nobody needs to know. The time is not right for this, okay? If you go through with this pregnancy, your life as you know it is over. Your dreams, your talent, your independent life in London will all disappear."

"Mam, I ..."

"Listen to me." Angela stared into her daughter's eyes. "What other choices do you have? I'll tell you what they are. If you have this baby in London, you will have to drop out of college to work to provide for it and afford child care. And even if Joan allows you to stay, it will be hard making ends meet and you will have thrown away your dreams. If you come home here, everyone will know about it. That snobby mother of Danny's will want nothing to do with you even if Danny does. The whole town will be talking about you, looking down their judgemental noses at you and your child. You know how this country treats single mothers. You've heard the stories from those awful homes that some poor girls' families put them in. The time is not right for this."

"Oh, Mam, I don't think I could ..."

"Me and your dad love you and we will support you one hundred percent whatever you decide. But think about your future, Fern." Angela pushed back the wet hair that had stuck to Fern's face with tears. "You are so talented, pet. You have a fantastic career ahead of you. Choose life, Fern, choose your life. It won't be easy, love, but you will move on from this. You will pick yourself up, move on with your life, and grab every opportunity you can. The alternative takes all that away."

"I don't even know how I would organise something like that."

"Joan does."

"Aunty Joan?"

"Pet, your Aunty Joan has been helping visitors from many parts of this county for that exact same reason. You are not the first and you won't be the last."

Fern's face dropped in shock.

"Women have been taking that trip to London for donkey's years. Some of them could be from this parish. It's not your fault and you are not a bad person, regardless of what the bloody Church says. It's your life, love, and it's your choice but just know that there are hundreds maybe thousands of Irishwomen going over on the boat to the UK every month for the same reason. It's nobody's place to judge. Sometimes it's the best thing to do all round. Joan knows the right people and she can organise everything."

"I'm ... in shock."

"It's a lot to take in, pet, but my advice would be to say nothing to Danny for now and if you decide to go this route maybe say nothing to him ever."

"Ever?"

"What good would it do? You two aren't even seeing each other. In this situation, the fewer people that know the better. If you even tell one person – even someone you think is your best friend now – you can't trust that word won't get out at some time in the future. Keep this between you, me and Joan, do you hear me?"

Fern nodded. "Oh god!" she said, putting her head in her hands.

"You look exhausted, love."

"I haven't slept properly in weeks."

"How about you get into bed and I'll bring you a hot-water bottle and a cup of tea?"

Fern nodded.

"It's your decision, pet, but have a good think about it. You worked hard to get into this college and you have your whole life ahead of you. As I said, you pass by people every day who made decisions about their futures that they can never tell anyone about. But it was the right thing for them at that time and that's nobody's business but theirs."

"Thanks, Mam." Fern stood up and hugged her.

"Go on off to bed and I'll get that kettle on."

Fern opened the door of her bedroom and looked around. All her favourite toys and books from childhood were still there. Nothing had changed since she left except it all looked so childish now. Even the Bon Jovi posters on the wall seemed so happy and carefree. God, life was so innocent just a few months ago, she thought, looking around.

She was in a different space now. Her head was spinning with all that her mother had said. She had no idea that Joan had helped all those women in complete confidence. Yes, she did have a lot of visitors from Ireland to her London home but Fern had thought nothing of it.

She had heard the awful stories that leaked out about Mother and Baby homes and she knew how single mothers were judged but the fathers of those babies never suffered the same fate.

"There you are now!" Her mother arrived with a mug of tea and a hot-water bottle. "Get some rest now, love. Everything will be fine, okay? You are not on your own in this, do you hear me?"

Fern nodded. "I love you, Mam."

"You too, pet," Angela said as she kissed her on the forehead and left, closing the door behind her.

As she put on her pyjamas, she tried to take in everything she had told her. She wasn't the first to be in this predicament and she wouldn't be the last but at least she had a mam and an aunt who could fix everything for her and for that she was grateful. But can I do this? Can I go through with this? She pulled the duvet over her head, willing sleep to come.

CHAPTER 41

When Fern finished speaking, Clo and Nora sat with their jaws open, shocked expressions on their faces.

Clo was the first to speak. "Oh my god, Fern!"

Nora's eyes filled with tears. "We would have been there for you ... we could have supported you."

"You two were off living your lives. I didn't want to drag you into it and at the time Mam said the fewer people who knew about it the less chance it would come out."

"I can understand that," said Clo. "I hate to think of you going through something like that on your own though."

Fern took a deep breath.

"Well ... I didn't."

"What do you mean?" said Nora.

"I didn't go through with it."

Nora looked confused and then her eyes widened. "You had a baby?"

"Yes." Fern nodded, looking at her two friends.

"Danny's baby?" Nora could barely get the words out.

"Yes. We got serious over that summer and obviously we weren't careful enough. We decided to go our separate ways, him to college in

Galway and me to London. We had both agreed that it was pointless to try to keep a relationship going and I was happy with that but, of course, I had no idea ..."

"But ... how did you keep this a secret? How did we not know? How did it not get out?" Nora was frantically trying to make sense of all this.

"With the help of my Aunt Joan. I decided to have the baby and my aunt arranged everything with an adoption service. I couldn't look after a baby; I was still a child myself. And, selfishly, I loved my course, I loved my life in London and I knew I would have to give all that up. It was better all round to put him up for adoption and give him the best chance at life. I carried on in college until I started showing. I then told the college and they let me defer the rest of the year. I got a part-time job in a hospital in the admin office and then for the last month I stayed in Aunt Joan's house."

"You said 'him'?" Nora asked.

"Daniel James O'Malley was born on the 10th of May 1996."

"What? I can hardly believe this," Clo said, shaking her head. "And what about Danny, did he know?"

"Yes. I tried to keep it from him but then I figured he had a right to know, so when I was eight months pregnant and everything was set up, I told him. I didn't want to tell him before that in case he tried to interfere or change things."

"And ... what did he say?"

"He was shocked obviously but he came to see me straight away. He made something up to tell his parents and he got the bus and boat and came over to London. We spent a lovely weekend together and we cried together. He just asked that his name be put on the birth cert and that I send him a photo. He offered me money too, but I didn't take it. It was sad but we both knew it was the right thing to do."

"Jesus .... I think I need another drink." Clo filled up her glass.

Nora was lost for words. She looked down at the table. A mix of emotions flooded through her. She couldn't help it. She felt angry and she felt so stupid.

Danny was supposed to be mine, she thought, trying not to let her feelings show. Yes, I was jealous when he dated Fern, but I knew they wouldn't last. I thought it was just casual. I never thought they went all the way. Oh god, I'm so naïve, so fucking delusional! She started to sweat, her breath quickening.

"Nora? More wine?"

"What? Yes, yes, please."

"I know it's a lot to take in," Fern said to Nora, "and I know you really liked Danny back then so I can understand that this is a bit of a shock."

A bit? Nora, grabbed the sides of her chair to steady herself. I thought we had a connection all that time, all those years waiting for him to notice me and he never said a word about this? Danny obviously never considered me enough of a friend even to confide in me.

"*Em* ... sorry, it is a shock," she managed to say. "I had no idea. How did you keep it a secret? You and Danny both?"

"We decided to put the whole thing behind us. Even when I came home here we never spoke about it but every year on DJ's birthday we sent each other a text with just a heart on it to mark the day."

"Oh, Fern!" said Clo.

Fern sighed.

"So does anyone else know?" asked Clo.

"At first it was just my mam and she told my dad after I went back to London. I told my Aunt Joan and Danny. I told Max when things got serious between us. But then everything changed just over a year ago."

Oh god, thought Nora, taking a gulp of her wine, what now?

"Both Danny and I left letters with the adoption agency just in case the day ever came when Daniel might want to find us. We were delighted that his adopted family kept the name we gave him. They just shortened it to DJ. I hoped it might happen when DJ turned eighteen but of course I had no idea if his adoptive parents ever told him he was adopted. When the years went by I presumed either they hadn't or he didn't want to find us, which I always knew I would have to accept. And then I received a phone call from the agency to say he had contacted them."

Fern swallowed hard as her eyes filled up.

"Hey," Clo said, reaching out to hold her hand.

"Sorry," she sniffled, pulling a tissue from her sleeve. "It was such a shock at the time and such an amazing moment that I get emotional every time I think about it."

"Long story short, he didn't know he was adopted until his adoptive mother died. She didn't want to tell him while she was alive – she was afraid that she'd lose him. So it took him a while to come to terms with his adoptive mam's death and then the news that he was adopted. But he left an email address and I emailed him and then he said he was coming to London to meet us."

"Us?" Nora asked.

"Yes, Danny and me."

"When was this?" Nora asked.

"He came to London six months ago just after Christmas, and we met at my house. I nearly fell over when I saw him. Do you want to see a photo?"

"Yes, of course," said Clo.

Nora felt sick as she watched Fern open her phone. She didn't want to see a photo of their love child but what could she do?

Clo and Nora gasped when she turned the phone around.

"*Oh my God!*" said Clo.

"I know," said Fern. "There's not a bit of me in him."

"Can I see?" Nora said, holding out her hand.

Taking the phone, she looked and felt tears come.

"Oh Nora!" Fern said. She pushed back her chair, came around to Nora and put her arm around her.

"Sorry," Nora said, wiping a tear away. "It's just ... he's the spit of him."

"It is uncanny. When they met, Danny and DJ just stood there looking at each other and then they fell around the place laughing at how similar they looked."

"You said he came to London," said Clo. "Where was he living?"

"Sydney, Australia."

"No way!"

"Yes, his adoptive parents moved to Australia when he was still a baby so that's home to him. And like Danny he's a top sportsman. He plays

Aussie rules football for a top Sydney Team. He is a professional football player and by the sounds of it he makes a great living out of it."

"Jesus, Danny must have been thrilled," said Clo.

"Over the moon." Fern smiled, remembering how the two men got on so well and how proud Danny was of his son.

"But what about Rossa?" asked Nora. "Did she know?"

"Ah yes – well, this is where it gets complicated. Danny never told Rossa about DJ until he contacted us."

"That must have been a shock."

"Yes, I mean they had three kids by then and I suppose, like me, Danny didn't know if DJ would ever contact us. And Danny and I never spoke about it so I suppose he didn't feel the need. I never asked him how Rossa took it. That was his business. But, yes, it must have been a huge shock."

"And his parents?"

"His mother always knew."

"The whole time?" said Clo.

"Yes. I had no idea. Danny only told me that when we met DJ and, believe me, I was shocked."

"You mean she knew all these years and never said anything to you?" asked Nora.

"Yes, and when I think of the amount of times I saw her here when I came home. But it's worse than that – she never told his dad."

"*No way!*"

"Yes. From what Danny tells me he told his mother everything when he came back from visiting me in London. He wanted to see if his mother would mind the baby. Now, I wouldn't have let that snobby cow do that anyway but I suppose he was just emotional about the whole situation. Anyway, she swore him to secrecy. Told him that if it got out it could affect his dad's political standing and possibly ruin his career – which was bullshit but, sure, Danny believed her."

"What a bitch!" said Clo.

"But after we met DJ in London, Danny wanted him to come back here and meet the family. He was so proud of him. We couldn't do it then and, in fairness, his dad still had no idea, and neither did Danny's kids. DJ had to go back for football season anyway so we said we would do it the next time he came back to Europe."

"So does DJ know about Danny's passing?" Nora asked.

Fern took a deep breath. "Yes, I rang him and told him and, of course, he was shocked like the rest of us – and it has to be so disappointing for him because he was just getting to know us. He didn't know whether to fly over because, apart from being in the middle of the football season, we didn't know if it would be too much for him to show up here, so we agreed that it was best for him not to come at this time."

"Is that why Rossa wants to talk to you?" asked Nora.

"I'd say so. I did message her from London to tell her that he wouldn't be showing up. She has enough on her plate and I still don't know if her kids know about DJ."

"Oh dear!" sighed Nora. "But at the wake when you saw Rossa – was it weird or anything?"

"No. I just felt terrible for the woman."

"I get that," said Clo. "And you still don't know if the dad knows?"

"Well, that's where things have turned feckin' crazy ..."

"What do you mean?" asked Nora.

Fern sighed heavily. "Kevin knows."

CHAPTER 42

Fern looked at the shocked faces of Clo and Nora.

"*Fuck off! How?*" Clo couldn't believe what she was hearing. "If we didn't know, how did he know?"

"Oh, believe me, he didn't hear it from me," Fern said. Her jaw tightened as she recalled their conversation earlier. "I met Kevin today in the supermarket. We chatted and then he said he needed to talk to me. So I said grand and we went to the tidal pool and ... well, you're going to need another glass of wine when I tell you this ..." She rubbed her temples with her fingers.

Fern recounted the conversation with Kevin word for word.

"So Danny told Audrey," said Nora.

"Yes, and I get it. DJ lives in Australia, so does Audrey and she is his aunt. But Danny didn't tell me! I'm so angry at Danny for not telling me that! He could have warned me. And I would have been okay with her meeting DJ – she is his aunt and his only blood relative in Australia. I just wish I knew. And I had to hear all this from Kevin of all people!" Fern shook her head. "I'm afraid I completely lost it, when I suppose Kevin was trying to do the right thing by letting me know."

"And what a week to find all this out!" Clo said.

Nora just stared into the distance.

"Nora? You okay?" asked Fern.

"Yeah, I'm just taking it all in. Do you think Audrey will say something? She's not staying with her parents so they have obviously had a falling-out. Do you think Audrey wants to expose Danny and ruin his image as well as embarrass her parents?"

"I can't believe she would do such a thing at this time," Clo said. "At the end of the day, her parents have lost their only son, and Rossa and the kids' lives have been devastated by what has happened. They don't deserve to find out now either. But how do you feel about the word getting out, Fern?"

"I don't know," said Fern. "I had planned on just telling you two. I hadn't thought about the whole town knowing about it and talking about it and, regardless of how I feel, now is not the time. Danny is just buried and we have the memorial on Saturday. It would be too much for his kids and Rossa to have people talking about this rather than honouring Danny. It would take away from the memorial." She ran both hands through her hair. "I don't care what people say about me. I will be returning to my life in London and by the time I come back here again it will have blown over. But Rossa and the kids have to go on living here. I don't know if I should talk to Rossa first and warn her about Audrey or try to talk to Audrey first. What do you think I should do?"

"Well, I think you should talk to Audrey and see what she plans to do," Clo said. "Rossa is in mourning and is consoling the kids. If you could talk to Audrey you might stop her from taking it any further, for now anyway."

"It's so bizarre," Nora said. "What are the chances of Kevin who hated Danny meeting Audrey who hates her parents, and the two of them dating each other now?"

"It is crazy," said Fern. "And the fact that they kept their relationship a secret from Danny and her parents. I mean, I thought she and Danny were close. But Kevin said that they wanted to walk in and surprise him."

"Rub his nose in it, more like," said Clo.

"And they met with DJ in Australia?" Nora asked.

"Yes, they travelled to Sydney to one of his matches. She contacted him through his football team. Now that I've calmed down, I can see that DJ is an adult and he can see who he wishes. I understand why he would want to meet her and I can see why she would want to meet him. She can also tell him things about Danny growing up that I can't and I'm sure that's valuable to him. I just feel so left out of it all, and he is my son."

Clo reached over and squeezed Fern's hand.

"If she wants to confront her parents then there is nothing I can do about that," said Fern. "What I don't want is a big showdown while everyone is still mourning Danny. This week is for him."

"If Rossa doesn't know about Audrey meeting DJ, then maybe she wanted to talk to you about something else," Nora said.

"Yes, I should have rung her today but I can't do that now, knowing what I know."

"And you don't know how she took the news about DJ?" asked Nora.

"No, I don't. All I know is that Danny was on a high when we met DJ, we both were, and we got on so well with him. I know that Danny wanted him to be part of his life and he was going home to sort all that out. He really wanted to bring him back to Belmullet. It might have been just as well that DJ had to return to Sydney for football season because that gave Danny a bit more time to decide how to tell Rossa. He knew I'd told my parents about DJ getting in touch and coming to see us, so he did ask me to tell them to say nothing to anyone from here until he had that sorted. After that, I didn't hear from him before the accident."

"Well, then we can take it that Rossa knows but her kids may not," Clo concluded.

"Yes," said Fern, "and they've just lost their dad, their hero, so now is not the time for this bombshell."

Fern stood up and went into the kitchen where she opened a kitchen press. Taking out some matches, she returned with two candles, lit them and placed them on the table. It was getting dark outside now.

The three friends sat looking at the flames.

"I'm going to need you guys over these next few days," Fern said. She stretched out her arms across the table and Clo and Nora took a hand each. "I spoke to Max and Otto and they really want to be here but filming will go on into next week. I told them to extend their stay there and I'll fly out there to meet them. I'm desperate to see them."

"We will be here for you," Clo said.

"One hundred percent," said Nora and they both squeezed Fern's hands as the sun went down in Blacksod Bay.

CHAPTER 43

Friday

Nora had a terrible night's sleep. She tossed and turned all night. She had come to terms with Danny marrying Rossa years ago but this revelation about Fern and Danny's baby shook her.

It also made her think about her friendship with Fern and Clo. They were her closest friends, her oldest friends, and yet they had kept these secrets, huge secrets from each other for years.

Clo and Rory's five-year affair was a revelation she didn't see coming but it was not as shocking as Fern's big secret.

And Danny. She thought she knew him. All the cosy chats she had with him every time she came home and he never said a word to her. She had confided in him about her sham of a marriage, more than she had told the girls, and yet he said nothing to her about his huge secret. It felt confusing and sad. She had built a relationship with Danny in her head. She was never going to be anything more than a friend to him.

Millie mooched in the bed beside her.

"Time to get up, sweet pea," she whispered in her ear as she snuggled into her.

Thank god for Millie, she said to herself as she gave her an extra squeeze.

"Mummy!" Millie giggled as she brushed Nora's hair from around her face.

"Where are you going with Granny today?" Nora asked.

"Ball-in-a."

"That's right, you're going to visit Aunty Martha. You and I will give Penny a little walk and then we'll get your overnight bag ready for you. You might be late getting back from Ballina so I think Granny wants you to stay over. Is that okay with you?"

"Yes! Sleepover in Granny's!"

Nora laughed. She was delighted that Millie loved staying with her mam. They would be returning to Dublin on Sunday so her mam deserved to see Millie as much as she wanted to.

"Are we going to Pavel's house again?"

"Pavel's? I don't know. Why do you ask?"

"He's funny and I want to see Milis again."

"*Hmm*, we'll see."

"Granny said he likes you, Mummy."

"Really? What did she say?"

"She said it to Ralf. She said, 'Did you see the way he looks at her?'"

"*Hmm*, well, I think Pavel likes everyone. He likes me and you and Penny. Now let's get washed and dressed."

"Okay," Millie answered, jumping out of bed and running into the ensuite.

The way he looks at her. Nora couldn't help smiling. They'd had a lovely night at his house. Millie ran around outside, playing with Penny and Milis, while she and Pavel sat sipping wine in the sunshine at the side of the house. The elevated position provided a view out over the town to the left and Blacksod Bay in the distance.

"This really is a sun trap," she had said, closing her eyes as she lifted her face to the sun.

When she'd opened her eyes he was looking at her and this time she didn't turn away.

"You're lucky – you tan naturally," she said, looking at his tanned arms.

"I get most of my tan from working outdoors. I used to sunbathe naked out here but Alek didn't like it."

Nora's face dropped.

"I'm joking!" He winked and then laughed at her.

Nora laughed too but now she had the image of a naked Pavel in her mind and she felt sure she would return to that image later.

"Sitting here is so much more enjoyable with company," he said, smiling.

I'm sure there are plenty of women around here who wished they were sitting here right now, Nora had thought as she smiled back.

It was just so easy to be in his company. His big size made her feel safe and secure. We have managed to work together for hours and sit quietly together too without forcing conversation. I could easily fall for him if I stayed here, she thought, but that wasn't something she was about to consider.

Maybe Clo was right. Maybe she should let loose a bit and have a fling. It's been so long, she thought, six years ago to be exact.

"All done!" Millie called from the bathroom, snapping Nora back to the present.

"Okay, I'll have a quick shower while you get dressed and then we'll have breakfast."

Pavel was working on his other jobs in the area this morning and Nora planned on meeting him at the school after lunch. They'd worked hard yesterday after the delivery arrived, finishing the mixed heather bed and securing the bench to the ground. The grasses that lined the driveway were in too. There wasn't much left to do with the school garden now. They just needed to weed and water and check that all the planting had settled well.

Mary Comerford and the school committee were coming down to decorate the sports hall and go over the plans for tomorrow and Pavel was digging out the hole for the hawthorn memorial tree.

Just two more days here, thought Nora as she pulled on a pair of leggings and an oversized T-shirt. She had dreaded coming here, thinking that she would be broken-hearted about Danny. But nothing had turned out like she'd thought it would.

She could barely keep it together for his wake and visiting the house he shared with Rossa and the kids had been torture. That was the life she thought she would have with him. The fact that he never told her about him and Fern and the baby just showed that he didn't share her idea that they had this special bond. She couldn't even be angry with him. He never promised her anything. All those years dreaming of a life with Danny had been such a waste of energy, she realised.

She felt stupid but feeling like a mug wasn't going to help her now. What's the point in looking back, beating myself up over this? I need to put all this behind me and move on. In a way, Danny's death has released me from my delusions.

I need to do something today, she thought as she slipped her feet into her Birkenstocks. A hike or a sea swim maybe to wash the past off and turn my thoughts to the future. It will actually be nice to get home to my little house – just Millie, Penny and me.

"No more drama, please, Universe," she said to her reflection in the mirror, tying up her long red hair into a high ponytail, pulling down a few strands of hair around her face. "Let's have a lovely calm day today. I just want to enjoy our last two days here."

CHAPTER 44

Fern was woken by the sound of Millie calling Penny and the front door shutting. I can't believe I slept so deeply, she thought, looking at the time on her phone. She lay in bed looking at the ceiling. Do I feel different, she asked herself. She had imagined she would feel lighter after telling the girls about DJ but it didn't turn out like she had imagined it in her head.

She had imagined calmly telling them and the three of them hugging and crying and smiling as they looked at photos of DJ. That's the image she'd played over and over in her mind when she'd asked them to stay with her.

But Kevin had robbed her of that scenario by confronting her at the tidal pool with the shocking information that he and Audrey had met DJ. It had felt like a horrible intrusion.

If only Danny had warned me that Audrey knew, she thought, but I have no choice but to deal with it now. Regardless of what has happened or how aggrieved Audrey feels, she has to consider Rossa and the kids. I need to get to her today and see what she plans to do. I need to stop her before she talks to Rossa.

She looked at her phone again. It was only eight o'clock. She didn't have a number for either of them. There's only one thing I can do then, she thought, pulling back the quilt and swinging her legs out of the bed. I'm going to have to go to the Talbot Hotel and try to catch Audrey there.

Hopping in the shower, she tried to think about how the conversation would go. How do you prepare for a topic like this, she wondered, as she turned down the temperature of the shower to cold. I need to be fully awake and sharp for this, she thought, and then gasped as the cold water hit the top of her head.

Fern got a parking spot right outside the Talbot Hotel. The town was waking up. Shopkeepers were opening as delivery trucks pulled up to deliver stock. It was still quiet enough as the primary school kids were off school this week and the secondary school students were preparing for the Leaving Cert, due to start on Monday. Building workers in hi-vis jackets and hard hats strolled into the Cake Queen Café for their breakfast.

Belmullet was changing all the time. New builds and apartment blocks had sprung up in the town and small estates of summer houses for out-of-towners had been built nearer the bay for those much sought-after sea views. It was good for the town, thought Fern, as she looked out the front windscreen. It was great to see new people move into the area and big supermarkets choosing to open there. The winters could be long, so having new life around the place and new investment in the town could only be a good thing.

"Right," she said aloud. "Let's do this."

Walking in the main door of the Talbot Hotel she said good morning to the receptionist and headed straight for the breakfast room.

"Good morning," a waitress said, smiling, and picked up a menu as she approached her. "Table for one?"

Fern glanced around the restaurant, spotting Kevin and Audrey at a table. "No, thank you, I won't be staying."

Kevin looked up and his face dropped as he saw Fern walk across the floor. He whispered something to Audrey who did not look up and continued to eat her granola.

"Fern," Kevin said, standing up.

"Good morning."

Audrey put down her spoon and slowly turned to Fern.

"We were expecting to hear from you today," she said. Even at this early hour, her hair was tied back in a tight bun, not a hair out of place.

"Sit down," Kevin said, pulling out a chair.

"No, thanks. I'll let you have your breakfast in peace – I don't think this is a good place to talk," she said, looking around at the room full of families and businesspeople enjoying breakfast.

"Where do you suggest?" Audrey asked.

"The Broadhaven Bay has a big lounge just past reception. We'd have plenty of privacy there. I'd like to talk there as soon as we can."

"We're almost finished here so we could meet you there in thirty minutes," said Audrey.

"Great." Fern nodded to the two of them, turned and walked out of the room.

CHAPTER 45

Fern walked from the Talbot to the Broadhaven Bay Hotel. It was only fifteen minutes away and the morning air was refreshing. She wasn't sure what she was going to say. Audrey was a funny cookie – she couldn't quite make her out. But yesterday Kevin had run after her and seemed genuinely concerned that she was upset by his news.

Even this morning she could feel his concern when he saw her arrive at their table. But Audrey had kept a very cool composure throughout their exchange. She didn't seem at all surprised to see her arrive this early in the morning.

The sun was high in the sky, its reflection shimmering on the water to her left as she reached the hotel grounds. It really is beautiful here when the weather is clear, she thought. You can see water from almost everywhere. But she also loved her terraced house in the centre of London and the busyness of the city gave her a different energy. I will need the comfort of my own things around me after this week, she thought as she entered the hotel.

"Good morning, Lorraine."

The receptionist smiled as Fern entered. Lorraine was a local woman and she and Fern had been in school together.

"Hello there," she said, standing up to give Fern a hug over the reception desk. "I heard you were home and I saw you at the funeral but I didn't get a chance to go over to you. That was some crowd, wasn't it?"

"Yes, one of the biggest ever, I'd say. How are you keeping?"

"All well, thank god, keeping busy. And yourself? Are you still in London?"

"Yes. I'm busy there too but it's lovely to come back even if it is under these terrible circumstances."

"Is your son back with you?" Lorraine asked.

"No, just myself. He's working with his dad on a film set in Morocco, would you believe? But Clo and Nora are staying with me."

"I heard that, yeah."

Word travelled fast in a small town.

"Nora's doing a great job, I believe, down at the school with Pavel."

"Yes. I haven't seen it myself yet but she's certainly putting the hours in. Listen, is it okay if I take a table up at the back of the lounge there." Fern pointed up the steps to a big open area with comfortable couches and low tables.

"Yes, of course."

"I'm meeting Danny's sister Audrey and Kevin – remember him?"

"Indeed I do. That was a turn-up for the books, wasn't it, the two of them getting together in Australia!" said Lorraine.

"I know. I couldn't believe it myself."

"Imagine going halfway around the world and ending up with someone who used to be your neighbour?"

"Yeah, it's nuts all right. They should be here in a minute."

"I'll send them up to you when they arrive. Can I get you anything?"

"Coffee for the three of us would be great, Lorraine."

"No bother at all. I'll organise that for you."

"Thanks, Lorraine, great to see you again."

"Likewise."

Fern picked a table with a couch and two big chairs around it at the back of the lounge. She could hear the sound of cutlery and delph coming from the breakfast room but it was far enough away for them not to be disturbed or overheard.

She had just picked where she wanted to sit, a big, wingback chair rather than the lower couch, when she heard Lorriane saying hello to Audrey and Kevin and sending them in her direction.

"I ordered coffee if you guys want any," Fern said as they walked up to her.

They both sat on the couch. Audrey perched up straight near the edge, Kevin sitting back a good foot away from her. The body language between them seemed frosty and Kevin appeared uneasy.

They've had a row, Fern thought. She could feel it.

"Here you are now!" A waitress arrived, carrying a tray with a large pot of coffee, three cups, saucers, and a sugar bowl and milk jug. They all watched her place them on the table as if it was their first time seeing it done.

"Thanks, Ann," Fern said, taking a cup and pouring herself some coffee. "Help yourselves," she said to the others with a smile.

"Not for me," Audrey said with a strained smile.

"Thanks." Kevin nodded to Fern as he leaned in for a cup.

"So," Fern began, looking at Audrey who was sitting directly across from her. "As you know, I had a very shocking chat with Kevin yesterday and, to be honest, it's taken nearly twenty-four hours to let it sink in. I was very taken aback by what he told me as I'm sure you can imagine. I wish Danny had told me that he told you about DJ. I would have been more prepared for Kevin's revelation."

"I'm so sorry, Fern." Kevin looked like he meant it.

"Well, it's done now and we are where we are." Fern shrugged.

"I wished that Kevin had waited until both of us were there to tell you," Audrey said coldly "But he changed the plan."

The plan? Was the plan to humiliate her too, she wondered. Did Kevin seek her out to avoid that?

"Well, I don't know what your 'plan' was or is but I would like you to tell me because this is a very difficult time for everyone and I don't want you making it even worse."

Audrey visibly stiffened at being spoken to like this. "Worse for who? What about DJ who we knew nothing about? You can't keep him from knowing his family. He needs to know where he came from and you can't deny him that."

"I am denying him nothing. Your mother wanted nothing to do with my son all those years ago. I believe she said it would tarnish the family name and damage your dad's career – so don't talk to me about denying him his family."

Audrey flushed a little. "I know and I am ashamed of my parents' attitude and –"

"Good," Fern interrupted her. "You should be."

Kevin leaned forward. "Look, I don't think we'll get anywhere talking about the past and we certainly don't want to fall out with you, Fern. But after Danny told Audrey about DJ, it's understandable that she would want to look for him, especially with him living in Australia too."

Fern took a deep breath. "I understand that," she said, looking at Audrey. "He is your nephew so I get that you would want to meet him. I just wish Danny had let me know what was going on."

Audrey nodded. "You must recognise that it's been disturbing for me too – and it's all been so recent – first finding out that Danny had a secret son and then finding out he was brought up in Australia. I had to find him. I'm sorry Danny didn't tell you that I knew. But now that I do know," she straightened her posture, "I think he should be recognised as Danny's son."

"When Danny and I met DJ in London, Danny was so delighted," said Fern. "They were like two peas in a pod. He told DJ he wanted to bring him to Belmullet to meet his own family first and then his grandparents. He wanted to show him where he came from. That was always Danny's plan."

"So why didn't he arrange something then?" asked Audrey.

"He was going to. DJ had to return to Australia for the footie season. You know how important that is. And Danny said they would keep in touch and come up with some dates that would suit everyone. But you have to remember that Rossa only found out about DJ after DJ contacted us."

"Well, I don't approve of that either," Audrey said, folding her arms.

"It doesn't matter whether you approve or not," Fern said, trying to remain calm, but Audrey's attitude was grating on her nerves.

"Did you tell your husband you had a son with Danny?"

"Yes, I did, but that was my choice and Danny made his. You have to remember that we didn't know if DJ would ever contact us at all, ever. Many adopted kids never look for their natural parents, especially when they have had a happy life which thankfully DJ has had."

"But Danny planned on bringing him here."

"Yes."

"Then he wanted people to know that he has a son."

"Yes – but remember he has three children who know nothing at all about this and that's why I wanted to meet with you today. I want to know what you planned on doing while you were here and who you planned on speaking to."

"Why?"

"Because I want you to stay away from Rossa and the kids."

"You can't tell me –"

"Oh yes, I can. They have suffered enough. They have lost their dad. Rossa knows about DJ and she will decide when it is the right time to tell the kids."

Audrey shifted uncomfortably on the couch. "I don't want to cause any trouble for Rossa or hardship for the kids."

"Then leave it."

"I just feel so angry. I'm angry that Danny never told me and I'm angry at my parents' reaction at the time, not offering you any support. I fell out with them years ago over other things and then when I found out about DJ I felt newly disgusted at their attitude."

"Audrey, remember that your dad probably knows nothing about this."

"*What?*"

"It was your mother Danny told and she called all the shots. She told him never to say it to your dad and never bring it up again. Danny had planned on talking to both of them after he met DJ but I don't know if that ever happened."

"*Oh my god! That bitch!*" Audrey said through her teeth. "Poor Dad probably has no idea." She turned to Kevin. "*He needs to know, he deserves to know.*"

Kevin nodded in agreement.

"Look, Audrey," said Fern, "Danny wanted DJ to come to Belmullet someday soon to see where he came from and that will happen. DJ will come to Belmullet. My own parents are dying to meet him. They have always known about him and when DJ came to London, we video-called my parents so they could see him and talk to him. But you have to move slowly with these things, Audrey. It's as much an adjustment for DJ as it is for everyone else. And now on top of everything he has lost his birth father after just connecting with him. There are a lot of feelings to unpack for him. And, whatever you think of your parents right now, they just lost their only son. But if you feel you need to say something in private to the two of them, then all I ask is that you wait until we get the memorial over with tomorrow. Let them have that. Then tell them what you want. But leave Rossa to decide what she wants to do and when.

Right now, DJ is the furthest thing from her mind as she tries to keep the kids together."

Audrey put her head in her hands and Kevin rubbed her back. It was the first time Fern saw her lose her composure.

"Okay," she whispered. "I'm just so upset about everything."

"Please don't be angry at Danny," Fern said gently. "He didn't know if he would ever see DJ, ever. We never forgot about DJ and we hoped the day would come when he would contact us. Every year on DJ's birthday Danny sent me a heart emoji." Fern's eyes filled up. "I'm going to miss that so much. It was a simple gesture to say that we never forgot DJ and he was never far from our thoughts wherever he was in the world."

Audrey's shoulders shook as she started to cry. Fern stood up, moved around to the couch and sat down beside her, putting an arm around her.

"You are mourning your brother, Audrey. He loved you so much – he thought you were amazing. He always thought you were way brighter than him and that you deserved to take over the quarry. I know that for sure."

Audrey took a tissue from her sleeve, wiped her tears and blew her nose.

"Thank you for saying that."

Kevin reached behind Audrey and squeezed Fern's arm.

"I want to develop my relationship with DJ and see more of him in Australia," Audrey said, straightening up. "If he is okay with that."

"I'm sure he would love that. He's a grown man and he will make his own decisions but I think it's nice that he has a family member on his side of the world and you can answer questions about Danny that I can't."

"Thank you."

"Rossa wants to talk to me. I won't say anything about you knowing or meeting DJ for the moment unless she asks me, okay? And if anything changes I can let you know. Can we swap numbers?"

"Yes, of course," Audrey said, taking out her phone. "I will be confronting my parents but I'll wait until after the memorial tomorrow."

Fern stood up. "I'll see you both tomorrow then."

Audrey stood up and they hugged and then Kevin came around to Fern and hugged her.

"Thank you," he whispered in her ear.

Fern walked back out into the bright sunshine, feeling absolutely drained.

CHAPTER 46

Clo woke and stretched her arms over her head. She checked her phone. She was meeting Pierre and Sophia at the tidal pool for a swim before breakfast. Apparently it was a 'cool insta spot' for photos, according to Sophia.

Sophia had dared her dad yesterday to give it a go and he reluctantly gave in. Being French, he spent the summer holidays of his youth in the south of France, swimming in the warm Mediterranean sea. He could never understand how Irish people could throw themselves into the freezing cold waters of the Atlantic but he agreed to do it today. As a compromise, Sophia agreed to book a one-hour slot in the Sona Sauna overlooking the pool.

Things were still strained between Clo and Pierre but 'you got to fake it till you make it', she reckoned. She couldn't think too far into the future right now.

"Okay, show time," she said, getting out of bed and putting on her turquoise bikini that was drying on the bathroom radiator from her swim with Rory the day before.

Applying some eyeliner, lipstick, and waterproof mascara, she finished off by running some hair serum through her hair, spiking it up on top. It was just an outdoor dip in the town's tidal pool but she needed to look her best to feel her best. She was still on shaky ground with Pierre so she needed to feel good about herself.

Throwing a sundress over her bikini, she picked up a fresh towel, slipped her feet into her sandals, and headed out the door.

She had offered to pick them up but the tidal pool was only a ten-minute walk from their hotel so they said no. As she pulled up in her car beside the log-shaped Sauna, Pierre and Sophia came walking around the corner.

"Good morning!" She waved, getting out of her car.

Sophia kissed her on both cheeks and so did Pierre.

"I'll just check in with the sauna guy," Sophia said and went over to the sauna.

"How are you?" Clo asked Pierre.

"Well, I'm not looking forward to this," he said, smiling, as he looked out towards the pool.

"You'll be fine once you get in."

They stood for a few seconds, looking at each other.

"You look great," he said, reaching out and rubbing her arm. "Let's go back to normal when we get home, yes?"

Clo felt a shiver at his touch. He leaned forward and kissed her gently on the lips. She kissed him back and relief flooded through her. It *is* possible to love two men, she thought, as she placed her hand on his chest.

"*Hey, you two, cut it out!*" Sophia shouted as she walked back to them, shaking her head. "The sauna is all set up so let's go. I want to take a few photos now while there is nobody else in the pool." She walked ahead.

Pierre took Clo's hand as they went down the steps together.

"I can't believe the weather we're getting while you two are here," Clo said, putting her bag down on a bench. "Half of my summers here were spent dodging rain showers. Also, where Fern lives the fog could come in and just hang over the peninsula all day, making it cold and damp while it was sunny and warm up here in the town."

"Okay, Dad, can you take my photo, please?"

"Sure," Pierre said, putting down his towel.

"Sorry, Mum. Dad is just better at it."

"No problem." Clo smiled, watching Sophia pose at the side of the tidal pool while Pierre, who had the patience of a saint, took as many photos as she wanted.

"Okay, let's get in," Sophia said as she lowered herself down the steps.

Pierre followed, letting out a yelp with each step.

Sophia burst out laughing. "Dad, it's not that bad!"

"It is!" he replied as he finally let go and swam in a circle, moving his arms as fast as he could, still yelping at the cold.

Clo lowered herself in next. "It *is* freezing!"

"But it's gorgeous!" said Sophia as she swam across the pool.

They laughed and swam around a bit before Pierre had enough.

"I need to get out before I die," he said, hurrying up the ladder and over to his towel. "I will see you in the sauna."

"Your father hates the cold – he's not built for it."

"Let's try the sauna," Sophia said, "but then I'm getting back in again."

Once out of the pool, Clo took out her big towel and wrapped it around her.

"I love your bikini, Mum," Sophia said, fishing her towel out of her bag.

"Thank you," Clo said with a smile.

"That colour is all in this summer. I saw someone wearing the same colour bikini yesterday on a beach here."

Clo froze. "A beach? Which beach?"

"I was going to ask you the name of it for my insta post, because I couldn't see a sign," Sophia said, taking out her phone and flicking through her photos. "We just came across it when we drove back from the lighthouse."

Oh, Jesus, thought Clo, it couldn't be! She managed to remain very calm when Sophia turned the camera around to show her the beach photo. The beach that she and Rory thought they were alone on yesterday.

"That's Belderra Beach."

"Belderra – okay, I'd better type that in," Sophia said, holding out her hand for the phone. "It was stunning there."

"Where's the bikini woman?" Clo asked, giving it to her. She held her breath as Sophia scrolled to the next photo.

"There. You can't make it out too well – they were at quite a distance – but it was definitely the same colour as yours."

Clo looked at the photo of herself and Rory as they headed towards the sea.

As Sophia turned away to put her sliders on, Clo deleted the photo and quickly swiped to see if there were any others.

"*Oops*, I think I might have pressed the wrong button and deleted one of the photos."

Sophia took back the phone. "Oh, that's okay, I have enough from there," she said, dropping the phone into her bag. "Come on, let's get warmed up," she said, walking off.

Clo sat down for a second, her head spinning. Oh Jesus, that was close! Letting out a deep breath, she stood up to join her family in the sauna.

CHAPTER 47

Nora stood up from the flower bed, stepping back to check that she hadn't missed any weeds. She had spent the whole morning weeding, putting down bark and making sure all their planting had settled.

That's the last bit done now, she thought as she pulled away some loose grass. She checked her watch. Millie should be enjoying her tea now in Aunty Martha's house.

She smiled as she thought about how excited Millie had been, heading off on her little trip. It was so nice to have family around. Her mother and Ralf doted on her and now she would be spoiled by Aunty Martha today.

I only hope she won't be bored when it's just the two of us back in Dublin, she thought with a sigh. Arching her back, she stretched her arms up over her head and wiggled her hips to loosen them out.

"Nice view."

Nora dropped her arms and swung around to see Pavel with a big grin on his face. She laughed.

"Hey, cheeky! I didn't hear your jeep."

"It's around the back."

He smiled as he approached and she felt butterflies in her stomach.

"You finished work?" she asked.

"Yes, just now. I'll dig out that hole now for the hawthorn and put some fertiliser down. Do you need help with anything else?"

"No, I think it's all pretty much done now. Mary and the committee were here earlier. They are delighted with how everything looks. We were supposed to go over the running order for tomorrow but there seems to be a storm threatening so we will do that tomorrow morning in case things have to be changed around. I told Mary we'd meet the committee here tomorrow morning for that and to help with any last minute bunting they need putting up. I hope that's okay?"

"Of course. What are you doing now though?"

"Now? Packing up and then I thought I'd go for a swim."

"Can I join you?"

Nora's heart quickened. "I'd love that," she said before tearing her eyes away from his.

"Let me dig out that hole while you pack up. I need to go by the house and get my swim gear. Do you want to follow me there or would you prefer I skinny dip?"

Nora faked a shocked face. "I'll follow you there."

Nora packed her tools away in the school shed while Pavel dug out the hole for the memorial tree. They had already marked it out together so it took no time at all to dig out.

"Okay," he said, walking around from the sports hall with his shovel over his shoulder. "Ready?"

Nora hopped into her jeep and followed him to his house.

"No point in taking the two cars to the beach so we could just go in mine?" she suggested, getting out of her jeep.

"Sure," he said, disappearing into the house.

Nora felt giddy. If she drove him to the beach then she would be driving him back here afterward. And then what?

I am child-free tonight, she thought. I need to channel my inner Clo and just be open to whatever might happen.

"Which beach?" he asked, opening the passenger door of her jeep.

"I was thinking Cross Beach."

"Okay, let's go," he said, turning to smile at her as he sat into the passenger seat.

When they arrived, they pulled up beside a group of paddle-boarders packing up their van.

"You know, when I was growing up around here there was nothing much to do in the summer," Nora said, getting out of the jeep and pushing her beach-bag strap up onto her shoulder. "And now people travel here to do all sorts of water sports. I think you take your environment for granted when you grow up in a place. Sometimes you don't appreciate it until you see it through someone else's eyes."

"*Hmm*, yes, this is true," Pavel said, shutting his door and then walking beside her. "It gets very busy here in July and August. And even in the bad weather people still take to the water. It's great."

"If you waited for the weather to get good around here, you'd never do anything," she said, looking up at him. "We have been so lucky this week."

"Yes, we have but I think there's a change coming tomorrow."

"My mam said something about that. Some storm rolling in from the Atlantic. I hope we get the memorial over with before it begins."

"I think it is to come at lunchtime and the memorial is at eleven so we might be okay."

"You would never think it now," Nora said, stopping to look at the view.

The white sandy beach curved around the bay. The turquoise and blue sea was calm but further out it looked a bit choppy. The sun was high in the sky and there was a lovely warm sea breeze. Two dog walkers greeted each other as they passed and a mother sat on a blanket while her kids made sandcastles with buckets and spades.

"I can't wait to get into that water," Nora said, walking towards the sea. "Is here okay?" she said, dropping her bag on the sand.

"Yes, perfect." Pavel put his towel down and peeled his T-shirt off over his head.

Nora couldn't help but look at his firm chest. She turned toward the sea as she took off her T-shirt – she was wearing her bikini underneath. She then quickly opened her gardening combat trousers, letting them fall to the ground. She could feel Pavel's eyes on her and she didn't mind at all.

"I really need this swim," she said.

She wanted to wash off the past and her delusions about a romance between herself and Danny. Time for a fresh start, a brave one.

"*Race you!*" she shouted and ran off. She felt giddy with excitement, hearing him running behind her.

She ran into the water. The icy waves made her catch her breath but she kept going. When the water got to waist high she dived underneath. She needed to feel that cold water at the top of her head, washing old feelings away.

When she came up for air Pavel was just a few feet away from her. She felt electric.

“It’s so cold but fabulous,” she said, looking at the water running down his chest and arms. His eyes moved from her eyes down to her bikini top, the cold water pushing her hard nipples against the thin material.

Old Nora would have turned away embarrassed but not today, she thought, as she waded the few steps between them and pressed her body against his. His arms reached around her waist as he bent his head to meet her waiting lips.

His kiss was gentle at first and then deep and slow. Then he pulled back.

“I have been wanting to do that all week,” he said, placing his hands on either side of her head before kissing her again. “Shall we go?” he asked when he stopped.

“Yes,” said Nora. She didn’t need to ask where.

They waded out of the sea hand in hand and towel-dried themselves before dressing and heading back up to the jeep.

“I should have brought another towel for my hair,” Nora said, sitting into the jeep as water from her hair dripped down her T-shirt.

Pavel looked at her and smiled. “I have many towels.”

They drove, not saying much. The sexual tension in the jeep spoke for itself.

Nora parked the jeep in his driveway and they both got out.

He opened the door and stood aside for her to enter. Then taking her hand, he said, “I will show you the shower.”

The bathroom was just past the main bedroom. Pavel leaned in over the bath and turned the shower on, testing the temperature with his hand.

He nodded. “Now it is good. I can wait outside ... or ...”

Before he could finish that sentence Nora took her top off. She was naked underneath.

“I want you to stay,” she said, stepping close to him. She pulled his T-shirt up while keeping eye-contact with him.

He quickly took it off. He held the back of her head while he kissed her.

Oh my god, Nora thought, feeling her knees go weak.

Moving his hands down he unbuttoned her combats and pulled down the zip. She responded by undoing his jeans.

She pulled back and took her combats and underwear off. “How about that shower?” she said, stepping in under the water.

A smile crossed Pavel's face as he shed his clothes and joined her.

CHAPTER 48

Wrapped in a cosy blanket on Pavel's couch, Nora felt every part of her body tingle with delight. She had never had sex with anyone that came close to what she had just experienced with Pavel. She took a sip from the glass of red wine he had poured for her.

"Your clothes won't take long," Pavel said, walking into the living room barefoot, wearing only a pair of faded jeans.

The clothes they had discarded on the bathroom floor became saturated as the shower water sprayed out over the side of the bath. Nora vaguely remembered her foot hitting the shower screen, forcing it to swing back when Pavel lifted her legs up onto his hips. Her back was pressed against the shower tiles and her arms wrapped around his neck as she clung to him for balance.

Knowing they were alone and in a detached house, Nora let herself go completely. She cried out when she came, feeling all the sadness of Danny's death, the lost dreams, and the tension of the past few days flood out of her body.

"Can you stay the night?" Pavel asked as he sat down on the couch, lifting her legs and placing them on his lap.

Looking at him, Nora couldn't remember the last time she felt this aroused.

"I can but I need to be in Fern's house first thing tomorrow to change – and I think we're going to go to the ceremony together."

"And after the ceremony, when do you plan to return to Dublin?"

"Sunday, I'm afraid."

"Afraid? You don't want to go?"

"No, I do … I mean, I have to. I have a business to run and people who rely on me. It's just … despite the sadness and coming to terms with Danny not being here anymore, this week has been very good for me and Millie."

Pavel sighed and looked away.

"You have been good for me too, Pavel, so good," she said, reaching out for his hand.

"And you have been good for me," he said, picking up her foot and kissing it. "*Aw*, Nora, I wish we had more time."

"Me too," she said and she meant it. I was meant to meet him this week, she thought, looking at him. He saved me.

"What are you thinking?" he said, gazing at her while stroking her calf.

Nora smiled suggestively. "I'm thinking that it's sad that we didn't get more time like this but … we have time now …" She pointed her toe while rubbing her foot up and down his chest. She threw the blanket open and stretched out her naked body, raising her arms over her head.

His breath quickened as his eyes took in everything before him. His hand moved from her calf to her thigh as he moved his body to hover over hers.

The alarm on the dryer went off to signal that the clothes cycle was finished but neither of them heard it.

CHAPTER 49

Saturday

Nora stood back and looked at herself in the bedroom mirror. She was delighted that she had thrown in her jade-green jumpsuit at the last minute. It was crease proof so it was easy to roll up and pack with her other clothes. The colour highlighted her green eyes.

Pavel had made her feel like a woman again. She spent so much time in gardening gear and the only socialising she had done since having Millie was occasional after-work pints in her local pub, the Pebble Beach, after a long day working on a gardening project.

When she was married, she and Greg dined out a lot, at least once a week. Greg loved fine dining and most of the nice clothes she had were from that time.

Wearing this now, she felt feminine and sexy. She hadn't felt like that in years. She smiled when she thought back to last night. It was the most amazing sex she had ever had.

I didn't know sex could be like that, she thought. She didn't want it to be the last time either but she was leaving tomorrow and they were literally at the opposite sides of the country.

Pushing that thought out of her mind, she applied some lipstick and headed out to the kitchen.

"Oh *wow*, look at you!" Clo's mouth dropped open when she saw Nora approaching. She couldn't remember the last time she saw Nora in anything other than casual attire.

"You look ... stunning," Fern said, standing at the worktop. She had chosen a long, black, net skirt and a red chiffon blouse to go with her trademark Doc Martens.

"Thank you both," Nora said, smiling. "I decided to put in a bit of effort." She sat down at the kitchen table.

"Coffee?" Fern asked.

"Yes, please."

"There's fresh toast on the table too."

"You look ... different," Clo said, eyeing Nora suspiciously.

"Well, you've only seen me in comfy gear since I came here," Nora said, reaching out for a piece of toast.

"No, no, no, it's something else," Clo said, squinting at Nora.

Nora blushed.

"*Oh my god, did you get laid?*"

"*Clo!*" gasped Fern.

"You did! Didn't you?" Clo insisted.

Nora laughed. No point in hiding anything from Clo.

"Yes, I did."

Clo clapped her hands excitedly. "Good for you, girl!"

Fern brought the coffee pot to the table. "Okay, I'm presuming we are talking about Pavel here?" She poured the coffee into their three mugs.

Nora nodded while she buttered her toast.

"Come on, spill the beans!" Clo said.

Nora paused and looked from Fern to Clo. "All I can say is that I have had the best sex of my life. I never imagined it could be like that."

"He is a big ride, in fairness!" Clo said. "I'm delighted for you. So what now?"

"Now? Well, I'm meeting him at the school shortly to make sure everything looks okay and –"

"Not that! What now with you and him?"

Nora sighed. "I have to go back to Dublin tomorrow. I have a business to run and he has work here."

"At least you're both in the same country," said Fern.

"Well, look, we didn't say anything about seeing each other again so maybe I was a one-night stand to him."

"Ah, don't say that!" Fern said.

"No, honestly I wouldn't mind. He has his life here, I have mine in Dublin, maybe that's it. He made me feel like a woman last night and, yes, it was fabulous but I have no right to ask for anything more."

"You deserve to have some gorgeous man mad about you," said Clo.

"Well, we'll see. He helped me get rid of the ghosts of the past. Today I feel on top of the world and I'm grateful to him for that. And now I must go." She took another sip of her coffee and stood up.

"Well, we're delighted for you," Fern said. "We'll see you down there shortly."

"See you there," Nora said as she left.

A heavy fog was hanging over the peninsula and dark clouds were looming. The storm was due by lunchtime and was forecast to bring strong wind and rain with it. Nora pulled out of the driveway.

Nothing can dampen my mood today, she thought, smiling to herself, feeling excited at the thought of seeing Pavel again.

CHAPTER 50

Pavel was already there when she pulled up. His eyes widened as she stepped out of her jeep and walked towards him.

"You look ... gorgeous," he said, his eyes taking in every curve of her body.

She wanted to reach out and pull him to her but Mary Comerford was waving excitedly to her as she rushed out the school door.

"*Hello, Nora!*" she called. "I'd hardly recognise you out of your gardening gear! You look beautiful, love."

"Thank you, Mary."

"Well, let me start by saying you two have done a fabulous job," she said,. "There was not a bit of colour here before and now look at it!"

Nora looked around the transformed forecourt. The green, grey and black grasses lined the driveway up to the main school entrance where the heather bed burst with different shades of pink, violet and purple. The seat was a perfect resting spot to rest and enjoy the colour and the scent. She was very happy with how it turned out.

"So let me tell you the order of the day," Mary said, fumbling around with a pile of papers in her hands. "This wind isn't helping, is it?"

"No," Nora answered, looking around at the bunting flapping in the wind. "Hopefully we'll get the ceremony done before the storm comes in."

As she spoke Pavel placed his hand at her lower back, sending a shiver through her body. She turned to look up at him and he ran his hand up her back.

"Ah, here it is!" Mary said, pulling out a sheet of paper. "Okay, we have thirty minutes before we kick things off so people will be arriving soon. Given the weather forecast, we have moved up the tree planting to the first thing. So," she shuffled the pages together, "the headmaster was going to give a speech outside before the tree planting but now we'll start with the tree planting as soon as the family arrives. I'll introduce you both and thank you and then you help Rossa and the kids plant the tree and we'll head inside the sports hall for the speeches. The women are set up in there with tea, coffee and cake so we can have the speeches and then refreshments and then we're done."

"Very efficient," said Pavel.

"Yes, poor Rossa must be exhausted so she and the kids can leave whenever they want. Will we move inside? Hang on," she said, looking over Nora's shoulder, "I think that's Rossa now."

The three of them turned around to see Rossa get out of her car.

"She's on her own," Mary said. "Hello, Rossa," she said, moving towards her, "are the kids not with you?"

Rossa walked straight up to Nora. Her face was like thunder. "I'm going back for the kids in a minute," she answered Mary but her eyes didn't leave Nora. "I just need to talk to Nora first, alone please."

"Oh right," Mary said, looking confused. "We'll be just inside."

Pavel looked from Rossa to Nora, sensing something was wrong.

"Go ahead, I'll follow you in," Nora reassured him.

Rossa waited until Mary and Pavel had reached the door before looking back at Nora.

Nora's mouth went dry. "What can I –"

"*Millie Cunningham.*"

Nora's stomach sank.

"I felt there was something about your daughter when I met her the other day and again when I met her with your mother yesterday but I couldn't put my finger on it." Her face was drained and stoney as she spoke.

Oh, Jesus. Nora felt weak.

"And then I found this," she said, holding up a bank book. "I was looking for documents in Danny's office, a cheque book to pay for his funeral actually, and I found this. And then it all made sense. Millie may have your red hair but she looks so like my Hannah when she was that age."

"I ..." Nora tried to speak but the words would not come out.

"Do you know what this is?" she said, holding the small blue bank book an inch from Nora's face.

"No ... I ..."

"It's a savings account in your daughter's name that my husband has been paying into since the fourth of April 2018. Does that date ring a bell, Nora? I bet it does. It's the date your daughter was born, isn't it?"

Nora felt dizzy. Her mouth went dry and she broke out in a cold sweat. "Rossa ... I knew nothing about ..."

"*You fucking whore!*" Rossa hissed in her face. "*She's Danny's daughter, isn't she?*"

"Rossa, I don't know what to say ..."

"*Isn't she?*"

"Yes," Nora said in a whisper.

"*You desperate slut!* You always wanted my husband, didn't you? The whole town knew you had a crush on him. *But he chose me, Nora.* He was married to me, had children with me but that didn't stop you, did it? You must have caught him unawares, when he had a load of drink on him, and laid it all out for him on a plate." She looked Nora up and down in disgust. "*I want to know where and when and how long it went on for!*"

"I'm so sorry," Nora said in a whisper, looking down at her feet.

"*Where and when?*" Rossa spat the words out, stepping closer to Nora.

"It was a once-off. My husband had just left me and I was upset and it was just that one time. I swear. I never meant to ..."

"*Never meant to? Yes, you fucking did!* You were besotted with him! When he chose me and you knew you couldn't have him, you waited and waited until he had a weak moment and you pounced, you pathetic slut!"

A gust of wind blew through the car park. Nora started to shiver.

"My children have suffered enough. I have suffered enough. You will get nothing from me or Danny's estate, do you hear me?"

Nora nodded. "I don't want anything. I didn't know about any savings account, I swear."

"I don't care what you tell me. Who else knows about this?"

"No one."

"Nobody else knows? Nobody?"

"No. I swear."

"Not even your mother?"

Nora shook her head.

"And what about those slutty friends of yours, whose do they think she is?"

"My ex-husband's. Everyone thinks she's Greg's."

"The queer?" Rossa sniggered. "Well, if they believe that, they are even more dumb than I thought."

Nora shook her head as the tears came.

"Cry, little slut, cry all you like! I will not let you ruin my children's image of their father, do you hear me?"

Nora nodded.

"Take this book," she said, slapping it against Nora's chest. "Do what you want with the money. That is the last penny you will ever get, do you hear me? If you tell anyone that she is Danny's, I will destroy you and your business and your reputation. Never, ever reveal who her real father is, do you understand? I don't want you anywhere near this service today. Get back in your truck and fuck off back to Dublin!"

"I ..." Nora tried to find some words..

"Oh and one last thing ..."

Nora looked up and took the full force of Rossa's hand across her face.

Nora's hand flew to her face as she stumbled sideways from the force of Rossa's slap.

"That's from me," Rossa said as she walked off and got back into her car.

"*Nora!*" Pavel ran from the sports hall where he had watched the encounter. "Jesus, what happened?" He held her and helped steady her.

Nora could hardly get the words out through her sobs,

"I'm ... sorry ... I have to go."

"*No! You can't go*. What happened?"

"I ... can't ..." Nora pushed away from him and ran to her jeep.

"Nora, please!" Pavel said as she shut the door.

"You must stay here for the ceremony," she said through the open window as the tears streamed down her face. "Please, Pavel, you cannot say anything to anyone. Please just say I felt sick and had to go."

"I'm coming with you," he said, putting his hand on the door.

"No, please, stay here. Please ... do that for me. I ... have to go ..."

"*No, wait! Nora, please!*" Pavel called after her as she sped out of the car park.

CHAPTER 51

Six years previously ...

Nora pulled up the collar of her jacket against the wind and rain as she quickened her step down Lower Barrack Street to McDonnell's pub.

"Ah, welcome home, Nora," Pádraig the bar owner welcomed her as she shook the rain off her jacket.

"Thanks, Pádraig, how's things?" Nora said. She nodded to a few older local men sitting at the bar, nursing their pints.

"Not too bad. It's good to see you. Are you home for long?" He started to pull her a pint of Guinness. Pádraig had a reputation for remembering everyone's orders.

"Just a flying visit," she answered. "To clear the head, you know."

"I do indeed," he said as he put her pint down to settle.

"Well, there's a sight for sore eyes!"

Nora didn't need to turn around to recognise the familiar voice of Danny O'Connor.

"You're looking well," he said as he placed his arm on the bar beside her, turning his body to face her.

She could see by his eyes that he'd had a few pints already.

"How're things with you?" he asked.

Looking into the eyes of the man she had a crush on most of her life, she felt tears come to the surface.

"Hey, hey," he said, leaning toward her and gently taking her arm. "Come sit down in the snug, I'll take care of this." He pulled out his wallet. "Can you put another one on for me, Pádraig?"

He led Nora through the small crowd to an empty snug at the back. McDonnell's had a few quiet corners and snugs if you were looking for a bit of privacy.

"Sit down there now in front of the fire," he said, before going back to the bar for the drinks.

"Thanks, Danny," she said when he returned.

He pulled up a stool and sat beside her.

"Now, tell me what's up," he said.

Nora let out a big sigh. "My marriage is over, Danny, Greg is leaving and moving away."

"*Aw*, no," Danny tilted his head as he looked into her eyes. "I'm genuinely sorry to hear that, Nora. Is there nothing you can do to save it?"

"No. Not when your husband leaves you for another man."

"Jesus!"

Nora gave a quiet laugh when she saw his shocked face. He was the first person she'd told. I suppose I should get used to that reaction, she thought.

"Please don't tell anyone," she pleaded with him. "You're the first person I've told and I'm not sure if I want people to know the real reason. Promise me you'll say nothing?"

"Of course. I won't say a word."

A silence hung between them.

"Come here," he said, opening his arms and pulling her to him. She moved along the seat until there was no space between them.

He always gave great hugs, she remembered as she inhaled his scent – a mix of cologne, fabric softener, and the bitter scent of Guinness. He kissed her gently on her temple.

"Well, all I can say," he said, leaning back and lifting her chin with his finger, "is that any man would be lucky to be with you, Nora." He kissed her on her forehead before releasing her from the hug.

"The heart wants what the heart wants," Nora said, turning away to take a sip of her pint. When she turned back to him she met his beautiful blue eyes.

She didn't look away.

"Had you no idea he was ..."

"Gay? No, Danny. If I did I wouldn't have married him, would I?"

"I'm sorry," he said, shaking his head, "That was a stupid thing to say."

"No, you're alright. It's a ridiculous situation. I thought we were trying for a baby. But he had other plans, it seems."

"A woman like you," Danny said, "deserves to have her needs met."

"Are you drunk, Danny O'Conner?" Nora teased.

"No. Well, maybe a little."

Just then a microphone was plugged in and a musician and a singer started to test it.

"1-2, 1-2. Good evening, everyone, the music will start in five minutes."

"Oh god," Nora said, "I don't think I can handle listening to a singer tonight."

"Do you want to go somewhere more quiet to talk?"

"Where do you suggest?" she said, almost in a whisper.

She looked at him. He was tipsy all right. He reached across and stroked the back of her hand with his fingers, his eyes not leaving hers. Is he coming on to me or is he teasing me now?

"Why don't we go to my place? I have a nice bottle of wine in the fridge and it will be easier to talk there. What do you think?"

Oh my God, thought Nora, as a rush of desire swept through her. *He wants me*. She felt dizzy. The chemistry was undeniable. Does he feel it too? Is this the moment – could this be it?

She swallowed hard. "Won't your family be there?"

"No," he said, looking at her as he licked his lips. "Rossa took the kids to her parents in Wexford for the weekend."

"I see," Nora said, keeping eye contact with him.

Her heart was pounding. She quickly weighed up her options. She could go back to her mother's house and sit there depressed while Margaret and Ralf watched TV – or was this the moment she had been waiting for all her life? Did he realise now that they had an undeniable connection?

"Well?" he said, openly flirting with her now.

She could tell by his eyes that if she said yes there would not be much talking done. He was making that very clear. *He wanted her.* At last, Danny O'Connor was sitting here asking *her* to come home with him. She looked into his eyes. Her breath quickened with desire for him.

"Let's go," she said, finishing the rest of her pint in one go.

Nora woke first. She squinted her eyes against the sun coming in through the open curtains in the unfamiliar bedroom. Turning on her side, she smiled as she watched him sleep. They barely made it to the bedroom after she drove him home from the pub. They pulled each other's clothes off as soon as they shut the front door behind them, leaving a trail of clothes behind on the stairs.

She knew it was wrong. He was a married man with three kids but she didn't care. She had loved Danny O'Connor all her life and she had given up hope that anything might happen between them. He wanted her and she was so hungry for him.

She thought he had always seen her as a friend but that changed last night.

Her marriage was over, Greg was leaving her and she hadn't had sex in so long. What did she have to lose?

He was a quick lover. She would have liked them to have taken more time but reminded herself – this is what she always wanted, what she had dreamt of for so many years: to make love with Danny O'Connor.

He had fallen asleep straight after but she managed to rouse him again for round two. They collapsed in a sweat after that and this time there was no waking him.

"Morning," Nora whispered in his ear.

Danny opened his eyes.

"Oh *eh*, yeah," he said, pushing himself up to sitting, placing his head in his hands. "Jesus, my head hurts!"

Nora sat up beside him, naked in the bed, and ran her hand across his chest.

"*Eh*, I need to get a glass of water," he said and stood up.

Grabbing his jeans from the floor, he pulled them on quickly, keeping his back to her. "Can I get you anything?" he asked over his shoulder as he walked to the door. "A glass of water? Coffee?"

"Coffee would be nice." Nora pulled the quilt up over her bare chest, suddenly feeling self-conscious. The atmosphere had changed since last night. It felt ... awkward.

"*Em,* Nora," Danny said, stepping back into the room. He sat on the corner of the bed, the furthest place away from where she was sitting. "Look, I'm sorry but ... what happened last night ... should not have happened."

Fuck, she thought, *fuck, fuck, fuck*.

"I'm married and I want to stay that way. If Rossa ..."

Nora sighed, completely deflated. "Don't worry. I won't say a word," she said, holding back the tears.

Danny's head dropped with relief. "Thank you, Nora. I'm so relieved," he said, placing a hand on his chest. "I knew you'd see it that way. Good girl." He tapped her leg through the quilt, stood up and then went downstairs.

Shit! Nora could see in his eyes that he so regretted what had happened between them. Gathering her clothes, she quickly dressed, picking up her check shirt as she went down the stairs and pulling on her trainers that were abandoned in the hall. She could feel that the tears weren't far away.

She walked to the kitchen door.

"Oh, you're up. I was going to bring this up to you," he said, holding out a mug of coffee.

"Thanks, but I'm going to go. I don't want things to be awkward between us, Danny, so let's pretend this never happened, yeah?" she said, pressing her nails into her hand to stop herself from crying.

"Oh, that's great, you're so right," he said. "I wouldn't want to ruin our friendship."

He walked towards her and held out his arms. She stepped into his hug, breathing in his scent for the last time.

"I'll be off then," she said, pulling away.

Opening the front door, she looked back down the hall to the kitchen where he was standing with his back to her, pouring her coffee down the sink.

She waited until she drove out of his driveway before letting the tears come.

Twelve weeks later the tears came again as she stared at a positive pregnancy test.

CHAPTER 52

Fern and Clo parked in the car park at the back of the school. A stream of people walked ahead of them towards the sports hall.

"The planting looks great," Fern said as they walked up to the door.

The hall was packed. Rossa and the kids were at the top of the hall, standing beside Mary Comerford and other members of the committee.

"God, Rossa looks awful," Clo said.

"She looks grey. Maybe the shock is setting in now and it has been a long week," said Fern.

"I see Pavel up there but I don't see Nora," Clo said.

"Yeah, that's strange, she should be up there too." Fern looked around the hall. No Nora.

"Good morning, everyone," Mary Comerford began. "Due to the bad weather forecast, we are going outside now to plant the special tree that our wonderful gardeners, Pavel Nowak and Nora Cunningham, chose especially for the climate here and to honour Danny. Unfortunately, Nora had to leave, so Pavel will be facilitating the tree planting. So if you would like to follow us outside, we'll do that now."

Clo and Fern looked at each other.

"What the hell?" Clo said. "She was all dressed up for this. Why would she leave?"

"God, I hope Millie is okay. Maybe she's sick – she was out visiting relatives yesterday."

"That must be it. Will I ring her?"

"Let's do the tree thing first, everyone's heading out," Fern said, leading the way.

Mary Comerford said a few words before Pavel helped Danny's children plant the tree. Rossa's face was unemotional. She just nodded her thanks to Pavel and when the ceremony was over she said a quick thank-you to everyone who came, before leading the children away.

Everyone returned to the hall where the committee had a huge spread laid on. Tables of sandwiches, cakes, and homemade biscuits and beverages lined the back wall.

"How long do we have to stay?" Clo asked.

"We can't be the first to leave," Fern said, looking around. "Will you get me a coffee and a bit of cake while I ring Nora?"

"Sure," Clo said, heading to the back of the hall.

Fern rang Nora's number but it rang out. She was just about to leave a message when Rossa appeared in front of her.

"Oh Rossa, hi. How are you?"

"Can we talk, in private?"

"Yes, of course," Fern said.

Rossa headed for the door.

Fern looked around for Clo but couldn't see her but she did see Pavel stare over in her direction as she left.

Fern followed Rossa down the corridor and was surprised when she walked into the boys' changing room.

"This is the only place we won't be overheard," Rossa said, closing the door behind them.

"Is everything okay?" Fern said nervously.

"Not really, no. It's about Danny." Rossa sat down on the nearest bench and Fern joined her.

"About a month ago, Danny's GP sent him to see a cardiologist in Dublin to have some test done," she began. "He had been having occasional heart palpitations and sweats with them and they had become more frequent. Of course I was at him for ages to see the doctor about it but ... anyway we were waiting on the results on those tests when he collapsed on that road."

"Oh God, Rossa!" Fern reached out, placing her hand on Rossa's arm.

"The letter from the cardiologist arrived, confirming that Danny had Long QT Syndrome, a serious heart condition. It arrived the day of the funeral, can you believe that?"

"Oh Jesus!" Fern's hand flew up to her mouth.

"So it seems his heart gave out because he had this condition. That he never knew he had. If he had known, then they could have put him on medication to try to prevent something like this happening."

"Oh no!" Fern's eyes started to fill up.

"It's called Long QT Syndrome, Fern," Rossa continued, "and the reason I'm telling you is because it is a *genetic* condition which means each child of a person with Long QT has a fifty percent chance of having the condition."

Fern felt the blood drain out of her as her jaw fell open.

"I don't want the word to get out yet. We're still trying to get our heads around him not being here but there is a test and I'm getting the kids tested for it. They test for it in a special unit in Tallaght Hospital in Dublin. I've booked the kids in to be tested next week. They don't even know it yet, so, please, I need you to keep this news to yourself. I don't want his family or the whole town to know until I sort this situation with my children out."

"I understand." Fern's mind was racing.

"I believe your DJ plays professional football in Australia, so he should get himself tested too." Rossa took a card out of her pocket. "This is the name of the doctor I'm dealing with and I wrote down the name of the condition on the back, so you can look into it yourself."

"Thank you," Fern said in a whisper. "I'm so sorry, Rossa."

"So am I. Maybe if he had gone to the doctor earlier he'd still be here. But he isn't, is he?"

"It's just terrible," Fern said, trying to take the shocking information in.

"Audrey called me yesterday and she told me about your chat, so thank you for stopping her from causing more distress. She was always jealous of Danny and so bitter against the parents. She has a lot of emotional baggage to unpack. That mother of theirs is a right weapon. Anyway, thank you for dealing with her."

Fern nodded. "I did tell her not to contact you, you know."

"I need a break from that family. I'm taking the kids to Canada for a bit. I need to get away from the O'Connors and from this place. I have no family here now. My brother and his wife live near Toronto and I was born there myself."

"Oh, I didn't know that."

"Yes, I have a Canadian passport and dual citizenship. My parents lived there for twenty-five years and I went to primary school there. We go there every summer and the kids love it. Ed applied and got into a college there so he was moving in with my brother over there next month. And ... after what has happened now ... I am considering it myself."

"Oh right. Do you mean permanently?" Fern said, realising she knew nothing at all about Rossa.

"Yes. My brother does very well over there and he has sent us open tickets so I'm thinking of going next week after our appointment in Dublin. I just told the kids this morning and they want to go. They think that we're going for a break but I don't know if we'll come back but keep that to yourself too, will you? I won't be telling that wagon of a mother-in-law until I'm in Dublin airport."

"Of course," Fern said.

"You'll be heading back to London, I presume, so I just have one last favour to ask."

"Sure."

"I know your DJ will probably want to come here at some stage to see where he came from. I don't think my children could handle that, so could you give me notice, if and when that happens? Like I said, I mightn't even come back from Canada but I don't think I will be telling them about DJ for a good while. But if he comes here the news will get to them no doubt, so I'd appreciate the warning. My email address is at the back of that card."

"Of course," Fern said. "I'll let you know immediately if that is about to happen."

"I will tell the kids someday about DJ but it won't be for a while, okay?"

Fern nodded. "I completely understand that, Rossa."

"Good luck, Fern," she said, standing up and holding out her hand.

"Take care," Fern said, taking her hand and shaking it.

And with that Rossa left the changing room and Fern fell back against the wall in shock at what she had just been told.

CHAPTER 53

Nora was pulling clothes off hangers and shoving them into her bag when she heard the knock on the door. She had raced back to Fern's house, stunned by her encounter with Rossa, and right now she wanted to get as far away as possible from this place. She just wanted to go home.

The knocks on the door were louder now so she couldn't ignore them. Walking out into the kitchen, she could see Pavel's shape through the porch door glass. She took a deep breath and walked across the kitchen to open the door.

"Nora, thank god," he said, stepping in and closing the door behind him. He went to put his arms around her but she backed away.

"Pavel, I have to leave." She could hear her voice quiver as she spoke. "I have to leave right now. I can't stay."

"Nora," he said, opening his arms and moving to her.

"Please," she whispered but she was unable to move. He put his two strong arms around her and she rested her head on his chest and cried.

"Come with me," he said, taking her hand and leading her to the door.

Nora stopped. "I can't. I have to ..."

"I know," he said, turning to her. "But right now you're upset and your friends will be back here soon. Let me look after you."

Nora felt so drained. She surrendered and followed him out the door.

They drove in silence. When his hand wasn't on the steering wheel, it cradled her hand.

When they arrived at his house, he got out and opened his front door, then came around to Nora's door, opened it, and carried her inside in his arms. He carried her into the bedroom and placed her gently on his bed.

He then lay down beside her and pulled the big quilt over the two of them. She snuggled into his chest and cried and cried and cried.

Lying in his arms, she felt a weight lift.

"I know we may not see each other again," she said. "But I need to tell someone something in total secret and I feel that person is you."

Pavel traced her hairline with his fingers.

"Whatever you tell me, there will be no judgement. I hate to see you like this so I know that this is very important to you." He kissed her forehead. "Whatever you tell me, I will take it to my grave, you have my promise."

Nora looked up at him. She hardly knew him a week but she trusted him. And so she began to tell him the whole story.

Pavel didn't interrupt her once.

"I never wanted Rossa to find out. I'm so stupid to think that my secret wouldn't get out but today was ... just horrible. I don't blame Rossa at all for her reaction. To lose your husband and then to find out about this. I feel so ashamed. I just want to get Millie and go."

Pavel nodded.

"Who does Millie think is her father?"

"Greg , my ex. She knows that I was married to Greg and I'm not now. I'm going to have to change that story or I'll mess her up for life. You see, when Greg told me he was leaving me for another man, I was so shocked. I left the house and drove straight here. That's when it happened. Greg was still there when I got back and we shared the same house for another three months, so he was there when I found out I was pregnant. We told our families that he had taken a new job in Tuscany. He's English and all his family live in England and mine are here so we didn't say anything about the pregnancy. Once he was settled in Italy with Luigi, he told his parents that we had separated. I haven't heard from his family since. I waited as long as I could before telling my parents I was pregnant and separated and that I would be bringing the baby up on my own."

"How did they take it?"

"Well, they badmouthed Greg for abandoning me because they thought he was the father, and I let them." Nora winced. "It wasn't long before word got around and after Millie was born Danny called me. He did the maths and wanted to check with me. So I told him the truth, that yes he was the father but that I wanted nothing from him and that I didn't want to upset what he had with his family. A few weeks after that he rang to say that he wanted to send me some money for the baby but I said no. I didn't need anything from him. Millie was my miracle baby and I was quite happy to stay in our little bubble forever."

"So did he get to meet her?" Pavel asked. "Surely he saw her when you visited?"

"Yes. He asked me to message him whenever we were coming home to Belmullet and I'd arrange to meet him in secret for him to spend a little time with Millie, but it wasn't too often."

"But you would have to tell Millie someday, no?"

"I know it sounds stupid but I refused to think that far ahead."

"But now Rossa knows."

"Yes, but I swore I would never tell anyone ever. I need to leave and god knows when I will come back."

"*Hmm*. This is a lot."

Nora sighed. "I know and I don't blame you if you never want to see me again."

"No, I meant that this is a lot for you to deal with on your own." He held her face in his hands. "I want to be there for you. I want to help you with this."

"But you hardly know me and I'm a complete mess-up."

"I don't see a mess-up. I see an amazing and beautiful woman that I would like to stay in my life."

A tear ran down Nora's face. "I would like that too, Pavel, but I don't see a way." She pushed herself up to sitting. "I have to get Millie and leave Belmullet."

"Don't go today, you are too upset. Also, your friends will wonder why you are leaving early. I am sure they are concerned for you."

"What did you tell them?"

"I didn't get to speak to them but Mary announced to everyone that you had to leave. But something strange did happen. Rossa came up to me and said tell Nora she needs to speak to Fern. Before I could say anything, she just turned and left."

"Fern? Oh god, what now?"

"*Shhh,* whatever it is I am here for you, okay? So please don't leave tonight."

"You are right. I'm in no fit state to drive and I was going home tomorrow anyway."

"Let me feed you and make you feel better and then I can drive you to get Millie, yes?"

Nora nodded.

"Then you can have your last night with your girlfriends."

"Okay, you're right. It's such a long drive back to Dublin and I'm exhausted."

Pavel lifted her chin with his forefinger and kissed her gently on the lips.

"I'm so happy I met you," she said and returned his kiss.

"Let me look after you," he whispered as he kissed each of her eyelids.

"Yes," she whispered as she wrapped her arms around his neck, sinking into his arms.

CHAPTER 54

"There you are!" Clo said as Nora walked in the door with Millie.

"Can I have an ice cream, Mummy?"

"Check with Fern first, yeah?"

"You go ahead, lovey," Fern said, coming out from her bedroom.

"Are you okay? You look white as a sheet?" Nora said.

"Well, tell us about you first," Fern said, helping Millie reach the ice-pops. "What happened this morning?"

"Millie, will you go outside and throw the ball for Penny? She hasn't had her walk yet."

"Yes!" Millie ran around to where Penny was happily sleeping in her bed and took a ball from her doggie bag.

Penny perked up immediately and wagged her tail.

"Here, I'll open this door," Fern said, sliding across the door to the back of the house.

Millie and Penny ran outside.

Nora, Clo, and Fern sat down at the kitchen table.

"So, Mary said you had to leave. Were you sick or something?" Clo asked.

"Oh god, it was awful. I felt perfectly fine leaving here and then as soon as I arrived at the school I started feeling sick. I thought I was going to throw up. I don't know if it was something I ate or a bug but I started sweating and feeling dizzy so I had to leave."

"We rang a few times," Fern said.

"I know. I'm sorry. I came back here and went straight to bed, turning my phone off."

"Back here?"

"Yes, and after some sleep and some paracetamol, I felt better."

"But ... Pavel dropped you back."

"Yes. Bless him, he came to check on me and I asked if he could drive me to pick up Millie. I still felt wobbly and I didn't trust myself driving."

"And how are you now?" Clo asked.

"Just a little weak. Honestly, it came on so fast but I feel much better now," Nora said, feeling surprised and a little guilty at how easy it was to lie to her oldest friends.

"Well, you were thanked and everyone said the school grounds looked great," Clo said.

"I can't believe I missed it. I don't know what happened ... it's been the strangest of weeks."

She looked at Fern and realised she looked awful, her face drawn and pale-looking.

"Are you feeling okay, Fern?" she asked.

"No. I'm not okay."

"It's Rossa," Clo said.

"Rossa?" said Nora.

"Yes, Rossa grabbed Fern for a chat. You were white as a ghost after you spoke to her."

Fern let out a big sigh. "Yes, it's Rossa. And I'm sorry I couldn't explain, Clo, but I wanted to wait until you were both here. I'm still getting my head around it."

Nora felt sick. *No, no, no,* don't tell me she told her about Millie.

"This is between us at the moment," Fern said, laying her hands on the table.

"Jesus, what is it?" asked Clo.

"Rossa called me aside to tell me that Danny had a heart condition. He had been for tests in Dublin but the results only came back after ..." Fern paused. "The results arrived the day of his bloody funeral, can you believe that?"

"Oh my god!" Clo and Nora said together.

"The results of his tests showed that he had a heart condition. It's called Long QT Syndrome. It caused his heart to stop and that's how he collapsed on the side of the road. It could have happened anywhere. He never knew he had it. He was probably dead before he hit the ground."

"Jesus!" Clo gasped. "So that explains his cause of death – it wasn't from a fall or the head injury, it was his heart."

"I don't understand, this condition, would it have made a difference if he did know?" asked Nora.

"Yes, he could have been monitored and had regular checks and medication, so it probably could have been prevented."

"That's just so sad," Nora said, placing her head in her hands.

"But why does Rossa want it kept quiet?" asked Clo.

"And why did she tell you if she wants it kept quiet?" asked Nora.

Fern's eyes filled up. "Because the condition is genetic which means it can be hereditary. It means that any children of Danny's have a fifty percent chance of having the same condition."

Nora froze. She felt like she'd been punched in the gut. Oh Jesus, no! Rossa knew this but never said anything to me, she thought, trying to figure things out in her head. But of course she knew Fern would say something.

She looked out to the back garden where Millie was giggling and playing with Penny. My beautiful baby. Her heart ached. She wanted to run to her but her legs couldn't move.

"She gave me this card," Fern said, taking the card out of her pocket and putting it on the table. "It has the name of the condition and the name of the doctor dealing with it. There is a special centre for cardiac risk in Tallagh hospital. Rossa rang Danny's GP for an emergency referral and she has an appointment for next week for her kids. To get tested."

The three friends sat in silence. Nora picked the card up. "I ... I've never heard of it," she said, trying to keep it together. Taking out her phone she took a picture of the details. "Maybe we should look it up?" She felt nauseous as she turned to look at Millie running up and down outside without a care in the world.

Clo reached across and looked at the card,. "I've never heard of it either, I'll google it. Rossa's email is on this too." She took a photo of both sides.

Fern nodded. "Please don't tell anyone this either."

Nora felt dizzy. She didn't think she could take any more.

"Rossa is going to Canada," Fern said. "She plans to book flights from Dublin and leave next week after the kids are tested. Apparently, she was born there and has dual citizenship. She went to primary school in Canada before her parents moved back to Wexford. Her parents are dead now and her brother lives in Canada – they visit him every year and he has sent them all open tickets. Ed is actually going to college there, moving next month anyway, and now she wants them all to go."

"To move permanently?" Clo asked.

"She's not decided. But probably. It turns out she wants to get away from Belmullet. I suppose there are memories of Danny everywhere here and maybe a new start is for the best. The only family she has here are Danny's parents and she hates them. Anyway, she has to do what's best for her family and I have to do what's best for DJ. I'm terrified that he might have this heart disease ... he plays sports ... and ..." Fern started to cry.

"Oh Fern!" Clo said, leaning over to place a hand on her arm.

"I have left a message on his phone so if it's okay with you guys I'm going to go to my bedroom to wait until he calls me back."

"Of course. I think we've all had a shock," said Clo.

Nora just nodded. Her chest was tightening and she felt faint. She couldn't say a word but her beautiful Millie could have this too.

"Are you okay, Nora?" Clo asked.

Nora shook her head. She then got up, ran to the bathroom and threw up.

Clo sat alone at the kitchen table, staring at the doctor's card in her hand and her hands started to tremble.

CHAPTER 55

Sunday

"Morning," Fern said as Clo entered the kitchen.

"Good morning to you," Clo said as she yawned and stretched her arms over her head. "Did you get through to DJ?"

"Yes. He rang me back just before midnight and it was awful having to give him that news."

"I can imagine."

"Luckily he was staying with the team in a hotel somewhere so he was going to contact the medical team and tell them straight away. He's lucky that he has that service to hand. He was due to play today so he's dropping out of that until they can find out about the condition and test him for it."

"Maybe they can fast-track his results for him."

"Yeah, maybe. If he has it though it could affect his whole career."

"We don't know that yet." Clo put her arm around her friend.

"I just feel ... you know ... we had him put up for adoption, then Danny died just as they were getting to know each other and now this.

If he had never contacted us then he would never have known he could be at risk, just like Danny. We've been so unlucky for him."

"Are you kidding me?" Clo said, hugging her friend. "You gave him up so he could have a fantastic life. And he wouldn't have his great football career if he wasn't Danny O'Connor's son. And he may not have this condition. Come on now!"

"Yeah, it's just hard, you know."

"Life is fucking hard and complicated and messy and I should know because I keep fucking up all the time, but you? You have kept this secret and you have a wonderful family who love you."

"Thanks, Clo."

"Have you spoken to Max?"

"Yeah, for hours. I can't wait to see him and Otto."

"*Morning!*"

"Good morning, Miss Millie!" Clo said as Millie skipped into the kitchen.

Nora followed, looking the worse for wear.

"Would you like pancakes, Millie?" Fern asked.

"Oh yes, please!"

"Pancakes, everyone?"

"Yes, me too," said Clo. "How are you feeling, Nora?"

"Well enough for pancakes," she said with a smile. "Can I help you with anything, Fern?"

"No, I'm grand. I made up the mixture last night."

"Lovely. Millie, will you let Penny out, please?"

Millie opened the front door and Penny got up and walked out to relieve herself.

"*Hello?*" someone called from outside.

"It's a man! Two mans!" Millie said, running back in.

"Rory," said Fern. "Come in and ... Kevin?"

Kevin walked in behind Rory.

"Hi," Kevin said shyly. "I hope you don't mind us calling in like this."

"No, not at all," said Fern "In fact, I'm delighted."

"Millie, this is Rory and Kevin. They are old school friends of ours."

"I'm just making some pancakes," Fern said. "Will you have some?"

"No, thanks, I had an early breakfast," Rory said. "I just wanted to catch you girls before you all leave. Kevin and I had a few pints last night and I convinced him to come with me today to see the house again."

"Well, do you have time for a tea or a coffee?"

"I think we can manage that," said Rory. "Tea for me."

"Me too," said Kevin.

"Nora, will you look after the pancakes while I make the tea," Clo said, beaming as she looked at Rory.

"I'm going out the back with Penny," Millie said, bored with the adults already.

Kevin stood looking around the familiar house. Fern caught his eye.

"Come on, let me show you upstairs," she said.

He smiled and followed her lead.

"*Wow*, it hasn't changed," he said when they entered the studio. "Your mam still painting?"

"Yes, and Dad is still holding bogwood workshops. They are in the south of France at the moment."

"And you really did achieve your dream too," said Kevin, turning to look at her.

"I guess," Fern shrugged.

"You're being modest." Kevin grinned. "I've been following you on social media."

"Really! Why didn't you reach out?" she said, playfully hitting his arm.

"Ah, yeh know." He shrugged.

Fern nodded. "Kevin, I'm so sorry about how things ended with us and everything that went on that summer."

"You've no need to be sorry, Fern. I was a jerk. I was mad about you but I pushed you away. I'm really happy that you got to live your dream and that you have a happy life now."

"Thanks. And you? Are you happy?"

"Happy? I think I am. I was screwed up over a lot of things but Australia really has helped. Meeting Audrey definitely has helped, as bizarre as that probably seems. And this trip ... I was dreading coming back here. I had all this bitterness against Danny but ... it was all such a waste of time. And now Rossa is a widow and the kids have no father. Life is too short for bitterness and resentment. And I want to thank you."

"Me?"

"For how you were with Audrey the other day. She has a lot of issues around her family and you were ... well, you were kind and that meant a lot to both of us."

"Hey," Fern said, walking to him. "Give me a hug."

Kevin stiffened and then relaxed and let Fern hug him.

"Give my boy a hug for me when you see him, will you?"

"Ozzie men don't hug, Fern," he said and then smiled. "I'll pat him on the back. Will that do?"

Fern laughed. "Yes, I suppose. And let's connect on socials, okay?"

"Sure."

"*The first pancakes are ready! Get them while they're hot!*" Clo shouted up the stairs.

They all sat around the kitchen table as Nora placed a plate stacked with pancakes in the centre. "Help yourselves," she said.

"This is surreal," Fern said, passing around the maple syrup. "The school players back together again."

"Yes," Clo said, looking around the table. "Some of the happiest days of my life were in this house, around this very table." She ran her hand over it.

"I thought about those days so many times when I moved to Oz," Kevin said.

"We did have some laughs," said Rory.

"I've loved seeing you all again," said Nora.

"Okay, before any of us start crying, I'm off to Shannon to pick up my girls," Rory said, finishing his tea.

"Oh, how lovely! I hope the weather stays good for you," Fern said.

"Sure, don't you know it won't," said Rory. "It's been too good all week. It'll probably start raining as soon as they get off the plane. You can see the mist rolling in already."

Kevin and Rory stood up and hugged everyone.

Clo walked them out to the car. Kevin got in the passenger side and shut the door.

"This was a nice surprise," Clo said quietly to Rory. "I thought we said our goodbyes last night?"

"Well, after you visited my old bedroom, I had to go and drown my sorrows, didn't I? And when I walked into McDonnell's Kevin was there on his own, so he joined me."

"Does he know?"

"That you are the love of my life? Sure everyone knows that, Clo Kennedy."

Rory smiled and gave her a peck on the cheek. "Until the next time," he whispered in her ear before getting into the car.

Clo swallowed hard as she watched him drive away. Turning to look across the bay, she took a deep breath of the salty sea air before going back into the house.

CHAPTER 56

"So I think that's everything," Nora said, looking around the kitchen. "Millie and Penny are strapped into their seats and I think I picked up all the toys. Thank you so much for having us."

"I'm ready to go now too," said Clo, picking up her car keys.

"It was an absolute pleasure having you both here," Fern said. "I don't think I could have got through this week without you two. I only wish we could have had longer to just sit around and talk but so much has happened this week."

"Yes, it has." Nora nodded. More than I can ever tell you guys, she said to herself.

"Will you see Pavel before you go?" Clo asked.

"Yes, we have to call into my mam's and then Pavel's place. It could be a while before we actually leave Belmullet. What about you?"

"Well, Pierre left for Dublin yesterday afternoon and Madam wanted a night in the hotel by herself so I'll go and pick her up. I think she wants me to take her back into Westport for some more shopping so basically I'm her chauffeur for the day." Clo smiled. I'm lucky my daughter is even speaking to me after this week, she thought.

"And my flight is at two so I have to get a move on," said Fern.

"Have the best time in Morocco," Nora said, hugging her friend.

"I just can't wait to see them! And as soon as I hear from DJ, I'll let you know."

"Please do," said Clo. "And we've agreed to more WhatsApp messages and Zoom calls because I really need you guys in my life."

"One hundred percent!" said Fern. "And you both need to visit me in London and maybe we can meet back here again."

"I'd love that," said Clo, "although I have no idea what way my life is going at the moment."

"And I'd love that too," said Nora, "but I have no idea what way my life is going either."

The three friends laughed and hugged for the last time before Clo and Nora headed on their way.

Fern shut the door behind her and walked around the house one last time. This house has seen so much, she thought. This week was such a rollercoaster and not the way I thought it would be but my secret is out and that burden has lifted.

Please God, let DJ be okay! she said to herself before blessing herself with water from her mother's holy water font at the front door and shutting the door behind her.

CHAPTER 57

Two Weeks later

“Is this the place?” Pavel asked as he pulled over to the side of the road and put the hazard lights on.

Nora craned her neck, looking up and down the street from the front seat.

“They said it’s across the road from the main entrance to the hospital so ... oh, there it is! “ She pointed. “See the blue poster with a picture of kids on it?”

“Well spotted,” said Pavel.

“I can see the CRY sign over the door. It stands for Cardiac Risk in the Young,” she said, lowering her voice.

As soon as Nora got back to Dublin she called their GP and explained that Millie needed a referral as she might have inherited Danny’s condition. He wrote a referral immediately. The cardiologist suggested by Rossa worked in the clinic three days a week.

“I can turn around and use the underground car park over there,” Pavel said, looking over his shoulder.

"We're very early though, our appointment isn't for another forty minutes."

"Do you want to go in and wait while I park?"

"I think it would make me more nervous to go in and wait. Can we stay here for a bit?" she said, slipping her hand in his.

"I don't see why not, there's very little traffic here."

"Mummy?"

"Yes, Millie."

"Where is Milis going to sleep in our house?"

"We'll put her bed beside Penny's."

"And how long are they coming for a holiday?"

"I told you, sweetie – one week."

Pavel surprised Nora by changing all his work appointments this week to come to Dublin and accompany her to this appointment.

"You'd come to Dublin?" Nora had said, shocked and delighted.

"Yes, I can't bear the idea of you going on your own and these Zoom calls are not the same as having you right beside me."

"Oh, I can't wait!" Nora had said, feeling butterflies just thinking of having him in her bed.

"I have rearranged jobs so I can come for a week, if you'll have me?"

"Oh, I'll have you alright," Nora replied suggestively and Pavel threw his head back and laughed.

They had zoom-called every night since she returned to Dublin. Even though it was only two weeks since she left Mayo, she missed him desperately.

Nora leaned over from the passenger seat and gave him a juicy kiss.

Pavel kissed her back.

"And where will Pavel sleep?" Millie said from the back of the jeep.

Pavel and Nora looked at each other and smiled.

"Maybe in Mummy's bed?" said Nora.

"Okay," Millie said and went back to playing with her dolls.

Nora looked nervously towards the clinic. "Thank you so much for being here," she said.

"I want to be here," he said as he lifted her hand to his lips and kissed it.

"Pavel kissed Mummy's hand!" giggled Millie.

"Yes, I did!" Pavel laughed. "And now I'm kissing Mummy's nose," he said, giving Nora a peck on her nose, "and now I'm kissing Mummy's eyes."

Millie squealed with laughter.

"And now Mummy's neck."

Nora giggled and then she froze.

"Oh my god," she whispered. "Don't move!"

"What? What is it?"

"I ... I ..." Nora couldn't finish her sentence.

Across the street she saw Clo and Sophia come out the door of the underground car park and walk quickly to the clinic door. Clo looked up at the sign and then she and Sophia walked inside.

"What?"

"How can that be?" said Nora, looking at Pavel whose face was just as shocked as hers.

"Why are we here again?" Sophia asked, sitting down with a sigh on the couch in the waiting room.

"I told you. Your granny decided to tell me last week that some cousin of ours has a heart condition and it might be hereditary, so we're just here for a test. It's a quick in and out, I promise."

"But why aren't you getting it then?"

"Because it skips a generation," Clo lied, looking at her watch.

"You're very jittery, Mum."

"I just want to get it over with, that's all. But while we're here I need you to promise me you won't tell your dad about this, all right?"

"But why not?"

"Because he will only worry, love, and right now he has a lot on his plate with the new shop so let's not add to the stress, okay?"

"But what if I have it?"

"You won't. This is just a precaution, darling. We'll be on our way soon. Have a look at your phone there, I heard there is a new designer shop opening in Brown Thomas today. How about we go and check it out after we're done here?" Clo asked. "I will treat you for dragging you here today and keeping this between ourselves, okay?"

"Cool!" Sophia said, her face lighting up as she started typing on her phone.

This is going to cost me a pretty penny, Clo thought, fidgeting with her car keys. Sophia had expensive taste but she didn't care – she just wanted to get this over with.

This test better be bloody negative, Clo thought nervously as she looked around at the cardiac posters, or I am completely fucked. I had completely blanked that night from my memory and now this? She looked up to the ceiling.

Dear Jesus, if you exist at all, she thought, *please, please, please let this test be negative* – and then she found herself praying for the first time in thirty years.

CHAPTER 58

Eighteen years previously

"Well, well, well, if it isn't Clodagh Kennedy!"

A familiar voice made Clo turn around as she walked into the Horseshoe Bar of Dublin's 5-Star Shelbourne Hotel.

"Of all the bars in all the world ..." he continued.

Clo had to laugh as she walked over. "Well, if it isn't yourself, Danny O'Connor."

He stood up from his barstool and kissed her on the cheek. "You're looking great, Clo."

"You too, Danny, you scrub up well."

"Sit down," he said, pulling out the barstool beside him. "Are you on your own?"

Clo sat up beside him, placing her bag on the bar. "I am, and you?"

"Yes, just up for a bit of business. Don't you live in Paris now?"

"Yes, but I'm moving back."

"Here, let me get you a drink," Danny said, nodding to the barman. "What'll you have?"

"Do you have a champagne menu?" she asked the barman.

"Oh, are you celebrating or do you just have expensive taste?" Danny asked.

"I'm celebrating," Clo said, accepting the champagne menu from the waiter. "Will you join me?"

"Well, I couldn't have you drinking on your own, now could I?" he said with a grin.

Clo couldn't help noticing that his eyes were still as blue as when they were younger when every girl in the school fancied him.

"A bottle of Laurent Perrier La Cuvee and two glasses," Clo said with perfect French pronunciation.

"It's very sexy when you say it like that," Danny said with a wink.

"It's French, Danny, don't get too excited."

Danny laughed. "So what are we celebrating?" he asked as the waiter returned with the bottle, an ice bucket, and two glasses.

"We are celebrating me signing a lease on a property. It will soon become my business, a vintage designer clothing shop to be precise," she said, raising her glass. "To business and prosperity!"

"To business and prosperity!" Danny said, clinking her glass before the two of them took a sip.

An hour later they had moved to a more comfortable spot in the bar. The bottle of champagne was finished and they had moved on to cocktails.

As they sat side by side, Danny moved his leg to touch hers.

The barman called for the last orders.

"Why don't we continue this celebration in my room?" Danny whispered in her ear.

"I am very happily in a relationship with my partner," Clo said, looking him in the eye.

"And I'm a very happily married man," he said, placing his hand on her knee under the table.

"What do you think you're doing?" she asked but she didn't push his hand away.

"I'm just helping you make up your mind," he said as he moved his hand right up her thigh and then between her legs.

Clo gasped.

"Is that a yes?" he said, manoeuvring his fingers inside her underwear.

Clo felt dizzy. Danny had never looked at her in that way when they were teenagers. She had always wondered what it would be like to be with the famous Danny O'Connor. And ... she was celebrating ... so ...

Clo stepped out of the shower and dressed quickly. Her taxi was due any minute to take her to the airport and back to her beloved in Paris.

Pushing thoughts of Pierre out of her head, she leaned into the mirror to apply her lipstick.

"Danny O'Connor," she said to her reflection.

She had left his bed in the early hours to sleep in her own room. She had wondered over the years if Danny would be any good between the sheets and now she knew. Although enjoyable, sex with Danny had been a bit frantic and certainly nothing special.

I'd give him a six out of ten, she figured. That was for the teenage me, she said to herself, the teenage me that he never would have been interested in.

Picking up her handbag, she pulled her small suitcase behind her as she left the room to meet her driver.

Twelve weeks later she and Pierre announced their delight and surprise that they were expecting a baby.

Epilogue

Fourteen Months Later

Saturday 02 August 2025

Mullet Peninsula, County Mayo

Fern opened the door with a big smile.

"Look how you've grown!" she said as Millie jumped down from Nora's jeep.

"Hello, neighbours!" she added as Nora and Pavel walked up the drive hand in hand.

"It's crazy, yeah?" Nora said as she went in for a hug.

"Not crazy at all," Fern whispered in her ear. "I am so happy for you."

They all walked into Fern's parents' kitchen. It was a beautiful sunny day and the big sliding door was open letting the sea air in. She had set up a long table in the back garden decorated with flowers and bunting.

Strings of fairy lights looped along the washing line all the way down to the sea wall.

"This is beautiful, Fern," Nora said, looking out at all the decorations.

"Well, I'm only fifty once," Fern smiled.

"Yes, Happy Birthday! Pavel, I left Fern's present in the jeep ... can you ...?"

"Of course," he said, kissing her on the head before he left.

"You two are so adorable together. How has it been moving back here?"

"It's a big change from Dublin but we had to do something. We were spending all our time driving across the country to see each other. So when Alek got accepted into Trinity College we decided to let him live in my cottage and for me and Millie to move here."

What Nora didn't tell her was that her decision to come back to Belmullet was very much based on the fact that Rossa and the kids had decided to stay in Canada. They had only come home once in the past year, for Danny's anniversary Mass in June, when Rossa put the house on the market.

A few days after Nora arrived home to Dublin, her mam rang to say an envelope addressed to her had been dropped in her letter box. Margaret posted the letter to Dublin. It was a typed note from Rossa, although she hadn't signed it, containing the details of Danny's condition and the same details she had given Fern. She obviously couldn't bring herself to tell Nora face to face but presumably couldn't leave Ireland without informing her. Or perhaps she'd been so angry she initially intended to leave her in ignorance? Was Rossa capable of such a thing, Nora wondered. Surely not?

Finding out that Millie's tests were negative and that she had not inherited Danny's heart condition lifted a huge weight of guilt off her shoulders, making her feel like she could settle in this place now, her home, their home and start again. Yes, she would one day have to tell Millie everything but for now she wanted to stay in this bubble of joy and love with her new family.

"And what about your business?"

"I still own it but Mairead manages it. It's working well so far. Pavel and I plan to set up our own company here."

"I couldn't be happier for you," Fern said as she squeezed her friend. "Come on, Mam and Dad have started drinking already and Max and Otto are at the barbeque marinating all kinds of things. They both thought they were the best at barbequing until DJ arrived."

Nora stopped in her tracks when DJ turned around and smiled at her. He was the image of Danny.

"You must be Nora," he said, walking towards her with his hand extended.

"I ... I'm delighted to meet you. You are so like Danny."

"Yes. I'm getting that everywhere I go here. People keep doing a double take when I walk down the road or into the pub."

"We sent Danny's parents some photos in advance so it wouldn't be such a shock," Fern said, slipping her arm through DJ's.

"So you've met them?" Nora asked.

"Yeah, it was very emotional for them, especially the old lad as he didn't know about me at all until last year when Audrey told them," Danny said.

"Do you see much of Audrey and Kevin?"

"We keep in touch and they have already asked me to be godfather to their baby."

"I'm so happy for them," Fern said. "A baby will be the making of them."

Fern had kept in touch with Kevin and Audrey and they sent fabulous photos every time they met up with DJ.

"Happy Birthday," Pavel said, handing Fern her birthday gift.

"Thank you so much," she said, leaning in for a kiss on the cheek. "I honestly didn't expect any presents – I'm just so happy to have everyone here."

"*Anybody home!*" a voice called out from the porch and Clo walked in carrying the biggest bouquet of flowers and a bottle of Moet Champagne. She looked fantastic as usual, dressed head to toe in expensive designer brands.

"*Clo!*" Fern ran and hugged her friend.

"This is for you, darling," she said, kissing her on the cheek and passing her the champagne.

"You still have expensive taste, I see."

"Oh, there's more where that came from. Rory!"

"Coming, dear," Rory mocked as he carried in a large box containing more Moet Champagne. "For the birthday girl, I believe," he said, holding it up.

"Thank you so much. You both look amazing for two people who just got off a flight."

"Well, we did stop on the way to freshen up," Clo said with a wink.

Fern just laughed and shook her head. "The same old Clo," she said as she led them out to the back garden.

"Well, I don't have to ask who you are," Clo said as she hugged DJ. "And Max and Otto, great to see you again."

As Clo walked over to hug Nora and Pavel she could hardly believe it was just over a year since her life changed completely.

Fourteen months since she left this house not knowing what the future held. Twelve months since the test results came back positive.

The worst days of her life followed as she had to tell Pierre about her one-night stand with Danny and that Sophia not only had a heart condition but was not his biological daughter. She watched him crumble in front of her and she knew then that their marriage was over. Sophia's condition was completely treatable. She had no symptoms and would be monitored every year. They then had the horrible task of telling Sophia – who as Clo suspected sided with her dad. Their bond was thicker than any DNA test.

Clo left the family home that night. The only correspondence she had with Pierre now was through lawyers. He bought out her share of the house and the business, leaving her a wealthy woman but with no family and no home.

There was nothing left for her in Dublin so she boarded a plane to New York. The story she told Fern, Nora, and Rory was that the marriage was over and that Sophia, blaming her, chose to stay with Pierre. Lies,

lies and more lies, but she couldn't bring herself to ever tell Rory or her friends the truth.

"So how is life in New York?" Nora asked.

"Oh, wonderful. I'm busy managing an upmarket boutique and Rory's business is doing very well, so things are good."

Nora wasn't convinced by Clo's insistence that everything was wonderful. She saw her go into that clinic with Sophia. And then the fallout afterwards was very fast which could only mean one thing. But who am I to judge? Look at the secrets I'm keeping, she thought as she watched Millie sit down beside DJ.

They have the same dad. They are half-brother and sister and they don't know it. And I'm guessing Sophia is too. She swallowed hard.

Was it right to keep all this a secret? Would Rory stand by Clo if he knew? Or would that be the last straw for him? Would Fern stay friends with either of them if she knew her two best friends also had children by Danny O'Connor? The risk was too high.

The truth would have to be told someday – for the children's sake – but Nora knew that now was not the time. When that day comes, she thought, I can only hope that the strength of our friendship, and the love we share, will carry us through.

"Let's get this party started!" Max said, opening the first bottle of champagne, filling the glasses on the table outside.

Otto passed around the filled glasses to everyone.

"I would like to make a toast!" Max said, raising his glass. "To my beautiful wife, in this beautiful place! Happy Birthday!"

"*Happy Birthday!*" everyone said, raising their glasses.

"Thank you," said Fern, smiling and looking around at all the people she loved. "Thank you all so much for coming today. Thank you to Mam and Dad for this beautiful home where I spent some of my happiest days with these guys here, writing and rehearsing our awful plays that we thought were wonderful. I can't believe that most of us are standing here today, still the best of friends. Here's to Danny who we remember today and to Kevin and Audrey getting ready for their new arrival! To my wonderful Max and Otto and to DJ who complete my world! And to my two best friends, Nora and Clo! We have shared some crazy times and we have told each other our darkest secrets. I love you both. You are my soul sisters!"

Fern raised her glass.

"To everyone I love!"

Nora and Clo raised their glasses to Fern who they loved to bits. But when, if ever, could they reveal their true secrets and lies?

THE END